# ROUGH

BLOOD RUNS DEEP. JUSTICE RUNS DEEPER.

# COUNTRY

HAT CREEK
*an imprint of*
Roan & Weatherford Publishing Associates, LLC
Bentonville, Arkansas • Heber City, Utah
www.roanweatherford.com



Rough Country
Description: First Edition | Bentonville: Hat Creek, 2026
Identifiers: ISBN: 979-8-89299-111-7 (trade paperback)|
ISBN: 979-8-89299-112-4 (eBook)
FICTION/Westerns | FICTION/Crime |
FICTION/Thrillers/Action & Adventure

Hat Creek Trade Paperback edition April, 2026

Cover Design and Interior Design by Casey W. Cowan
Editing by Reavis Z. Wortham, Don Money & Rachel Santino

# ROUGH

BLOOD RUNS DEEP. JUSTICE RUNS DEEPER.

# COUNTRY

# TABLE OF CONTENTS

# PREFACE

MY FIGHT-OR-FLIGHT response kicked in when Casey Cowan, my publisher at Roan & Weatherford, called and asked me if I'd be interested in editing an anthology of short stories for "a good cause."

While Casey talked on speaker, I crossed my fingers and made a *mal ojo* sign to ward off evil. He kept talking, and I ran to the kitchen for garlic, which I intended to smear all over the phone to ward off anything that might make me agree. I quit when reality set in, and I remembered how much I dislike garlic.

Casey is persuasive, and after a few minutes, I heard about the U.S. Marshals Survivors Benefit Fund, a private nonprofit organization that provides financial and educational support to the families of U.S. Marshals and Marshals Service employees killed in the line of duty. It offers immediate death assistance for funeral costs, provides education benefit grants, and supports programs that honor fallen heroes.

I've always been a strong supporter of first responders and am honored to call a number of law enforcement officers friends, and that includes bestselling author Marc Cameron, who is a retired U.S. Marshal now living in Alaska. The idea of this anthology came from a conversation between he and Casey, two of the most giving people I know.

I also owed Casey for signing me on to his publishing company to produce *Comancheria,* the first weird horror Western in a new cutting-edge series, followed by *The Sound of a Dead Man's Laugh* (October 2026) and *What We Owe the Dead* (October 2027).

Putting together an anthology isn't like writing, where I simply sit down at the computer and start hammering out words while making up stories about my imaginary friends. To assemble all the parts, you have to somehow get authors to commit their time, creativity, and open hearts to submit stories that would provide no personal monetary return on their investment.

What I've come to realize is that almost every mystery, thriller, and Western author out there loves to give. There's no sense of territory among these people, and very few are standoffish. To prove that, go to any writer's conference and find a group engaged in conversation. They'll welcome you into the fold.

After Casey and I hung up that day, I made a list of writing friends and authors I've come to admire since I launched my first novel back in 2011. Soon I had about a dozen names written down on a legal pad and began reaching out to those I knew, and they offered their own suggestions.

Soon I had commitments from bestselling and quite famous authors I'd never met. Some told me they'd seldom produced short stories, but they wanted to join this worthy cause. When the stories came in, I was blown away. No matter the length of their project, each of these authors are storytellers.

Stories are as old as breath. Before the first words were carved into clay tablets, or printing presses, or on glowing screens that scramble one's electro neurons, people gathered around fires and glowing coals to share history and their imaginations. In every era, stories have been the compass points by which we navigate the real world.

This collection had certain parameters, the hard West, rough country, between 1900 and today. I was delighted to see that some of our writers clawed their way out of that box and presented us with both tales of ancient hardships in the 1800s, and postapocalyptic challenges that blended old stories with new.

Within these pages you'll find tales spun by some of today's most celebrated literary voices and bestselling authors who have captured readers around the world. They range from freshmen authors establishing their place in the world of fiction, to million-selling novelists, and even one Pulitzer Prize finalist. We finish our second volume, *Hard Country,* with the haunting lyrics of a song that captures the spirit of the West. They've all earned a place in the world of literature.

Here in shorter form, their craft sharpens, condenses, and surprises. The brevity of the short story offers an intensive and personal level in only a few pages and distills the idea of *Rough Country* and *Hard Country* to its purest note.

Each author brings a distinct voice, their own fresh twist of imagination, and unforgettable plots and characters. We invite you to read slowly—or quickly—in or out of sequence, or even aloud if that fills your bill. However you choose to relish this anthology, we hope you find moments of delight, horror, unease, and even humor, all of which are part of life in the old and new West.

Remember, tales of the West have changed. None of these folks attempted to write like Louis L'Amour, Zane Grey, Max Brand, or Donald Hamilton (in his many pseudonyms). They brought their own style to this campfire of ours, and we're all glad they did.

Enjoy!

—Reavis Z. Wortham
Editor

# REAVIS Z. WORTHAM

## WHERE THE ROAD FORKS

### A TOM BELL STORY

"SEEMS TO ME that bank robbery is becoming a pretty popular pastime these days." Texas Ranger Captain Tom Bell hung his elbow out the window of a borrowed Model T Ford and steered down a hard-packed dirt road on the way to the Rio Grande border town of Cottonwood Springs.

Dust rose in a thick rooster tail behind them. After a pause, waiting for Ranger Jack Patton to answer, he continued. "I despise a man who prefers to steal from honest people instead of working."

They were on the trail of Red Schaefer, a small-time Texas outlaw who murdered a bank manager during a robbery in Salado and got away with nothing more than a bullet hole in his own shirt, but it was the blood on his hands they were most interested in.

This was likely the last official Ranger duty for both men. Only months before, the Texas Rangers as an organization made a miscalculation and backed Ross Sterling against Miriam "Ma" Ferguson for governor. Sterling lost, and Ferguson had already indicated she'd disband the historic law enforcement agency that dared to square off with her.

"Only a man born in this godforsaken part of the world would run to ground here." Jack tilted his hat back to cool his pale forehead and flicked his fingers at the surrounding dry country filled with cactus and thorny brush. "But most dogs run under the porch when they're chased."

"I grew up a good ways downriver." Tom slowed and dodged a deep, axle-breaking pothole. "Most of the people down here won't have much to do with us Rangers. They all came up hard and this life can make or break a man. That may be the reason Red turned bad."

"This old boy's the last of the old-time bandits," Jack said, his voice revealing his reluctant admiration for the man they were after. "The rest of these no-goods are called public enemies these days, 'cause they dress like the bankers they're robbing, I suppose."

In the six months they'd been working together, he'd taken the lead as the elder of the two, even though Tom was only six months younger and had seen more hard action in France during the Great War than Jack, who'd been a Ranger at home during that time.

"He's used every old owlhoot trick in the book." Jack waved at an annoying fly that buzzed under his hat before buzzing back through the open window. "Who'd have ever thought about pulling off a robbery on horseback here in 1933."

Their investigation revealed how Red doubled back, crossed and recrossed rivers and creeks, and swapped out horses more than once without asking honest farmers and ranchers for the trade.

The swollen carcass of a brindle cow blocked the road, forcing Tom to steer around it and past a thick growth of prickly pear. "He's done what I would have. Stay off the paved roads, travel dirt tracks at night, and likely making cold camps during the day when everyone's out looking for him."

Jack patted the telegram in his inside coat pocket. "He's not as smart as we give him credit for, though. If it was me, I'd shave that red beard for sure and maybe cut my hair short. That's what's caught folks' attention and they remembered him."

When they rolled into the drought-stricken town, they were surprised to find several businesses including three churches, two banks, two hotels, an ice plant, several grocery stores, a butcher shop beside a barber, and a real estate office across from a title company.

As a courtesy, Jack and Tom stopped by the marshal's office to find him gone. Not a deputy was to be found, either, much to the annoyance of Jack who felt there should always be someone with a badge close by.

"Hell, old Pancho Villa could ride across the Rio Grande and carry this town off."

"You know as well as I do that he's been dead for years," Tom said, smoothing his new mustache in thought. He shifted to adjust the Colt riding on his hip. "And besides, everybody here in town has a gun, and most of 'em would love the opportunity to put a hole in any old bandit that comes looking for trouble."

Jack snorted in disgust. "Well, it'd have to be civilians, since the local laws are off fishing somewhere."

Under bright blue skies providing no hint of moisture, they walked down the brick street, still another surprise to the men who expected to find adobe buildings and hard-packed caliche underfoot. They passed a livery and blacksmith shop, remnants of a time soon to be gone.

With their big hats, gun belts, and self-confident demeanor, the hard-eyed Rangers drew looks from townspeople who watched with caution. Jack nodded his hat brim at a sign reading *Café.* A faded rose was hand painted on the left of the door along with *No Cerveza, But Ask Anyway* on the right.

He raised an eyebrow. "That there's the best place in town to get the information we're looking for."

Tom squinted one eye, thinking. "I believe we can just ask for a beer and get one in there, even though they say Prohibition is still in effect."

"You, a law, asking for alcohol?" Jack chuckled and pushed through a heavy door into the cool, dim interior. Sand crunched on the worn boards underfoot.

A raven-haired young woman came around a makeshift bar. Bottles lined the shelves behind her. Coke, Nehi, Dr Pepper, and Chero-Cola were displayed, along with empty whiskey and beer bottles. Her eyes sparkled when she saw Jack. Tom had seen it before. Women quickly fell for his square chin, curly hair, and dimples.

They introduced themselves and she put one hand on a hip designed to hold toddlers. "You boys look hungry, and thirsty."

Jack removed his hat to reveal thick curly hair, pressed flat on the sides from his hatband. "You're pretty smart."

She didn't take her eyes off of him, apparently ignoring the *Cinco Peso* badges on their shirts. "How about tortillas and tamales, washed down with a little *cuba libre?"*

"That have alcohol in it?" Tom asked, testing the waters.

"Who would put alcohol in tortillas?" Her dismissive voice changed when she took Jack's arm and led him to a table, leaving Tom to follow behind. "This is the best table in the house, *mi vita."*

"Already, *my life."* Tom rolled his eyes and spoke only to himself. "Good lord."

She stayed close while they ate and even pulled up a chair to pour real Bacardi Oro rum for Jack, virtually ignoring Tom. The rare liquor was a treat they rarely saw once Prohibition settled over the country like a pall.

When they finished eating, she ran her fingers through the wavy hair on the back of his neck. "For fifty cents, I will draw you a warm bath. It will make you more presentable."

"That's a fine idea."

"Sounds good to me." Tom leaned back and crossed one leg over the other, absently spinning the rowel on his spur. Though they were in an automobile, such habits were hard to break. "We've been on the trail for some time."

She turned her shoulder to him, keeping her attention on Jack. "There is a barbershop across the street. If you have a bad tooth, *Señor* Tom, Eustolio can pull it at the same time." Seated like a man with her feet splayed on the gritty floor, she turned back to Jack. "I meant you can come home with me and I will heat some water."

It wasn't the first time Tom had been rebuffed by a woman doting on Jack. He took it in stride, finished his meal, and listened to a guitar player's attempts to pick out a tune on a gutstring guitar between shots of tequila. The instrument was missing the E-string, and the others were so old the instrument wouldn't stay in tune. It was an exercise in futility, but he admired the man's determination to make music.

From time to time, Tom visited with the few local customers, seeking information about Red Schaefer. Most refused to talk, not daring to trust the Rangers or their reputation in that part of the state.

Toward midnight, Tom grew tired of watching Jack and the waitress and slid his chair back. "Jack, I'm not going to get in the way of true love. I believe I'll get me a room in the Excelsior Hotel down the street. You can find me there in the morning."

Jack held up his glass in a salute. "Don't be jealous."

"It's far from that." Tom leaned close so only Jack could hear. "I just hope you don't get Cupid's disease from this hot little pepper."

Throwing his head back to laugh, Jack repeated Tom's warning to the girl, and she laughed as well, a sign that she'd lived a hard life among many men.

Tom couldn't resist. "Oh, and while you're whispering in her ear, why don't you tell her your Choctaw nickname."

Pursing his lips, Jack cut his eyes at Tom in a brotherly look. "Keep that to yourself."

"All right, but with your lips all puckered up like a cat's ass, that old Choctaw was right. Butthole Leather is a perfect name."

Jack threw half a cold tortilla at Tom's back as he dodged and headed for the door.

There were few lights in the little town when Tom stepped outside, but the nearly full moon washed the quiet town in a bright silvery light. The scent of a lit cigarette drifting in the cool air reminded him of his grandfather who enjoyed smoking in the dog-run of their little country house after supper.

He was about to round the windowless adobe building when an old man sitting under the *estabo de librea* sign drew deep on a hand-rolled, the cherry bright as a campfire.

*"Buenos noches, Señor* Ranger. I heard you were inside, and I've been waiting for you."

Tom's hand dropped to the butt of his Colt before he saw the stranger was friendly. *"Buenos noches, viejo."*

"Ah. *Viejo.* I guess I *am* an old-timer, for I have seen many things in my life." The man drew on a small jug and Tom caught the distinctive oily odor of mezcal. "I still feel the same inside as I did when I was young and listening to my grandfather who saw Santa Anna ride past in all his glory on the way to slaughter those men in the Alamo."

Interested in a good story, Tom squatted beside the old man whose face could hold a three-day rain. "He should have shot the son of a bitch when he had the chance."

The old man passed him a little clay jug and Tom took a sip. *"Gracias."*

*"De nada."* The old man chuckled. Missing most of the teeth on one side of his head, the others were surprisingly white in the reflected glow of the café's windows. "Ah, it would have changed the world had he shot him, but then I would not have been here to see it or to enjoy this wonderful night. The general was surrounded by hundreds of men who were hard as the road they trod." He offered the jug again. "This is good mezcal. My cousin makes it down in El Indio."

"I went down there once after a couple of horse thieves. It's pretty rough country."

"Rough country makes a smooth drink."

Tom accepted the jug and took a second swallow before passing it back. "That's as good as any I've ever had."

*"Bien. Como te llamas?"*

"I'm Captain Tom Bell. Texas Ranger."

"Ah. I could tell you were a *guardabosque.* We don't see many of you here, but when you come, many of our people die."

"I'd reckon that's because they shoot at us first."

"Sometimes." The old man dismissed the statement with a world-weary sigh. "I am Juan Carlos Cabral."

"Good to meet you, Mister Juan."

"What brings you to our humble little town?"

"Captain Patton in there and I are looking for a man named Red Schaefer. Wanted for bank robbery and killing a man in Salado."

"Was it a fair fight?"

"The law says it wasn't."

"Was the law there?"

Tom had to study on that one. "There were witnesses. Good people carry the law with them, so I suppose so."

"I am of the belief that stealing from a bank is no sin." Juan took a long swallow and chased the drink with a long drag on his cigarette, blowing smoke in two thick streams from both nostrils. After stating his opinion, he switched stories.

"I once knew a man who killed another in a fair fight. The people there liked the dead man more, so they hung the other."

Familiar with *frontera* justice, Tom nodded. "It happens like that sometimes."

Oiled up from the mezcal, Juan rolled another cigarette. "A few years ago, there was a family who lived that way named Schaefer." He pointed to the west with a gnarled, crooked finger. "They had a boy with red hair who went away after he killed Diego Cabral over a pig."

Tom considered the surname and understanding dawned. "Is the family still there?"

"No. One of my people killed the father who let his boy run wild. The mother left, taking another child."

"Is the house still standing?"

"It wasn't that long ago. Ten years maybe, and yes, the roof has fallen in, but the walls are still there. Adobe lasts forever if it has protection from above. If not, it is melting back into the earth it came from."

Tom considered the information. "So if he came back this way, the house might be a place to go back to, then."

"*Sí.*"

"Did you know the boy?"

"*Sí.* His name was Fred, but we called him by his hair color, Rojo."

"Red."

"That is what I said. He was a good boy when he was young, and I would see him in town from time to time. He was well behaved until one day he wasn't."

There was that Rio Grande philosophy that permeated the existence of those who scratched a living from the hardscrabble earth there on the border.

Tom eyed the old man. "You know what turned him that way?"

"When he was a pup, he took up with an *hombre* who worked there in the absence of the father, but Smith was *muy malo,* very bad, and some of my friends said he was hiding down here from *los rinches.* He acted very tough, and beat up anyone who was smaller than him there in the *cantina,* whether he was drunk or not."

Tom ignored the mild insult for Texas Rangers, figuring the old man was talking about others who came before, and not him. "So you think the boy took after him."

"That is what the whole town thought. The man was more exciting than Rojo's father, who was always gone and seldom came home. I heard he had another wife in Fredericksburg where his people lived."

"Sounds like a sorry son of a bitch to me."

"To me, too. Rojo tagged along behind the bad man he idolized, watching and learning."

"What was that fellow's first name?"

"I do not remember his first, but he insisted on being called Mister Smith, which I could not abide, so I called him nothing and avoided him like a scorpion. No, I would have killed a scorpion for being what it is, but I was not mano enough to crush him out."

"What happened to Smith? Is he still around?"

"No." Juan pointed south of town. "I heard he is buried down across the river in a shallow grave. He angered someone meaner and tougher than he was."

"There's always someone meaner and tougher. Tell me how to find this house, *por favor.*"

Juan waved a hand. "Follow this road out of town. You will come to an old live oak with limbs that soar down to touch the ground. It is a cool, green cave in there to rest in the shade. The road circles around this delight, and about a mile after that is a cutoff to the northwest. The house is another mile farther on, beside a little spring creek. It is a fine place to water your horses."

"We're in an automobile."

Another deep sigh, as if the changing world was a weight on the old man's shoulders. "Then you can fill your machine's radiator, or your water bag if you need."

Tom thanked him and pressed a *cinco* peso into the old man's hand for his help. *"Buenos noches."*

He weighed the coin in his palm for a moment. "This is too much for a few swallows."

"Probably not enough, considering." Tom rose with fluid ease and left.

Their car was parked to the side of the livery and Tom opened the trunk and took out a Winchester carbine and his grip. He strolled through the cool darkness filled with the scent of animals and fresh spices from someone's supper.

The square stucco hotel was the only two-story building in town. A drowsy manager with hair sticking up like a rooster's comb signed him in. "You don't need to be so heavily armed here."

"It's not just here." Tom leaned the rifle against the counter, took up a pen, and signed his name while the man selected a key from the cubbyhole. Most were filled with dusty yellowed paper curling in the heat.

The manager had apparently mastered the art of reading upside down. *"Bien,* Mister Bell and room ten. Far end of the hall."

"My partner'll be here looking for me. Another Ranger by the name of Jack Patton."

"There's be an extra charge of course."

"He'll be around at dawn. It's just me."

The room was sparse with just a bed, washstand, and a warped wardrobe made from old, cast-off lumber. There was no rug, and dust bunnies lived underneath the bed. He raised the stained paper shade and opened the window to admit the breeze, making the stuffy room tolerable.

Stretching out on top of the quilt with his Colt close to hand, Tom drifted off to the distant music of the gutstring guitar down the street.

JACK UNLOCKED THE door at daylight and kicked the metal bedstead's footboard. "Get up. We need to get back on the trail."

"I was awake half an hour ago, but I was enjoying the quiet." Rising, Tom rubbed the sleep out of his eyes, marveling at how fresh Jack looked after being up all night. "You're lucky I didn't shoot you for an intruder."

"You were snoring so loud you didn't hear me knock."

"The manager gave you a key, I suppose?"

"Didn't need one." Jack pointed at the iron doorknob. "Lock's busted."

Tom sighed and pulled on his boots. He'd slept in his clothes on top of the bed. He poured water from the pitcher into the bowl and washed his face. The thin towel barely had enough threads to soak up the water.

Taking his hat from the washstand, he turned to see Jack staring down into the street. "I'm surprised you can make sense this early in the morning, but you smell like a woman."

"Dallying with a young whore ain't no chore, and she put some kind of perfume in the bathwater to freshen me up."

"You're lucky she didn't rob you blind while your eyes were closed."

"My pistol was against me when I got sleepy, and my money was stuck down the bottom of my holster. No one would think to look there."

Jack led the way down the hall and stairs.

Tom pitched the key onto the counter. "You need to get the lock fixed on that door."

"Nothing works around here," the dour manager said, trying to smooth the hair on top of his head. "Besides, you have more guns than half of the town. No one would have bothered you."

"The point is, a man needs to sleep sound, without worrying about being murdered in his bed."

The manager shrugged. "No one has ever died here—unless it was by natural causes."

Tom smoothed his thick mustache in thought. "If they're like you, they likely died from a lack of ambition."

Grinning, Jack held the door. "Did you ask him if he knows Red Schaefer?"

"Didn't need to." Tom told him what he'd learned from old Juan the night before.

When they came to the car, Jack slipped behind the wheel. "My turn to drive. I'm likely to doze off just sitting there."

He advanced the spark as Tom gave the machine some gas with the thumb throttle at the same time Jack turned the key. He gave the crank a half turn and the engine coughed to life.

Tom joined his partner in the seat. "You just don't like twisting that crank on a cold engine."

"Broke my wrist once when I used the wrong hand." Jack pushed the throttle with his hand and they pulled out.

"I'd rather ride horses anyway." Tom watched the buildings as they passed. "These things are loud in the morning, and they stink."

"Well, we can move faster in these, and that's the only reason we're close to catching Schaefer."

When they turned onto the street, the old man was gone from his wall, leaving behind the twists of two tiny cigarette butts he'd smoked down to the nub.

The sun rose as they followed the old man's directions and found the crumbling house an hour later. They stopped at a distance, considering the abandoned ranchero surrounded by a waist-high stacked rock wall. Smoke from a hidden campfire rose in the still air.

Jack adjusted his seat. "You see anything?"

"Nothing but smoke." The sun was to their back and Tom didn't need to squint in the soft light. "Roof must be caved in enough he couldn't get inside and use the fireplace."

"If he's still there this morning, his horse must be out back." The whipcrack of a shot startled the Rangers and Tom flinched as the windshield starred. "He's still there."

Men not unused to being shot at, they rolled out on each side and instead of taking cover behind the vehicle as most assassins would expect, they did the opposite. Snatching revolvers from their belts, the Rangers returned fire at a puff of gun smoke from behind the rock fence to force their adversary down and rushed at his position.

"I *hate* being shot at." Tom charged at the smoke rising from the bushwhacker's position, running and shooting to keep the other man's head down.

Jack separated with a few yards between them and did the same, splitting the man's attention.

Their fast shots echoed across the hardscrabble, slapping flat in the still morning air. A flash of red beard was all Tom saw as the shooter ducked below the low wall to dodge their return fire.

The figure behind the wall rose and shot twice more with a pistol before Tom came close enough to be sure they'd run Red Schaefer to ground. Unnerved by the full charge from two different directions, the fugitive dropped his empty pistol and rose to one knee to shoulder a rifle.

Apparently undecided about who to shoot at first, he swung on Jack who was closest and cranked off a round at the same time both Rangers' bullets found his chest from two directions, punching a pair of neat holes through a silk vest and his neckerchief. The carbine flipped away as Red collapsed with a gasp against the wall before rolling off and lying still.

The low wall was down in a few places, allowing the Rangers to easily rush through the openings. Pistols cocked and ready, they approached the still body as the gun smoke drifted away. From the curled position of the man's hands in the dirt, it was obvious he was dead.

Jack shook the spent rounds from his revolver and reloaded. He slipped it back into its holster. "This young man was no shot at all. Saved us a lot of trouble, though. I'll check on his horse."

"He was better than you think." Tom pointed at Jack's bloody side.

The surprised Ranger raised his shirt to find the bullet cut through the flesh of his waist. "It didn't even hurt until you said something. Now it's startin' to burn."

Tom examined his already bruising wound. Tiny yellow goblets of fat stuck out the seeping exit hole. "Went plumb through." He sniffed at the hole.

Knowing what he was doing, Jack swallowed. "Smell anything?"

"Nope. Didn't nick your guts, just what little fat you have on you."

Frowning, Jack twisted around to better see the damage from the back side. "Fat?"

"You're just gonna be sore for a while, though." Untying the red-head's silk scarf from around the dead man's neck, Tom put pressure on the wound and used his own scarf to tie the makeshift bandage around Jack's waist. "Looks like you'll live."

Relieved that the damage wasn't worse, Tom knelt and rolled the outlaw's body over to give his partner a moment to catch his breath. No matter how minor the wound, getting shot took something out of a man. This time, it took it all from the outlaw.

Jack rested one butt cheek on the wall and watched Tom pick up Schaefer's oiled Colt revolver. "Nineteen nine. Double action."

The .45 fit Tom's hand like a glove. "You want this pistol?"

"Naw." Jack's voice was a shade higher from being so close to death. "I have more than I need."

"This will be a fine one to keep in my bag, then." He tucked it under his belt and turned his attention to a rifle leaning against the wall. It was cared for as well. Not a speck of rust tarnished the barrel.

They must have surprised Red and relying on instinct, he drew the revolver instead of taking up the rifle. Tom figured the late Schaefer fancied himself a gunhand. Had he done the opposite, one or both of them might have died, if the man had the presence of mind to aim.

Tom studied the weapon for a long moment. "We're always out-gunned these days. I should have grabbed my rifle when we rolled out of the car, but it didn't occur to me until too late."

He looked down at the dead man. Schaefer died so quickly there was little blood, evidence that one of the slugs hit his heart.

"I think I'm gonna get me one of them drum-fed Thompsons and a Colt automatic pistol. At least a handgun like that's easy to reload in a hurry and I can lay down enough fire to get them off-balance."

"That'll only give you one more shot than a handgun, but since you were in the army, I guess you know that." Holding his side, Jack stood and glanced around. "I'll get his horse. It has to be around back of the house, or maybe inside."

"Can you walk all right?"

"It hit my side, not my leg." Jack made his slow way around the house.

Tom ignored Jack's surly comment since he'd been shot and shucked the live rounds out of the rifle's receiver. Picking them up, he slipped the bullets into one pocket and paused at the sight of a shovel laying nearby, obviously pitched aside when Schaefer finished digging up a bluish jar sitting upright on the ground. He studied the stacked fence, noting all the rocks were of similar color except for one that was about twelve inches above the hole.

The quart fruit jar had been wrapped in oilcloth to protect the contents and had been in the ground for years, proven by the circular imprint at the bottom of the hole.

Tom knelt and picked up the container as Jack came around, leading Schaefer's roan gelding and holding one hand against his bloodstained shirt.

"Damn this hurts. It feels like the time I cracked a rib when that gray mare pitched me off into a rail fence when I was a kid." Frowning in pain, Jack tied the reins to a well-established bridal wreath bush, likely planted there by the woman who tried to make a decent life for her family in the little house. "This is the first time I've ever been shot."

On one knee, Tom hefted the jar, checking its weight. "We've been lucky up to this point. Those bullets were close, and I suspect we'll suffer one or two more apiece if we keep at this job."

"I don't want to hear any talk like that. This one's bad enough." Wincing, Jack resumed his seat on the wall and planted his foot beside the hole. "What do you have there? Treasure, or corn liquor?" Despite the wound, he grinned at his own joke.

Crickets chirped from the damp bunchgrass around them as Tom unscrewed the rusty, gritty lid and frowned at the contents. For the first time in years he choked up. The lump in his throat might have been from how close they'd come to being killed, or jangling emotions. He didn't know and didn't care to study on it.

"You can call it that. It was treasure, I believe, to him." He carefully shook the contents onto the oilcloth that once protected them, probing at what a young redheaded boy with the given name of Fred Schaefer considered treasure.

Half a dozen glass marbles nestled against an old arrowhead knapped from flint, one silver dollar, and a large 1848 penny. A wooden button tied to the middle of a looped string was a common toy for children who pulled both ends and spun it fast enough to hum. Three polished deer antler points, an ivory cameo necklace, a metal soldier with all the paint flecked off, a turkey-bone call, a glass ambrotype of an old woman, and what he took to be a madstone.

The corner of Tom's mouth rose at the sight of a long, curved object almost four inches long he recognized as a coon's penis bone.

Jack frowned at the contents. "Wonder why he'd keep all that?"

Looking at his friend who seldom shared sentimental stories, Tom sighed. He picked up a small brass pocket compass. "This was a *kid's* treasure. The things he thought had value and made him happy." He opened it to see the needle was bent and stuck.

"I don't understand." Jack held his wound as he studied the items.

Tom did, though, because he valued the similar treasures resting in a San Antonio bank's safety deposit box. "Something happened to the boy who buried this little collection of memories and turned him."

"Something always happens to all of us as we grow up." Jack grimaced at the pain in his side. "We all learned to shoot, but he decided to rob and kill. The difference between the three of us is that he wanted to be like those dead bank robbers who tried to pull off that Cisco job a few years ago, while we went into law work."

"It don't seem like it could be as simple as that." Tom closed the compass with a quiet click. "Maybe if this compass hadn't broke, it would have led him down a better trail."

Replacing the contents, he rewrapped the jar and carefully put it back in the hole. Tom kicked the dirt and rocks over the top until he couldn't tell it had been dug up, then helped Jack load the outlaw's body over his own saddle to take him back. They had no intention of getting blood on the borrowed Model T's seats.

A sheen of greasy sweat on Jack's forehead stopped Tom Bell. Concern filled his eyes as he put a hand on his partner's shoulder. "You're hurt worse than you're letting on."

Jack grimaced. "I'm shot, and there ain't nothing we can do about it but go on and finish this job. It'll feel better when it quits hurting."

—New York Times *bestselling author Reavis Z. Wortham is the recipient of many awards, including two Spur Awards from the Western Writers of America and six Will Rogers Medallions. Kirkus Reviews listed his first novel in the historical Red River series,* The Rock Hole, *as one of their Top 12 Mysteries of 2011. Author of twenty novels, he also pens the Sonny Hawke contemporary Westerns, the Tucker Snow thrillers, and his newest Western horror series beginning with* Comancheria. *He and his wife, Shana, live somewhere in northeast Texas, but he doesn't even know the exact location from day to day. Visit his website at www.reaviszwortham.com.*

# CRAIG JOHNSON

## THE PERFECT A

### A WALT LONGMIRE STORY

*September 30, 1972*

I HUNG UP the phone and stared at the wall in the windowless office of the converted Carnegie Library that my new boss, Sheriff Lucian Connally, had assigned me, thinking more and more that it might be a converted broom closet. There was a curled and yellowed VFW calendar circa 1967 but no pictures on the wall because I wasn't sure I was going to stick with the job long enough to bother with it and, after the phone call I'd just hung up from—I wasn't sure I was going to be able to stick with being married, either.

I'd been a deputy less than a week when Lucian had handed off the payroll expense receipts for the department when the phone had rung. I'd told Martha that I would be home for dinner, but that was looking more and more unlikely, and the conversation with my new wife had kind of deteriorated from there.

The phone rang again, and I reached across the expanse of the battered surface of the surplus green metal desk and lifted the receiver with a great deal of relief. "Honey, I'm sorry...."

*"Excuse me?"*

I recognized the voice of Isaac Bloomfield, the chief and only resident over at Durant Memorial Hospital. I cleared my throat and tried again. "Absaroka County Sheriff's Department, Walt Longmire speaking."

There was a pause. *"Who?"*

With one week on the job, I had gotten used to that response. "Walt Longmire, the new deputy, Doctor Bloomfield. We met three days ago in the Emergency Room?" I nestled the receiver in the crook of my neck. "Can I help you?"

*"Is Lucian there?"*

I sighed, getting used to that response, too. "No, I'm afraid he's not—how can I help you?"

*"Well, there's a situation.... Um, Salvatore Ibarra was in town at the grocery store earlier today, and one of the cashiers mentioned to me that he'd had a spell while trying to carry his groceries out to his truck."*

"Ibarra, one of the shepherds for Extepare—interestingly enough, I've run into him twice this week." I scribbled down the name on a notepad, I'm not sure why, and then grumbled to myself. "What is he, like a hundred years old?"

There was the briefest of pauses. *"He's the same age as me."*

I cleared my throat. "Right."

*"They helped him get to his truck, but they called and said he was complaining of dizziness, chest pain, and discomfort in one of his arms."*

"Where is he now?"

*"I would assume back at his sheep camp up on the mountain."*

"Do you think he got back up there before the ice storm settled in?"

*"I don't know—it was very late in the afternoon when he was at the IGA."*

"So, you want me to go look for him?"

*"I hate to ask with the weather being the way it is, but I'm deeply concerned that he might've driven off the road or be lying on the ground somewhere near his camp."*

"I'll go take a look...."

*"One more thing?"*

"Yep?"

*"If you don't mind, I'd like to go with you."*

I thought about how much assistance the centenarian would be but kept my mouth shut—one of the many lessons I'd learned in the Marine Corps, one week in law enforcement, and a month or two of marriage. "I'll be by to pick you up in a minute."

I eased out of my tiny office and tromped down the steps past the painting of Andrew Carnegie and the photos of all the previous sheriffs of Absaroka County, thinking about the phone call with my wife and wondering if those men had faced the same problems as their newly minted deputy.

Probably.

Things just hadn't been going well between us lately, and it seemed as though everything we said or did lead to an argument. We had a baby on the way, money was tight, and neither of us was sure I'd made the right choice in taking the job or returning to Wyoming.

Pushing the front door open and then turning and locking it, I started down the steps and was immediately confronted with a world encased in ice. It was one of those invidious storms we all dreaded, a raw day just as September had ended and then a rain that turned into wind and a glaze of ice after the sun had abandoned us.

Cranking my hat down and making my way toward the tiny Bronco half-cab I'd been assigned, I slid on the veneer of parking lot ice like Sonja Henie. Grabbing hold of the side of the bed to save my life, I carefully groped my way around the tiny truck, locking the hubs on the front differential and then opening the door.

I fastened my seatbelt and started the small V-8, shifting the little truck into four-wheel drive, figuring to use any advantage I had in getting the thing to go in the direction I pointed it.

I thought about the man in question, thinking of the two times I'd seen Ibarra over the last week—a minor intersection fender bender, where when I arrived, he'd admitted to not having any insurance for but had nervously pulled out a wad of hundred-dollar bills the size of a Campbell's soup can from his pants pocket. He then peeled off bills until the man he'd crashed into was satisfied.

When he'd seen me staring wide-eyed at the cash, he'd explained that he didn't trust banks.

The other time was only two nights ago when Salvatore had been put out after the bars had closed and had decided to serenade the city of Durant with the Philip II aria from Don Carlo. I'd gotten out of my vehicle there on Main Street and stood listening as he hung onto a lamppost, the power of his bass voice vibrating the storefront windows. At the end, I'd applauded, and he'd bowed just before sliding down the post and passing out on the sidewalk. I'd loaded him into the bed of my truck like cargo and had driven him back to the office where I'd carried him in and placed him on the bench in the entryway under a blanket, just so he had known that he hadn't been arrested.

In the morning, Ibarra was mortified and offered to pay for any damages, but I'd waved him off and told him his performance had actually been pretty good and that I wasn't sure why anyone would've complained.

He'd mumbled something about some people perhaps not preferring Verdi and had apologized once again before going out the door—and that had been forty-eight hours ago.

Fortunately, there was no one else on the road to run into on the three blocks to the hospital, where Isaac stood under the portico of the emergency entrance, the picture of ridiculousness wrapped in a long raincoat, a hunter's cap with flaps up, galoshes, and holding an umbrella.

He walked out from the relative refuge of the covered area, opened my door, and climbed in, settling himself in the passenger seat. "Thank you for doing this, Deputy...?"

"Longmire." Pulling out, I drove carefully but could still feel the tires slipping on the glassy surface of the road as we headed west, gaining altitude. "Any idea where his grazing lease is?"

"Hunter Trailhead toward French Creek."

"That's pretty exact, Doctor. Did you speak with him recently?"

"No, but I've known him for quite some time."

Turning the first corner of the switchbacks going up the mountain, we felt the glissade as the utility vehicle, ignoring the direction I'd turned the wheel, continued sliding on the other side toward the guardrail and the thousand-foot drop-off. Gently pumping the brakes, I slid to a stop, spun the wheel farther, and started off again. "You mind if I ask how the chief resident of the hospital comes to be chummy with a Basque sheepherder?"

"We both play the violin."

I glanced at him.

"There was a recitation at the high school some years ago, and we sat next to each other and discovered we both played." His eyes stared through his thick glasses and the windshield into the night. "He plays very well—better than me, actually." He smiled to himself. "His occupation allows for a great deal more practice time than mine." The smile faded. "I received lessons as a child but then gave it up...."

"The war?" His turn to glance at me. "I don't mean to pry, but I saw the tattoo on the inside of your wrist."

He nodded and folded his hands in his lap. "Surprisingly, that's when I returned to it." His eyes went back to the windshield. "I was in a Nazi work camp, a slave camp really, where we assembled the components for V-2 rockets. Our camp commander took pride in having an ensemble, and when they discovered I could play, I was forced to join...."

"Sorry, I didn't mean to make you uncomfortable."

"No, no. It may have been the music that saved me." Placing a hand on the dash to brace himself as he turned. "Do you play any instruments?"

"I used to play piano but not for some time now."

"The war?"

I grinned back at him, shaking my head. "I guess so."

I took the cutoff toward Paradise Guest Ranch and was relieved to get off the pavement where we'd get a little more traction. I'd been careful to watch the roadsides, making sure Ibarra hadn't slid his aged International into the borrow ditch but hadn't seen anything in the frozen slush that might've indicated that he had.

"Are you all right, Deputy?"

I glanced at him again. "You can call me Walt."

"Walter. I like that name." He studied me. "I don't mean to pry, but you seem preoccupied."

"Oh, just some trouble with the wife."

"Ah."

"Ever married, Doc?"

"No, I never seemed to find the time." We rode along in silence, bouncing over the ruts until Isaac's expression became more wistful as he gazed at the dim light of the gauges recessed in the dash. "Ibarra actually had quite the correspondence with another famous musician."

"Who was that?"

"Toscanini."

I cut a glance at Bloomfield. "The conductor? The conductor?"

He nodded. "Indeed, the maestro himself."

"Arturo Toscanini, as in music director of La Scala in Milan, as in the Metropolitan Opera, as in director of the New York Philharmonic—*that* Arturo Toscanini?"

"Why, Walter, I think you've been hiding your light under a bushel." The doc also searched the sides of the road for any signs of the shepherd and his truck, finally breaking the silence with a question. "Did you know how he got his start?"

I took the turn at North Clear Creek and glanced up at the ice-encased lodgepole pines and laughed. "Toscanini, no—a little before my time, Doc."

"He was working with the orchestra of an opera company touring in South America, where they had hired a local conductor who proved to be inept. The show was only hours away, and in desperation, the company suggested the assistant chorus master. Without any conducting experience, he was convinced to take up the baton and led a two-and-a-half-hour performance of Aida entirely from memory. From what I'm to understand, his performance was astounding." The doc took off his glasses and took out a handkerchief in order to clean them. "He was nineteen years old."

Following the gravel road, I weaved between the great boulders and rock outcroppings as we drove ever upward. "Wasn't he beaten up by a bunch of Mussolini's thugs?"

"He was, at the Teatro Comunale in Bologna he refused to play the fascist anthem and was attacked by the Blackshirts. It was shortly thereafter that he left Europe and came to the United States for good."

"Kind of like you?"

"Somewhat." He sighed, guiding the glasses back onto his face. "The maestro was very open in his opposition to the Nazi persecution of my people all the way back in 1933 when he wrote Siegfried Wagner that he would not be conducting in a festival in Germany because the request had been made by an upstart politician—one Adolph Hitler."

Making the ridge, I turned right and followed Hunter Mesa Road. "Did they ever meet?"

"Toscanini and Hitler?"

"No, Ibarra and Toscanini."

He adjusted his glasses again, and the smile curled onto his face. "Once, but I'm sure only one of them would have remembered it. It was 1950, and the maestro was touring with his orchestra, and they happened to alight in Sun Valley, Idaho. Ibarra, a young man then, traveled all the way there and waited at the train station for four hours just to get a glimpse of the man."

"Did they get a chance to talk?"

"No, Salvatore said he was far too embarrassed to speak to him and simply watched as Toscanini waved to the crowd and then climbed into a motorcar and was swept away. He did say that when he waved back, Toscanini made eye contact with him. He said it was one of the most thrilling moments of his life."

Pulling to a stop where the road ended in a cattle guard, I could see the boxy outline of a battered truck shining with a thick coat of ice, where the door hung open and the headlight and running lights were on but growing dim. "Isn't that Ibarra's vehicle?"

Isaac peered through the darkness. "...Yes."

I cracked open the door, the ice covering the sheet metal splitting and falling like a cleaving glacier as I climbed out. Walking toward the truck, I reached in and turned off the ignition switch and the lights, then glanced at the bags on the floorboard. I looked across the hood at the doc who had followed me. "...The groceries are still in here."

We both moved toward the front, finding the barbed-wire fence that had stretched over the cattle guard still hooked at the bottom. Stepping over, I pulled out my flashlight and then stuck out a hand to help Bloomfield across the ice-coated pipes as we moved forward in the darkness of the lonely escarpment.

Nestled in the tree line, I could see the dim light of one of the sheep wagon's windows and the smell of a wood fire, probably from the stove inside.

Picking our way, we encountered a large number of sheep that parted in front of us only to re-cluster themselves as we passed. Once at the wagon, I placed a boot on the steps and rapped on the door with my glove-covered knuckles. "Mister Ibarra?"

There was no answer except for the tinny sound of a transistor radio softly buzzing with static. "Salvatore?"

With a final look at Isaac, I reached up and pressed the latch, allowing the door to slip open, revealing the soft, golden glow of a few candles and the tiny stove whose fire we'd been smelling.

At first, I'd thought the wagon was empty but could now see the aged shepherd lying in his bed, motionless, a motionlessness that I had grown to know from the battlefield.

Stepping up, I trailed a hand back and pulled Isaac into the wagon where we both stood for a moment looking at the man.

Quietly, the doc moved forward and retrieved the violin from Ibarra's one hand and then the bow from the other, ignoring the sheet music lying on the man's chest. Sitting on the edge of the bunk, he placed a few fingers at the Basque's throat. Still holding the violin and bow, he tucked Salvatore's arms under and then gently pulled the blanket over the man's peaceful but grizzled face.

I took off my hat and reached down, turning off the small transistor radio at the bedside, silencing the static. Out of habit, I glanced at the walls but could only see a small card that had been encased in a cheap, discount frame.

Reaching down, Isaac lifted the sheet music and studied it.

"What is it?"

"*Barber's Adagio for Strings*—it was one of Toscanini's world premieres and Salvatore's favorites."

I thought it odd that Bloomfield continued to mention the conductor and then watched as he turned the music toward him and did what seemed to be perfectly natural at that moment when he tucked the butt of the violin under his chin, positioning his fingers and carefully sliding the bow across the strings. The sound was one of desperate longing, a sadness so pure with a pathos that hung in the air with an enormity of soul and voice.

I'd never heard Ibarra play, but if he was better than Isaac then I doubt I could've withstood it. The tears slipped from the doc's eyes as he played with lengthened and loving strokes, the composition of passing that caused my breath to cut short.

Overcome, I reached out and steadied myself with a hand against the inside of the wagon, accidentally knocking loose an unnoticed piece of paper that had been tucked in the edge of the gilt frame. It fluttered like an autumn leaf, finally settling at the dead man's blanketed feet.

Reaching down, I picked it up and read the scribbled words on the brown paper, which was crumpled and aged.

> *Mr. Conductor: I have only two possessions—a radio and an old violin. The batteries in my radio are getting low and will soon die. My violin is so out of tune I can't use it. Please help me. Next Sunday when you begin your radio concert, sound a loud 'A' so I can tune my 'A' string; then I can tune the others. When my radio batteries are dead, I'll still have my violin.*
>
> *Salvatore Ibarra*

Isaac continued to play. Unable to help myself, I reached over and plucked the frame from the wall to discover a neatly typed response with a spiraling signature on the letterhead of the New York Philharmonic Orchestra in Carnegie Hall dated June 3rd, 1935.

*For a dear friend and listener back in the mountains of Wyoming, the orchestra will sound a perfect 'A' at the beginning of our next radio performance.*

*Arturo Toscanini*

Isaac continued to play as the deeply buried emotions were dislodged and carried away by the music, and by the time he finished I rubbed a thumb and forefinger across my own eyes. Overcome, I stepped to the door to find the hundred or so sheep now gathered around the doorway of the wagon, their faces uplifted in expectation as if the music had provided something beyond bereavement.

As Isaac finished, I watched as he once again took the glasses from his face, taking the handkerchief from his pocket and dabbing at his eyes. He rose, took the frame from my hands, and placed the ragged slip of paper back in the edge of the glass. He then rehung it on the wall and then stood there gazing at it, even going so far as to pat the tarnished frame.

He sighed, deeply. "You know, Walter, that's sometimes the way of things. Left to our own devices, we forget ourselves and fall out of tune, hopefully fearless enough to reach out somewhere to a higher power for that one note that will bring us back to an agreement within ourselves."

I watched as he carefully wrapped the music around the bow and then tucked it and the violin under his long coat, slipping past me and stepping down and out into the night without another word. He slowly walked toward my truck as the sheep made way like wet, wool waves, bleating, and then silently circling back and following him like a wake in a current.

Glancing around at the lonely confines of the tiny wagon, I thought of Salvatore Ibarra, the man who didn't trust banks and who had serenaded me while hanging onto a lamppost. A man who had devoted his life to such a solitary pursuit, spending so much of his existence in self-imposed isolation but who had found a concordance all those years ago through the kindness of a temperamental and exacting conductor and a Sunday afternoon radio program from a city far away.

I also like to think that it gave him a comfort and harmony in the last moments of his life, because that's simply the way of perfect notes, a resonance that never falters.

*—Craig Johnson is the* New York Times *bestselling author of the Walt Longmire mysteries, the basis for the hit Netflix original series,* Longmire. *He is a two-time recipient of the Western Writers of America Spur Award for fiction, multiple Will Rogers Medallion Awards, and his novella* Spirit of Steamboat *was the first One Book Wyoming selection. Craig is the 2025 recipient of the Owen Wister Award for Lifetime Contributions to Western Literature. He lives in Ucross, Wyoming. Population 26.*

# JOHN GILSTRAP

## DISTILLED CRAZY

DEPUTY UNITED STATES Marshal Ike Lincoln smelled the blood before he saw the body. He drew his Winchester Model 92 rifle from its scabbard near his right knee and laid it across his lap. Chambered in .44-40, the lever-action repeater could drop anything he might encounter. He carried it with the chamber loaded and the hammer on half-cock. Here in Indian Territory, most gunfights were settled with the first shot. There wasn't time to jack a round. For closer fights, he carried a Colt Bisley on his right hip and his issued Peacemaker in a cross-draw rig.

Ike clicked his tongue and Jefferson dutifully eased him up closer to the carnage.

The first body lay faceup at the edge of the tree line from which Ike and Jefferson were about to emerge. The corpse had the broad, hooked nose and narrow eyes of a Wycliffe. He also had a hole about the size of a silver dollar at the base of his throat—currently the feeding ground for flies. He imagined the hole to be the exit path carved by Deputy Walker Applebee's Sharps rifle.

The tree line marked the edge of a rise that afforded a clear view of the residence owned by Spiro Dodge, a Salina land speculator who'd agreed to shelter the Farmer boy until Ike could arrive and escort him to Muskogee to bear witness against the animal who'd murdered his parents.

Ike had suspected that word had gotten out about the boy's location, and he worried that the family might take action to silence the witness, but this carnage was of a different scale. Looked like Zeb Wycliffe had dispatched a whole branch of the family tree. At least three of them lay here as buzzard feed.

Judging from the damage done to the timber wall surrounding the house—the gray and white impact marks, the avulsed chunks of wood—there'd been a hell of a scuffle.

"Let's stay still and quiet for a spell," Ike whispered to Jefferson. The Texas quarter horse had a knack for knowing when a fight was coming or when there'd been one. Talking seemed to keep the beast relaxed. Ike pulled a telescope from his pommel bag and checked to make sure the sun was behind him before expanding it to better survey what lay ahead. He didn't want a flare from the glass to startle the defenders.

Spiro Dodge knew what he was doing when he built his log house. It sat high on its foundation so that its heavily shuttered window could provide an unobstructed field of fire from the interior. There'd been a heavy attempt to breach the main gate, as indicated by splintered wood, a corpse, and what appeared to be a battering ram.

Ike returned the telescope to its rightful place then reached behind to pull a spare kerchief out of his saddlebag. It was green.

"Because I don't have no white kerchiefs," he explained in case Jefferson was wondering. Ike tied the cloth around the muzzle of the Winchester. "If that's the difference that gets us killed, then we weren't meant to live in the first place."

Jefferson huffed.

"You're right. I shouldn't speak for the both of us." Ike settled himself with a deep breath, held the rifle aloft like a flag and gave Jefferson's withers a squeeze.

"It's Marshal Ike!" he yelled as he emerged into view. "I'm coming for the Farmer boy! Takin' him off your hands!"

Grateful not to hear any gunshots, he yelled again. "It's Marshal Ike!" He avoided using his last name on official business with strangers. While the War of the Rebellion was nearly forty years past on the calendar, it was just yesterday to a lot of folks out here in Indian Territory. Having the name Lincoln could sometimes cause a problem.

"If there's anybody hearing me, I'd appreciate you letting me know!" Ike said. "Walker Applebee, ain't you in there? Don't I recognize your handiwork on the top of the hill?"

"You look strange with that green flag," a familiar voice called from behind the gate. Applebee.

"Don't I know it!" Ike lowered the rifle and pulled off the rag.

"Reminds me of a whore I knew in St. Louis," Applebee said.

"If that's what I remind you of, then either she was ugly or you need glasses."

Jefferson stepped carefully across the open space, clearly aware of the bodies, but not spooked by them. Ike heard the throw of a heavy bolt and the gate in the timber wall swung open to reveal Walker Applebee. He looked a decade older than his thirty years, and older still, stained and smudged as he was with powder smoke.

"Looks like a mighty fight," Ike said.

"Mighty and more," Applebee said. "They's good fighters. Brave. Well, brave then stupid." He gestured with both arms at the bodies. "There's another one out back."

Applebee stepped aside to allow Ike and Jefferson through and then he closed the gate behind them. "Got fresh water in the trough."

Ike kept his rifle as he dismounted, and he gave the horse a light pat. "Where there's water, Jefferson will find it." He gave Applebee a stern look. "How did your side do in the fight?"

"Everybody's fine. Weary from the effort, but overall, we're good."

"And the Farmer boy?"

"He's tough for fifteen," Applebee said. He nodded toward the door and started to lead the way inside.

"Was he in the fight?" Ike asked.

"Wanted to be. We didn't have enough rifles to go around."

The interior of the house was dark, hot, and still. It smelled of sweat and a dirty chimney.

"How about we open the shutters?" Ike said. "Get the air moving."

He didn't wait for an answer but rather threw the locking bars on two of the windows and opened them himself. Instant relief.

With the new light, he saw three people in the crowd. All of them looked dirty and tired from the fight.

"I'm Marshal Ike Lincoln. Which one of you is Tommy Farmer?"

"Here." The voice belonged to a young man who was not the kid that Ike had been expecting. "Do you have an extra gun? Because I'm tired of being shot at and not shooting back." He looked two sizes too skinny for the ridiculous red-and-white striped shirt that drooped off his shoulders.

"Good morning to you, too. What is that you're wearing?"

"They call it fashion in parts of the world that aren't here," Tommy said. "This wasn't how I was planning to spend my night."

"That's true for all of us," said a tall cowboy in the corner with a crooked smile.

"This is Spiro Dodge," Applebee said. "The owner and my other gun. He heard there might be trouble and he offered to help."

Dodge gave a little wave and then stood. "Don't make me sound like a hero, Marshal. I rise to any opportunity to settle a score with a Wycliffe. If I can kill a couple and not get prosecuted for it, I call that a good day. Them sonsabitches are a cancer." He walked across the room to the door. "But now I must retrieve a very angry wife from the parsonage. These battle scars on our home will leave her unhappy."

Ike smiled. He knew more about angry women than he cared to. "So, it was just you two in the fight last night?"

"That's all I could round up," Applebee said. "And I was grateful for the help."

"What exactly is going on?" Dodge asked.

"Yeah," Tommy said. "Zeb Wycliffe killed my folks two years ago."

"They just caught him," Ike explained. "Now they need your testimony to put him away, and I am here to escort you to the court to do just that."

"That's thirty miles," Applebee said. He looked at Tommy. "You ever ridden thirty miles in a day?"

"If you can do it, I can do it."

That was good enough for Ike because there was no other choice. "How many Wycliffes got away after last night's attack?"

"Most," Applebee said. "At least seven or eight. I was too busy shooting to count."

Ike scowled and walked to the window. "They know what we need to do and where we need to go."

"You thinking there's gonna be a trap?"

"That's what I'd do," Ike said. This time, they both looked at Tommy.

The kid stood. "I want a rifle."

THEY NEEDED TO push through forty miles of unsettled territory to get to Muskogee, crossing from the Cherokee Nation into the Creek Nation. They traveled in a line, separated by twenty or thirty feet. Ike took the lead with Tommy in the middle.

They'd scrounged a Henry repeater off one of the corpses for Tommy, who seemed a little too anxious to have it, but given what likely lay ahead, Ike couldn't think of a reason to say no. If they stumbled into the ambush he anticipated, any extra firepower would be welcome.

Ike kept them to the woods as best he could, avoiding open spaces that would make them enticing targets. He'd considered following the tracks of the retreating attackers but dismissed the idea. The mission today was strictly about the safe delivery of Tommy Farmer to Muskogee. There'd be no attempt to track down and arrest the Wycliffes. That would be a mission for another day.

Ike raised a hand to draw the short column to a halt as they approached a natural draw that marked the beginning of a five-mile-long wooded canyon that rose above Little Sabine Creek. He waited for the others to form up around him.

Ike explained, "There are four homesteads over the course of the next five miles. If I was going to set a trap, this is where I would do it."

"Then why are we going this way?" Tommy asked.

"Because the hillsides are too steep," Applebee said. "I got no idea who lives in the cabins and shanties along the creek. We're gonna be in the wide open for a long time. For a few men with rifles, we'll be like a shooting gallery at a sideshow."

Ike had traveled this route just hours before. "It ain't all dour," he said. "Every one of them homesteads is on the west side of the creek, and they're spaced a mile or more apart. They're farming good bottom land. If we stay on the east side of the creek as close to the trees as we can, that'll give us as much as three hundred yards separation."

"Not that hard a shot," Applebee said.

"But not a cakewalk, either," Ike said. "And to make it even harder, I want us to cover the half mile that runs in front of the cabins at a full gallop. We keep a wide separation—at least five seconds between us."

Tommy shifted in his saddle, resting the butt of his Henry on his thigh, the muzzle pointing to the sky. "Am I hearing you right, Marshal? If those murderers start shooting at us—shooting at you, officers of the law—we're just going to ride off and let them live to shoot again?"

Ike said, "You heard the plan, Tommy. I expect you to follow it. Look at me."

Tommy pivoted his head to lock eyes with Ike, and the marshal saw something in that expression that chilled him. A hardness.

Ike leveled a finger at his nose as if it were a pistol. "Do not cross me, young man."

Tommy looked like he needed to say something in retort but Ike didn't want to hear it. "Here we go."

Ten minutes later, they rode up on the first clearing. Of all of the potential kill zones, this was the one that Ike was most worried about. This cabin sat closest to the stream, and the area between the front door and the streambed had been cleared for chickens and pigs.

"That is one pretty field of fire, Ike," Applebee said. "Almost looks like they designed it as such."

"You think the Wycliffes own it?" Tommy asked.

"No," Ike said. "But that doesn't mean they won't take possession of it for a day."

Tommy asked, "Do you think they're watching us?"

Ike answered, "I think that if this is the place where they set up a trap, then there's a good chance they've got a spyglass on us."

"Then I think we should go," Tommy said.

Ike cautioned, "Remember the plan. I'll run across first, then Tommy, then, Walker, you bring up the rear. Do not slow, do not return fire if fired upon. Our goal is to pass unscathed and get out of range. Are we clear?"

Nods all around.

Somehow, Jefferson knew in advance what was expected of him. As soon as Ike wheeled the horse around, he took off. Ike leaned in close to his saddle, presenting as low a profile as he could. He wasn't sixty yards into his sprint when he heard the sound of the first gunshot. It was deep and throaty, definitely a rifle. A second later, another, and then came the fusillade he was expecting.

He pressed lower into his saddle until the horn was against his stomach. Jefferson found more speed.

Without moving his shoulders, he dared a glance to his right, and he saw the muzzle flashes and clouds of white gun smoke launching not just from the house, but from an outbuilding on its left and maybe from a hay pile that had been pressed up against a fence only seventy-five yards from the edge of the water.

The haze of black powder smoke concealed the images of the individual shooters, but it was clear to Ike that his little posse was outnumbered. So far, he'd heard no whiz of a passing bullet, and he'd heard no cries from behind as others were hit.

"Hey! Tommy!" That was Applebee's voice. "Ike!"

Ike wheeled Jefferson to the right, not daring to present a stationary target. Tommy Farmer had pulled out of line and was charging straight into the ambush.

"Stop, goddammit!" Ike yelled, but either the kid didn't hear or he didn't care.

Tommy was standing in his stirrups, cranking the lever of his Henry and firing over his horse's head as he charged into certain death.

"Damn it to hell!" Ike cried to no one as he pulled his Winchester from it scabbard, cranked the hammer back, and kicked Jefferson into his war charge. Honest to God, this horse knew no fear.

And honest to God, that thing Tommy was doing was the bravest feat Ike had ever seen. But it was also stupid. The chance of hitting anyone from an unstable moving platform like that was close to zero.

Stupidity aside, it was Ike's job to not let him die.

As Tommy charged the center, Ike headed to the left, toward the shooters' right flank, intent on getting behind them.

Time slowed down in moments like these, and Ike had stayed alive by noticing details. Tommy somehow knew not to charge forward in a straight line, but rather to dodge left and right, but as the distance closed, the boy disappeared into the opaque cloud of gun smoke that clung to the ground.

No one paid attention to Ike and Jefferson as they raced past the right flank to move in behind Wycliffes along the fence line. He reined the horse to a stop and dismounted, taking his rifle with him.

"I'll take the outbuilding," Applebee said as he galloped past.

Ike gave Jefferson a good swat to encourage him to find a way out of the fight. He wouldn't wander far.

From the way the Wycliffes were shooting from the fence line, it seemed clear that they hadn't yet hit Tommy. Inside the house, the shooting had settled down, probably because they could no longer discern friend from foe through the smoke.

Ike ran toward the fence, in the open but staying low as he advanced on a pigpen with low rails that would provide some concealment but wouldn't do a thing to slow a bullet. He needed a target to shoot, and he needed to know that the target wasn't Tommy.

Crouched beside the pen, doing his best to ignore the pig stench, Ike pressed his Winchester into his shoulder and aimed down the fence line. Sooner or later....

For an instant, a breeze cleared the acrid cloud of smoke and he could see a Wycliffe shooter not fifty feet away, and another beyond him by another twenty. Then he saw a flash of Tommy's ridiculous shirt galloping along to his right. Best he could tell, he was racing circles in front of the shooters, taunting and firing and betting his life that God somehow favored him over the others.

Ike saw his opportunity. He settled his front sight just below the ear of that closest shooter and squeezed the trigger, launching a plug of lead clean through the shooter's head, erupting in a cloud of gore.

He racked his lever for a second round and fired at the center of the second man's belly. He thought he hit him, but he wasn't sure because Ike was already on the move. He'd just declared his location to however many Wycliffes wanted him dead, and this was no longer the place to be.

The closest window at the front of the cabin proved him right as two guns opened fire on him, their bullets chewing up the rails of the pigpen where he'd just been.

Ike crossed in front of the cabin, ducking low and cutting right, sprinting toward the fence, to catch the Wycliffe shooters from behind.

"Tommy!" he shouted. "Stop shooting! I'm in your line of fire." He had no idea if Tommy heard him, but at least one Wycliffe did. He turned from the fence and emerged from the gun smoke, searching for the source of the voice he'd heard. By the time he made eye contact, Ike's bullet was already on its way to his heart.

Ike was among the enemy now, and he didn't know how many there were.

"Tommy, do not shoot at me!"

"Watch out, Marshal!"

Tommy Farmer let out a war whoop as he galloped his horse straight at the fence, not ten feet in front of him and cleared it in an easy leap. "There's two more down there on the left in front of you. They won't be no trouble."

"Ride the hell out of here!" Ike commanded.

"The hell I will!" Tommy shouted. "Not as long as there's killers to kill." He pulled his horse to the left, but the animal didn't respond. It stumbled once, then collapsed, dead, spilling Tommy onto the ground. He sat there, looking confused.

Ike grabbed Tommy by his stupid, oversized striped shirt and dragged the kid along the ground as he scrabbled on his hands and knees trying to keep up. They found decent concealment behind another pen as every gun in the cabin tried to take them out.

"Good God, Tommy, have you lost your mind? What were you thinking? I told you—" He looked at the boy's empty hands. "Where's your rifle?"

Tommy stared back at the dead horse, where his Henry repeater lay where he'd dropped it.

"Shit," Ike said. He needed a plan. It was his guess that all the Wycliffes outside the house were dead, but that still left an unknown number of fighters inside.

"Why did they stop shooting?" Tommy asked.

"Probably because they can't see us. I wonder if there's a way to just sneak out of here."

"I'm getting my gun back," Tommy said.

Before Ike could respond, Tommy bolted out from behind their cover and sprinted back toward his fallen horse.

Instantly, the windows erupted with muzzle flashes.

Ike rose to his knees and cranked six rounds into those windows to keep the shooters' heads down and give Tommy a chance to live. Stupid kid was going to bleed him dry of ammo.

As bullets churned up dirt around him, Tommy stumbled and ran and tumbled toward the front wall of the cabin, finally throwing himself at the base of the stacked logs, between the two windows.

In his arms, he cradled his rescued Henry. His chest heaving for breath, he gave Ike a huge smile.

"Kid belongs in an asylum," Ike muttered.

*What the hell were they going to do now?* Ike wondered. Tommy was in a pretty safe position for the time being. He was too close to shoot, and Ike would shoot anyone who leaned out far enough to try to shoot Tommy. They were at a stalemate, but it couldn't last.

Movement along the right-hand side of the house drew Ike's attention to Applebee, who had worked his way to the front corner from the rear. He'd dismounted and he held his Sharps with the muzzle up, his finger poised near the trigger guard. When he knew he had Ike's eye, he motioned with his hand to ask if it was clear to cross the distance.

Ike scanned the windows over his front sight and motioned with his hand for Applebee to scurry over.

Applebee made it without drawing a shot. "Sounds like I missed the real action. The guy in the outbuilding is dead."

Ike motioned with his forehead to the front of the cabin.

"What the hell is Tommy doing up there?" Applebee asked through a snort.

"That's what insanity looks like. That is one crazy young man."

"He's in a pickle, I'll give you that."

Tommy waved to get their attention. He raised a finger.

"What is he—"

With the speed of a rattler, Tommy rose to his feet, poked his rifle through the window into the cabin, fired, and sat on his haunches. He levered out the spent casing then did it again.

Shouting and cussing erupted from inside the building.

"What did I just see?" Applebee asked.

"I'm tellin' you. That is pure distilled crazy. Tell me what you saw on the back side of the house?"

"There's no back door. There's windows back there, but they're boarded up. I guess we could get in if we had to, but not without announcing our intentions first."

Tommy rose and pulled the same rifle trick, but poking it through the other window.

"They're gonna be waiting if he does that again," Applebee said. "Gonna get his head blown off."

"I dunno," Ike said. "Kid's got a guardian angel."

"And I don't know why I'm complaining," Applebee said. "If he gets his head blown off, we got less reason to stay."

"Ain't you the cheerful one? You got an idea?"

"Yeah. We shoot the kid and call it a day."

Ike glared.

"I'm joking," Applebee said. "Well, mostly."

Tommy started bouncing on his haunches.

"Uh-oh, here we go again," Ike said.

This time, Tommy rose to his full height and exposed his full silhouette in the window frame to fire his rifle twice. Someone yelled and return fire knocked chunks out of the top and left-hand side of the window frame.

"Is he trying to get himself killed?" Ike asked.

On his haunches again, with his back against the wall, he grinned back at the marshals.

"Got a plan?" Ike asked.

"My plan is that that asshole never should have gotten us into this."

"What's another one?"

Applebee scowled. "We could smoke 'em out. Plug up their chimney."

"They're already thinking ahead of us," Ike said, pointing. "Look. There's no smoke. As crazy as it sounds, I think we need to join him up there."

"Oh, hell no," Applebee said. "Let him commit his own suicide."

"I can't think of anything better."

"So, you want us to go up there and join him up against that wall?" Applebee said. He seemed appalled. "What do we do then?"

Ike winked. "I'll tell you when we get there."

"How likely is it I'm going to die?"

"About as likely as staying here."

"Shit."

Ike smiled. "We'll wait till Tommy does his next parlor trick, and then we'll move."

They didn't have to wait long. This time it was the same window. As Tommy rose, Ike and Applebee made their sprint to the front wall and slid into place. They sat shoulder to shoulder under the windows, Tommy on the left, Applebee on the right.

"Meaning no disrespect, Marshal," Tommy said, "but wasn't that a stupid thing to do?"

"Son, you have no idea how close I am to killing you right now."

"You mentioned a plan," Applebee reminded.

"Right." Ike winced against the words he was about to utter. Barely above a whisper, he said, "We're all gonna do what Tommy just did."

"The hell we are," Applebee said.

Ike nodded. "Exactly." To Tommy: "How many did you kill in there?"

"I don't know how many I killed. Maybe none. But I know I hit at least four."

"How many are in there?" Applebee asked.

Tommy shrugged. "I was a little distracted."

"More than what you shot?"

Another shrug. "Dunno."

Through the open windows, the sounds of suffering were evident. Moans and curses.

"The ones that ain't hurt are gonna be tending to the ones that are," Ike said. "That's a break for us."

Applebee glared at Tommy. "Ain't none of this a break for us. We coulda been a mile and a half past here if he hadn't been stupid."

"And you'd be lookin' over your shoulder every step," Tommy said. "C'mon. Admit it. This is exciting."

Ike put his hand across Applebee's chest to keep him from tearing the kid's head off. "Don't," he said. "We're not done here yet." He turned his head. "That Sharps isn't gonna be much use to you in there, Walker."

"Really, Ike? Now you're gonna tell me how to do my job?" The Sharps was a fine rifle for long distances, but it was a slow loader. He laid the long gun on the porch and drew his Colt revolver. "Let's get on with it." His words sounded nearly like a sigh.

Ike said, "Listen, Tommy, you and me will shoot through that window—" He pointed to the opening on the left, above the kid's head. "—and Walker, that one's yours. Aimed shots if you can. Ready?"

"No," Applebee said. Then, "Yeah."

"Just say the word, Marshal." Tommy looked like a puppy with a treat.

"On three," Ike whispered. "One... Two...."

Tommy couldn't hold for the count. Halfway between two and

three he leaped to his full height and fired two shots into the window before Ike or Applebee could even take aim.

Return fire chewed at the wall, but it wasn't close. Ike saw a muzzle flash. As he took aim at it, movement from Tommy pushed him aside. "I'll take care of it, Marshal Ike," he said.

Then he launched himself headfirst through the window into the room.

"God damn it!" Ike yelled. Truth be told, he didn't know if his anger came from the fact that Tommy refused to obey orders, or that he'd just put Ike into the position that he had to climb through the window, too.

"You can always let him die," Applebee said.

"Let him die, my ass. I want to stand behind him." The kid was untouchable.

Ike's entry was ugly, but it was fast and it got him inside. Leading with his rifle, he put his belly on the sill and rolled over to hit the floor. The transition from the bright sunlight to the dimness of the cabin interior blinded him, so he made a point of crouching in the shadows until his vision cleared.

The air stank of gun smoke and blood. He hadn't heard another shot since he'd entered—or since Tommy had entered. From this vantage point, the cabin appeared to have three rooms—a big parlor and kitchen that spanned the width of the house—that's where he was now—and two rooms in the back, each identifiable by a closed door.

"United States Marshal!" Ike shouted. "Surrender yourselves. Come forward with—"

A rifle boomed from Ike's right and Tommy darted across the room from left to right, firing three more times in the same direction, at the same point on the floor.

"Oh, yeah, Marshal Ike. He's dead for sure."

Ike took in the scene around him. All told, he counted five bodies, four men and one woman. All of them had rifles at their sides. The plank floor shimmered with rivulets of blood.

"You think there's any more?" Tommy asked.

"You might want to look in those back rooms," Applebee said.

Ike shot him a look.

Applebee shrugged. "Why not?"

Tommy darted toward the door on the left.

"Wait!" Ike shouted. He left his rifle on the ground and rose to his feet, Bisley in his right hand, Peacemaker in his left. Inside the house, the rifle barrel was too long to maneuver the tight corners for clearing rooms.

But Tommy didn't wait. Maybe he didn't hear. Holding his Henry high and parallel to the floor he raced to the door on the left and pulled it open to reveal a boy about Tommy's age, only with a little more meat on his bones and barefoot. He held a Navy Colt revolver in both hands, and he was pressed up against the back wall, in the corner between a bed and a chifforobe.

Tommy pulled his trigger and clicked empty. His eyes grew wide with realization as the other kid's face bloomed in a smile. Ike didn't have a shot because Tommy was in the way.

He holstered the Bisley to free his right hand and grabbed Tommy by the back of his collar to throw him to the ground.

Ike whirled on the kid in the corner and was half a trigger pull away from killing him when the Navy Colt likewise clicked on an empty cylinder.

Ike broke his aim and pointed his revolver at the ceiling.

"I almost killed you!" he yelled.

The kid worked the hammer, trying to take another shot. Ike closed the distance in two strides and brought the barrel of his Peacemaker down across the kid's wrist with enough force that he thought maybe he broke the bone. The kid howled as his Navy Colt skittered across the floor.

"The other room is empty!" That came from Applebee.

"You broke my wrist!" the boy yelled.

Ike nodded. "Maybe. Have a seat." He nodded to the edge of the bed.

The kid sat.

"I'll get a rope," Tommy said.

"You're not doing anything," Ike said. "If I see a rope in your hand, I'm gonna hang you with it. What's your name, son?"

"Harley Wycliffe."

"How old are you?"

"Fourteen."

Ike looked at Harley's arm. It was swelling up quickly, but he saw no obvious break. "You're going to want to have that looked at by a doctor."

Harley fought tears. "You killed my family."

Ike patted his leg and stood. There was nothing to say. "Marshal!"

"Here." Ike appeared in the doorway.

"Do me a favor. Talk with young Harley here and get the names of all the corpses, will you?"

"Is he coming with us?"

"No."

"Wait!" Tommy said. "Ain't he under arrest?"

"For what? Hiding in a bedroom?"

"He was going to shoot me," Tommy said.

"Because you were going to shoot him!" Ike shouted. He felt his temper slipping.

Tommy wasn't done. "It ain't right that—"

Ike shoved him. Hard. He slammed into the wall, the back of his head thudding against the timber.

"Hey!"

Ike grabbed him by the front of his ridiculous shirt, pulled him close, and then shoved him again, this time through the door and out into the main room, where Tommy tumbled over his feet and landed in the blood smear flowing from one of the victims.

From behind, Applebee said, "Marshal Ike, you okay?"

"Mind your own," Ike said. "Do your job."

Ike strode toward Tommy, who'd turned to be on his butt, his knees up, his arms braced behind him. "What is wrong with you?"

Ike grabbed the front of the shirt again. This time, the button panel ripped and as the fabric pulled tight, Tommy raised his arms to be free of the shirt altogether.

Ike crossed the room, stepping over two bodies, to get to the front door, where he lifted a heavy locking bar out of its mounts and pulled it open.

"Get up," Ike said.

Tommy recoiled. "Have you gone crazy?"

Ike was having none of it. He stomped back over to Tommy and grabbed him by the back of his belt and his armpit.

Tommy tried to wriggle free. "Let go of me!"

Ike slapped him with an open hand. It was a slap for a petulant child, and as hard as he'd ever slapped anyone. For an instant, he saw the light flicker in the kid's eyes as he nearly lost consciousness. Ike took it as his opportunity to drag him into the sunlight, where he dropped him face down in the dirt.

Ten seconds later, Tommy jumped up, ready for a fight. He planted his feet and lifted both fists. "Marshal, I don't want to hurt you."

Ike took a breath and cocked his head. "You do whatever you think is best."

Tommy lowered his hands, then put them on his hips. "Why are you so ornery? We won!"

"Is that what you think?" Ike asked. "Is that really what you think?"

Tommy gaped. He clearly didn't know what to say.

"Look around," Ike said. "What do you see?"

Now that the smoke had lifted and the danger was gone and the sun was higher, the cabin's front yard looked like a battlefield. Four people that he could see, and maybe more lay sprawled in the grass and in the dirt. Overhead, the vultures had already begun to circle.

"I see dead Wycliffes. That's what I mean. We won."

"We won a fight that wasn't supposed to be fought," Ike said. He worked hard to keep his tone soft, his words measured. "You were supposed to ride past and not engage. If you'd done as I told you, these people would all be alive."

"They shot at you!"

"I'm trying very hard to talk myself out of charging you with manslaughter."

Tommy took two steps back. "You've got to be kidding. You killed people, too! Are you going to charge yourself?"

Ike stared. He didn't know how to formulate a response.

"They were just going to chase us down if we didn't engage them here," Tommy said. "This is what made more sense."

Ike brought his fingers to his head and rubbed his temples. This was going to be a very, very long day. "We don't know that," he said. "You can't kill people because—"

A gunshot exploded behind Ike at the same instant that a bullet hole pocked Tommy's right chest and his knees folded.

Ike stooped and whirled, drawing and cocking his Bisley.

Harley Wycliffe stood in the doorway of the cabin struggling with the lever of Ike's Winchester to chamber a second round.

"Oh, shit, Harley, don't—"

The boy got the bolt closed and started to raise the rifle when he was shot from behind. He pitched face forward onto the porch and an instant later Applebee appeared in the doorway, service revolver in his hand.

"Are you okay, Ike?"

Ike scooted over to Tommy, who lay flat on his back, eyes wide open despite the brightness of the sun. The chest wound was bad. Mortal. Little bigger than a pencil in the front, the flow of blood onto the ground told the real story.

"Am I dead?" Tommy wheezed through a liquid gurgle.

Ike took his hand. "Soon."

"Was it the boy in the bedroom?"

Ike couldn't bring himself to say it.

Tommy scoffed and launched bloody air bubbles from his chest. "Ow. The kid you wouldn't let me kill."

"Yeah," Ike said.

"Is he dead anyway?"

Ike nodded.

"Then this seems so unnecessary."

Tommy's pupils dilated wide. His grasp and features went slack. He was gone. Ike stood, holstering the pistol he didn't realize he'd still been holding.

"Damn crazy kid," Applebee said as he approached from the door. He carried Ike's Winchester. "I figure you'll want this back."

Ike took the rifle, looked at it, then looked up at Applebee. "Walker, what did you do?"

Applebee seemed amused by the question. "What do you mean?"

"How did Harley Wycliffe get his hands on my rifle?"

Applebee shrugged, held up his hands. "I guess maybe I got too caught up in gathering names from the bodies, and—"

"I told you to get their names from Harley."

"Oh, you did, didn't you? That's right. I decided to search their pockets and belongings first. I guess I looked away. The kid found your rifle under the window and—"

"How did you know my rifle was under the window?" Ike asked. "You were still outside the other window when I put it there."

"What do you mean? It was where it was."

"It was in the shadows, hard to find."

Applebee's demeanor changed. "Say what it is that you're afraid to say, Ike."

Ike couldn't say it, and they both knew it. Fear had nothing to do with it. Some words, some thoughts, some facts known between men need never be articulated. Especially when the words make allegations that could never be proved.

"Thank you for not letting young Harley shoot me, too," Ike said.

"I never woulda let that happen," Applebee said. "But I can't say I'm sorry to see that crazy son of a bitch Tommy Farmer dead. Anybody that puts me in that much danger on purpose deserves a spot in the ground."

Ike glared.

"Good news for Zeb Wycliffe, though, right?" Applebee said. "With no witness, he'll be a free man."

"Yeah, but he won't live long," Ike said. "When word gets out about all this, he'll come for us. He'll either die in that gunfight or after the trial that follows."

*—John Gilstrap is the award-winning,* New York Times *bestselling author*

*of over two dozen thrillers, including* Burned Bridges, *the first book in his new series featuring retired FBI Director Irene Rivers, plus* Zero Sum *and sixteen additional books in his acclaimed Jonathan Grave thriller series and half a dozen standalones. His nonfiction book,* Six Minutes to Freedom *is currently under development to become a feature film by Netflix. In addition, John has written four screenplays for Hollywood, adapting the works of Nelson DeMille, Norman McLean, and Thomas Harris. A frequent speaker at literary events, John also teaches seminars on suspense writing techniques at a wide variety of venues, from local libraries to the Smithsonian Institution. Outside of his writing life, John is a renowned safety expert with extensive knowledge of explosives, hazardous materials, and fire behavior. John lives in Fairfax, Virginia. Please visit his website at johngilstrap.com*

# KATHLEEN O'NEAL GEAR

## DYING ALIVE

THE HOLLOW THUMPS of distant explosions provide a velvet background to the sharp grating of my combat boots on gravel. Somewhere out there in the darkness a dog erupts in hysterical barks, and a little boy sobs.

I force myself to unclench my teeth. God, I hurt. The adrenaline is long gone. All that remains is the memory of screams and the stench of burning chemicals. Was the hospital bombed? Where is everyone else? Were they all killed when the building crashed down around us? I remember white walls exploding. I remember crawling out of the ruins.

As I walk, I try to focus. My movements have a strange surreal quality, as though I'm in shock, or dazed by a blow to the head. Soft voices float through the air. A few words are shouted, *Say again, say again.*

The endless night spins in strange smoky tornadoes as helicopters pass overhead.

*...bogeys... closing fast... get out, get out.*

That's Colonel Belden. Where is he? He may be standing right on top of me, and I can't see him because I'm actually still buried in the rubble, or my eyes were fried in a chemical attack.

I've seen that happen. Blind people wandering the streets, crying for help. Where was that? Outside of Saigon?

Dear God, I don't want to be blind.

On the other hand, there are a lot of things I never want to see again. I never want to pull bodies from a bombed-out building or stumble over small heads scavenged by dogs.

From out of nowhere, someone grips my shoulder hard, then the room fills with the odor of garbage smoldering in gutted buildings... or maybe furniture, old carpet? Am I still in Vietnam? Maybe I'm home. Maybe my house is burning to the ground around me.

A shout blasts through the roar of flames... fucking coward.

That voice must be coming from the other end of the galaxy. It's tinny and makes me feel like I have a stomach full of dynamite.

Another man shouts, "Dear God, pull her out of there!"

I'm just reliving the war, right? I came home. People with flags met me at the airport as I helped carry Jonny's coffin down the ramp. So... flashback? That must be why the pain is so intense. It always is when I relive the nightmares. My seared skin feels like it's being raked by electrified fangs.

"Where's the goddamned gurney?" the man yells.

I feel myself moving through the gauzy blackness and into a brilliantly lit room. What a relief. My eyes can perceive light. Maybe my blindness is temporary.

The smoke is gone, and the cool wind carries the scent of wet pines, but dear God it hurts to breathe. Float. Just float here and try to get air. When the room begins to move, thrusting me backward, it startles me. A vehicle. Where am I going? The Naval Station Hospital in Da Nang? I'm so scared I pee my pants, not caring about the pungent odor.

Rough hands flip me over, wrap me in a blanket. Maybe bandages. Voices suddenly come at me from all sides.

"Stay with me now! Can you hear me?"

Water thunders, splashes me like acid. Firehose? Am I on fire? Are they trying to put out flames?

"Have they found her husband yet?" a woman shouts.

"No, the police are still looking for him."

That startles me. I don't remember a husband. How could I forget something like that? There's a lot of noise. I need to listen harder to separate words from the cacophony. They may not be talking about me.

Metal doors slam, then I'm rocking and rolling, going fast with a siren wailing.

A woman says, "My god, look at the charring. She must be in unbelievable pain. It's a miracle she's alive."

"No way she's conscious. She's not feeling a thing, but in a few hours it's going to be agony," a man responds. "If she makes it that long."

I try to shout to tell them I am conscious but can't get the air to do it. Are they field medics? EMTs? If I'm home in America, I don't have to be afraid. No matter what happened to me, there are people who care about me. I have family in New Mexico. How can I remember that and not recall that I have a husband? Do we have children? Shouldn't I remember giving birth or hearing a child's laughter?

As if in response, that little boy starts sobbing again, but the dog has stopped barking. Probably clubbed by some irritated soldier.

"I guess he's the prime suspect."

"The husband is always the prime suspect."

If I had eyes, they'd be wide right now. The police are searching for my husband because he's a suspect? What did he do?

Did... did he hurt me?

The vehicle bangs and rattles over potholes. God, I have no idea where I am. Is it still 1969? When the truck swerves, I get tossed around and shriek in pain, except no sound comes from my mouth. I go on shrieking in silence.

Things haze in and out. Sometimes I'm back huddling in the darkness. "Say again, say again...." Other times, the cries of the boy rise and fall with the careening vehicle. Is the child in the vehicle with me? I have to find him. That little boy desperately needs me, and I know it.

"All right, get ready," a man says. "She has a cranial depression fracture, but I think her burns are more pressing. Most of her injuries are thermal burns, though I see evidence for chemical burns, as well, we need to—"

"I know, I know!" the woman shouts back.

If they're talking about me, I have chemical and thermal burns. No wonder the pain is god-awful. A fuel-air bomb? Could be phosphorous munitions or chlorine. The thermal burns are most likely from a flamethrower. I've seen them inflict horrific physical injuries.

*...forgive you?*

A shudder works through me. Who is he? Why can't I place that voice? Trying to remember makes me sick to my stomach, as though I don't want to remember. But it's vitally important. I'm sure of it.

The vehicle slams on its brakes and comes to a stop with the siren blaring.

I'm moving again, flying somewhere on the gurney, passing by a thousand squawking voices. If only I could see where they're taking me. Field hospital or hospital at home in America? Please, God, let me be home in New Mexico at the local hospital. They'll take care of me. I'll be all right. My family will come. The pain will eventually end, and I'll heal and go home and play with Jazzy, my beautiful seven-year-old cocker spaniel with huge brown eyes. But—but maybe Jazzy is the dead dog who was barking.

Did someone kill her?

"We'll get her stabilized, then she has to get to a specialized burn unit. We can't do much for her here."

"Just so you know, the patient may be pregnant," the woman says.

There's a pause.

"Dear God. How do you know that?"

The shock sends my heart slamming against my ribs. I'm pregnant and my husband tried to murder me? This is my worst nightmare, and I've had plenty. Especially the loop where I drag children out of the crumbling hospital. Tiny faces, mouths filled with dirt, a dead toddler clutching a red ball to her chest.

The woman says, "A neighbor found her. That's what he told the police."

"Did he say how many weeks along?"

"No."

The man expels a tense breath. "Christ. All right. We have to proceed with extreme caution, document every step we take to prep her for transport, and get her out of this hospital ASAP. Given the extent of her injuries, the fetus is probably already dying inside her. I don't want it to happen here."

Both are now silent, as though considering the ramifications.

"Besides," the doctor adds, "the woman is likely going to die anyway."

A bell clangs. It's a beautiful, deeply resonant sound. It could be inside the hospital, but maybe there's a church nearby. I want to think it's a church bell, because it makes me feel closer to God, and at this stage of the game that can't hurt. At least the trip will be shorter. It strikes me as a little bizarre that my gallows humor is intact.

"Let's get a morphine drip going," the doctor orders. "Just in case she wakes up."

As I float into the narcotic haze, I try to sway with the bell's rhythm. I've been near death a couple of times, but somehow this is different. It isn't just me dying. I can't decide if the fetus is my beloved companion along for the walk into the unknown... or an enemy sapping what little strength I have left.

I don't want to die.

Finally, the nurse says, "Are you going to warn the burn unit? They may not take her if they know she's pregnant."

"I'm not going to tell them anything, and neither are you."

IT'S SO QUIET, so still. Like the mountain cabin where I grew up.

Far back in the shimmers behind my eyes, a blanket of windblown larkspur covers the mountains. Every morning I trot outside with my little sister to gather bouquets, then charge back and present them to Mama, who showers us with kisses and arranges the flowers in an old Mason jar as though each blossom is a precious jewel. Mama tells us stories about how ancient peoples used larkspur to dye fabrics blue and someday we'll take white T-shirts and see just how blue we can turn them.

A powerful stench assaults my nose. It's not coming from the mountains. It's more like rotting pickles. What could possibly be generating that awful....

Wait a minute, I know that smell. Formaldehyde. Dear God, where am I? It's goddamned freezing in here.

Terror grips me.

A morgue?

I ponder that for a long while. It's possible. The gunfire. The explosions. And there was a fire.

When did that happen? How long ago?

I remember the war. Every moment seems etched into the fabric of my muscles. After I came home, did I marry a soldier? I think I wanted to. Someone I had served with? That might be right. Then again, there's always the possibility that everything I think I remember is simply the creation of a heavily drugged brain. Could be total crap.

The scent of rotting pickles gets stronger. Maybe I'm not in a morgue, but in a mortuary, and they're pumping me full of embalming fluid.

I try to call out, to tell them I'm alive, but my vocal cords must have suffered the same fate as my eyes. Oddly, I'm still in terrible pain. Do the dead suffer agonizing pain? Well, that's a silly question. They do if they're in hell. If God condemned me to eternal damnation I must be a really bad person, which is a stunning thought. What did I do?

I think back to the orphanage in New Mexico. I hated that evil old woman with the hardwood paddle. The other girls kneeled by their beds at night and prayed with all their strength to spout an eagle's wings and fly to heaven to find their dead or missing mothers, but not me. I huddled beneath my blankets and concentrated all of my strength on growing fangs like razor blades so I could rip out Anita's throat and leave her bleeding to death on the filthy wood floor.

God probably does hold that against me.

There's a rush of warm air, then metallic clashes erupt, as if someone stumbled over an instrument tray.

"The bastards! Why didn't they tell us?"

"Maybe they didn't know, Jeff. They were working fast, trying to get her stabilized and off to us. They probably didn't think to check for a second heartbeat. And maybe they figured she'd be dead before she got here."

"Well, this is a big problem for us. For God's sake—"

"Well, what do you want to do? Let her die?"

Jeff pauses and expels a breath. "Well. I mean, let's think about that. It would be an act of mercy. You know it would."

"You've forgotten your Hippocratic oath, buddy. First, do no harm. Remember?"

"Oh, come on, Mark. Can you imagine living like this? It's just a matter of time before we have to amputate. How would you like to live without arms or legs?"

"Jesus, what just happened? Her pulse rate shot up to one twenty."

The damned fools must be exaggerating for effect or even being metaphorical. They don't mean living without arms and legs, they mean living without the use of arms and legs. I'm not sure why I think that's better.

"You don't think.... No, it's not possible, right? She can't hear us. Her eardrums must be as fried as the rest of her body."

I'm spiraling down like a shotgun-blasted duck, falling out of the air with my heartbeat thundering in my ears. No wonder I can't feel my arms or legs. They're charred stumps. Is that possible? Surely, I would have bled to death or died from shock.

Maybe not.

...Saw a pilot once, shot out of the air, parachuted down with no legs, burned all over, flames had cauterized the wounds enough that he was still alive when he hit the ground screaming.

The dark cavern behind my nonexistent eyes starts flashing. Everything inside me vibrates with light. I glimpse a double rainbow hanging over a sunlit mountain cabin. I never wanted to leave, but they dragged me and Angie away. Where was that? Colorado? New Mexico? A herd of elk trots elegantly across a brilliant snowy trail. I see Mama hanging clothes on a line with old-fashioned wooden safety pins. Her hair is so black it seems blue in the morning glow, and she's laughing at something Angie said. Where is Mama? Long gone. I think there was an accident.

"Well, her bag of fluids is almost empty. You're in charge here, Jeff. It won't take much potassium chloride to end her torment."

"The police are on their way. Can't risk it."

"What the hell do they think they're going to do? It's not like she can answer any questions."

"They're looking for clues, I suppose." Jeff's shoes squeak as he shifts. "If they already know she's pregnant, the decision is out of our hands."

"Then let's shut off her breathing tube right now. In her condition, it's plausible she stopped breathing on her own. They won't be able to find any chemical traces."

"Well, if you're going to do it, do it fast. They'll be here soon."

"You won't help? I am not doing this alone!"

"You're the one who suggested it."

"Yeah, but I'm not taking the entire responsibility. This has to be a joint decision."

I'm lightheaded. Am I holding my breath or have they cut off my air supply?

Clanging, beeping, pinging alarms going off everywhere, and me so scared I can't think right. I'm not sure I disagree with their decision. If my condition is as bad as they say, my life is over. Death will be a blessing.

Feet pound the floor. There's another gush of warm air and a woman says, "They're here. Detective Sanders and his team are asking to see the victim."

The victim.

Not the patient.

THE SUBSONIC RUMBLE of approaching fighter jets shakes the ground. They roar overhead and soar off into the smoke-filled sky. God, it's hot. I'm roasting in my flak jacket. To the south, clustered on the summit of a towering mound of rubble, the fractured walls of Saigon hover as though suspended upon the heat waves like the sweet high notes of a requiem mass.

Someone wheezes.

"Please, keep your voices down." That's the woman I heard earlier, the one who said the police had arrived. What happened to Jeff and Mark?

"She's heavily sedated, isn't she, nurse?" He has a gruff voice.

"Yes, Detective Sanders, and we want to keep her asleep. By the way, it's doctor, not nurse. Doctor Marjorie Martin."

Shoes scuff across a concrete floor. The faint smell of cigarette smoke drifts through the air. There's a constant hacking of coughing and clearing throats as the detectives come to stand by my bed. Someone gags on the verge of vomiting.

"For God's sake, Mahoney, get out until you can control yourself."

"Yes, sir." Footsteps jog across the floor.

I try to decipher how many people have entered the room. Three or four?

A different man quietly asks, "Are you sure this is Lois Damien?"

Lois. My name is Lois.

Sanders says, "Nope. We just assume it is because the victim was found in the smoldering heap of Damien's home."

As my lungs struggle to get air, despair fills me. What is it about humans that they insist upon killing the innocent? In the war, most of the dead were not soldiers, they were farmers, women, and children—children lying on mounds of rubble, blown all to pieces. Damn all the politicians who create slogans, and the religious zealots who chant them and call themselves patriots and martyrs. God damn them all.

Papers rustle as one of the detectives flips through pages. "Lois Damien filed for divorce about six weeks ago," Pete says.

"Was her husband still living with her? Or were they separated?"

"Rhodes Damien. His address is different from hers, though, so probably separated."

"Any children?"

"Negative."

I search my memory. Rhodes. Rhodes. I don't have a single memory of him.

Doctor Martin says, "By the way, she's about twelve weeks pregnant."

"Jesus," Sanders says. "Do you think her husband knows?"

Dr. Martin's voice goes up in pitch. "Homicide is the leading cause of death during pregnancy in the United States. What do you think?"

"It's possible, Doc." Shoes move around the floor as the detectives pace. The odor of cigarette smoke rises again. "That's why we're searching for him. Happens a lot these days. Boys come home from the war and find their wives pregnant. Upsets 'em."

I'm fading in and out. It's dark and hot. There's a faint bugle playing out there in the moonlight, just a few notes, over and over.

I stand outside the hospital staring up at green tracer bullets crossing red tracers over my head. The whup whup whup of helos chatters my teeth. Lord, they're close. There's a sudden massive kaboom! The ground rises and slams me back down. Flying debris and chunks of plaster and wood cover me. I scramble away through the choking dust on my hands and knees.

Wounded soldiers scream—barely audible through the thunder of mortar fire and bombs falling. When I finally dare to lift my head and peer over the shattered walls, I glimpse people darting through the rubble like phantasms.

For a long time, I can't stop shaking. I lay on my back, sick and dazed, unable to do anything except gasp for air and watch the flares dropping in the distance. The air is filled with the awful smell of burning human flesh and the rattle of gunfire. I have to get up. Get up! Go find the patients who are buried....

"Well...." Sanders exhales the word. "That baby is going to need a father."

"A father?" Dr. Martin sounds shocked. "You mean the man who tried to kill its mother?"

"We don't know he tried to kill her. Not yet."

Pete says, "Come on, Doc, look at her. You kind of agree, don't you? She'll be pissing through a tube for the rest of her life, but in four months the baby might be able to survive outside the womb. Who's gonna take care of it?"

★ ★ ★

*MAJOR... DON'T LEAVE me, please don't leave me?*

In the background, Sergeant Jackson is shouting into the radio, "Say again... say again...." but I can't pay attention. I have my arm under Billy's shoulders, holding him up so he doesn't choke to death on the blood flooding up from his lungs. He's staring at me with wet green eyes.

Dear God, what purpose does this serve? This is no place for an eighteen-year-old ranch kid from Idaho. He ought to be home helping move the cows and calves down from the high pastures into the corrals for weaning. He should be smelling the crisp scent of aspens in the autumn air and riding his horse down the slopes hollering to keep the herd moving. What's he doing here? All he wanted was to be a rancher for the rest of his life, to marry his high school sweetheart, and have children grow up in the shade of the cottonwoods in the front yard. Yet here he is trying to be brave while life rhythmically pumps from the hole in his chest.

*Major? Am I dying?*

*No, honey. No, you're not.*

"Take it easy, Major. I know you're in a lot of pain. I'm going to take care of that. I want you to rest. That's your only job now. Rest."

I'm confused, not sure where I am. I focus on the clinking of instruments. Two people talk as though I'm deaf.

"I heard they found her husband," Dr. Marjorie says.

"Yeah." That's Detective Sanders.

So the police are back to stare at me. I hope the guy who gagged isn't with them today. That was pretty bad.

"Did they arrest him?"

"Can't. Don't have enough evidence. Doctor Damien says he was out of state at a conference, and he's got the receipts to prove it."

My husband is a doctor?

A medical doctor? Or a Ph.D. in basket weaving?

"Hell, if I was plotting to kill my wife, I'd book a hotel at a conference and hire some friend to check in with my ID and credit card.

Hotel clerks could care less about the photo on your driver's license. They just want to see your AmEx go through," Pete says.

Sanders replies, "Yeah, but he's got restaurant receipts and there are witnesses who saw him there."

"So?" Dr. Marjorie replies. "You obviously weren't a delinquent. Restaurant receipts are easy. Just ask a friend to walk out into the parking lot and start picking 'em up. They have to be cash receipts, of course. Are they all cash receipts?"

"You were a delinquent?" Pete sounds skeptical.

"A badass fifteen-year-old runaway."

"Uh-huh." Sanders sounds bored. "Well, Damien has witnesses—"

Dr. Marjorie breaks in. "Christ, do you know how many doctors I swear I saw at a medical conference who turned out to be home sick in bed? If you're used to seeing somebody at every conference, your mind just sort of places them there."

There's a small hesitation, then Sanders says, "Yeah, okay, true enough. Similar to people who witness a car accident. They each saw it happen, but their stories are so different it's like they witnessed different events."

Their voices drop lower and lower, and I'm sure it's the narcotics they're dripping into my IV. I fight to stay here, to listen to them for as long as I can.

"If he's innocent, why hasn't he come to see her?" Marjorie asks.

"How do I know? She filed for divorce. Maybe he hates her guts and is happy somebody tried to kill her."

Pete adds, "Jeez, I can't tell you how many times I've wished somebody would murder my ex-wife."

"You fucking son of a bitch," Martin says.

"Wow, you were a badass fifteen-year-old."

"I'm still a badass, Detective. Keep that in mind."

There's that roar in my ears again, fire burning hot, and I'm bobbing away through darkness. I shouldn't be dying in a hospital without even knowing what happened to me. That's the worst. Maybe I'm not as good a person as I imagine. Everyone has a grinning monster inside them. God knows, I've witnessed the best young soldiers suddenly metamorphose into something so terrible their actions seem incomprehensible. It's the darkness, you see? When the battle starts, daylight names shatter like broken toys, and the darkness gives us each a new name. One that no one would dare speak by day.

Pete says, "Jesus, did you know that Damien is a war hero? Three Purple Hearts, a Silver Star, and the goddamned Distinguished Service Cross."

My husband is a war hero? Did I know him in Nam? Is that how we met?

"Doesn't surprise me. When I spoke to him, Doctor Damien was impressive. Seemed like a good guy—"

"Not Doctor Damien. Major Lois Damien, our vic."

The room goes silent.

*...bogeys... closing fast... get out, get out....*

In an awed voice, Sanders says, "No shit."

Marjorie asks, "What's the Distinguished Service Cross?"

"Second highest award a soldier can get. Medal of Honor is number one." Sanders exhales hard. "Wonder what she did to get that?"

"Doesn't say." Pete rattles through pages. "She was just a nurse."

"Just a nurse!" Dr. Marjorie blurts. "I can't wait until you're in one of these hospital beds—"

"Yeah, yeah, okay. I was out of line."

That little boy is crying beneath the rubble. Suffocating, pitiful cries. I have to find him.

"So, I understand that you requested the right to be able to induce a coma. Is that correct, Doc?"

"Yes. She's getting weaker, and so is the baby."

"You're thinking of using sodium thiopental?"

"That would be my choice."

"But I read in your request that the fetal heart rate is so low it's risky. The lack of oxygen to the baby's brain—"

"That's right. I can't guarantee that the fetus won't be harmed."

"Well, then it's out of the question."

"Look, Detective, try to understand. I have no idea why Major Damien hasn't spontaneously aborted. She's in such bad shape—"

Offhandedly, Sanders says, "Well, Doc, if she's holding on to the fetus like a raft in a hurricane, maybe she thinks the baby's life is more important than hers, huh? Ever think of that?"

SOBS, I HEAR sobs. Twilight is settling over the devastation, turning the world that eerie shade of battlefield purple. Movement catches my eyes. A tiny arm sticks up out of the rubble. I'm exhausted, but I run to the arm, drag the boy out, and drop to my knees. He cries for a few moments and stops. He's not breathing. I work to resuscitate him. When I finally accept that my efforts are useless, I rock the little boy in my arms until it's over.

How is it possible that I have tears left?

*Lois, look out!*

Jonny hits me like a ton of bricks just as the Cobra gunship dives low over our heads firing rockets. The minigun chatters, six thousand rounds a minute, every fifth round a red tracer. Red death pouring from the sky.

Crazy voices. All around. Shouting orders that I can't decipher. I—I feel drugged. *Where...?*

I'm pretty sure I'm not supposed to be awake. They're shoving the bed around. The wheels whine, and I smell hot coffee-scented breath.

Someone stabs me. Little rhythmic stabs.

"Careful! For God's sake, nurse, haven't you ever worked on a burn victim before? Go slow!" Jeff's voice.

"Yes, Doctor, sorry," a young man responds in a shaking voice.

As the nurse works, I begin to feel my leg.

But what's the nurse doing to it? It feels as if he's puncturing my flesh with a red-hot needle. The needle keeps sticking, which forces the nurse to stab harder until the skin breaks free. After each stab, he tugs and exhales coffee breath, then inhales to prepare himself for the next ordeal.

"Is she going to make it, Doctor Randall?"

"Take a good look at her. What's your medical opinion?"

Cold fingers touch my leg. "I can't say, but...." His voice trails away into silence.

"What?"

"Well, it's not my place to ask."

"Ask anyway."

"I'm just wondering if we should we be trying so hard to save her?"

"That's our job, isn't it?"

"Yeah. I guess so."

Stab. Tug. Exhale. *Take a breath.* Sour coffee.... Stab.

I try to gauge exactly where the nurse is working. It's just below my knee, I think.

As though to remind me, Jeff's deep voice says the word amputate and it drifts around the chasm inside me like a crow floating on black wind.

Now it makes sense.

The nurse is sewing up the stump.

"All right," Jeff says. There's a *snap-snap* as someone pulls off rubber gloves. "You can finish the rest up by yourself, can't you, nurse? I need to go speak with her family."

Family. *Fam-i-ly.* The syllables feel transcendent, like the holy trinity.

I have family in the waiting room.

They're coming.

IT'S THE MIDDLE of summer. Sunday. No people are out and about, but there's a skin-and-bones puppy in the ruins, lying with a small shoe under his paws as though protecting it. Every now and then the puppy lifts his head, barks, and runs toward the bombed-out building with his tail wagging. For several moments, he stares longingly at the rubble, then his tail drops and he walks back to lay his head on the small shoe again. Is he waiting for that dead child to come out and play?

Two partial walls still stand. The windows resemble empty eye sockets.

Soldiers have to perform a strange kind of transubstantiation to make sense of things like this. They have to wave their hands and turn the filthy water into wine. It's a sacred mirage, upside-down seeing that gives soldiers hope they fight for what's right. Daily, hourly. You hope that all the dead children understand you didn't mean it. After all, you came here to save them.

A loud voice says, "You have ten minutes, Missus Spencer."

A door closes, and the sweet scent of vanilla hand lotion pervades the air.

"Hey, Lois," a trembling voice calls. "It's me."

I will know that voice a thousand years from now in my grave. My heart swells with emotion.

*Angie.*

Angie came to find me.

The legs of a chair squeal as my sister pulls it closer. "The doctors tell me that you may not hear me, and even if you do, you may not be able to understand my words." There's a heavy sigh. "They say you have a cracked skull. You may have fallen when you were trying to escape the fire, or it could be what they call blunt force trauma."

Angie is trying to tell me I have a traumatic brain injury. No wonder I can't remember things.

"I would have come sooner, but the giant storm closed every airport and road in northern Wyoming. You should have seen the eight-foot drifts in our front yard. The kids loved it. They've been sledding and throwing snowballs at each other."

Grief racks me. I don't remember Angie's children. How many does she have? How old are they? What's Angie doing in Wyoming? Those memories would be precious to me.

Will they ever come back?

"I wish I could touch you, but the doctors are afraid of infection. They have you bandaged from head to... to toe and sealed up in this big plastic tent."

Angie stops talking, and I hear my little sister stifle a sob, then blow her nose.

"They say you're pregnant. That stunned me. You said you couldn't bear the thought of bringing a child into this terrible world. I guess I thought it was never going to happen. Who's the father?"

...Dark clouds rise from funeral pyres and trail across the night sky like ghouls on a mission, flying to the next battle.

Jonny's body curls around mine in the dark. I can feel him breathing against my shoulder. We managed to pull twenty-eight people out of the rubble, ten of them children. I feel hollow, like I'm not really in my body. But I'm not alone. He's here. He's holding me. I finally feel safe enough to sleep.

*You didn't even write to tell me? You fucking coward!*

The words bounce around inside me, echoing in the empty chambers where I so often hide and cower from the memories. Coward. Oh, yes, dear God, I am. I want to hide forever.

"The reason I asked...." Angie heaves an unsteady breath and pauses for a long while, before she says, "I'm not sure I should tell you this, but you have a right to know that Rhodes has already hired a lawyer to force the hospital to keep you alive indefinitely."

I feel the air pressure change when a door opens. "One minute, Missus Spencer."

"Yes, of course. Thank you."

A cacophony of voices floods the room, then fades as the door slowly closes.

"Lois, we've always been honest with each other. The doctor says that if she can't terminate the pregnancy, you and the baby will both die. I—I don't know what to do. Rhodes is a prominent community leader. People respect him and look up to him. I'm just a housewife with three kids. They'll never listen to me."

Three kids. I clutch that knowledge to my heart like a Bible. It's salvation. Angie has three children. Despite all the death and horror, there is love in the world.

"Time's up, Missus Spencer. I'm sorry."

Angie's voice is clear when she says, "I love you, Lois. I'll be back as soon as they let me."

I want to shout, Don't go! Please stay and talk to me. Tell me more about your life.

Angie's steps move away.

Sanders's gruff voice announces, "Her husband is here. He wants to see her."

"Finally?" Dr. Martin says. "Where has he been all this time?"

"Give the guy a break, Doc. He probably had to work up the courage. Looking at her isn't the most pleasant thing on earth, you know?"

There's a long pause. The door closes.

Then. *Clack, clack.*

What is that?

I try to imagine what could cause it. Does he have taps on his shoes?

While the clicks and clacks slowly circle my bed, closing in, my mind plays tricks. Drumbeats. Rain falling.

*Taps.*

The mournful notes of the bugle drift over Arlington. They are too agonizingly beautiful to be of this earth. As Jonny's shiny aluminum coffin is lowered into the ground, I know I'll never escape this moment. For the rest of my life, I'll be standing here waiting for the bugle to stop playing, but it never stops... it never stops... never.

Someone laughs.

I'm jerked back to the hospital bed surrounded by the smell of the plastic tent. Rhodes walks to the left side of my bed and fiddles with something that jiggles the morphine IV in my arm. It hurts. An alarm beeps, then abruptly ceases.

He shut off the alarm.

How long before I'm in agony again?

He must have leaned closer to me. His distinctive aftershave is suddenly powerful, nauseating.

I start shaking.

That's trauma. Even when the mind forgets, the body remembers. Sometimes it's triggered by a scent. Other times by a sound. The stomach muscles clench. You long to throw up. The body knows something your brain does not.

"You actually thought I would forgive you?"

*—Kathleen O'Neal Gear is an award-winning archaeologist and* New York Times *bestselling author or coauthor of sixty books and more than 200 nonfiction publications. In 2015, the United States Congress honored her with a Certificate of Special Congressional Recognition. That same year the California State Legislature passed Joint Member Resolution #117, saying, "...the contributions of Kathleen O'Neal Gear to the fields of history, archaeology, and writing have been invaluable...." The United States Department of the Interior has twice awarded her a Special Achievement Award for outstanding management of America's cultural resources.*

*She has been inducted into four halls of fame: The Western Writers Hall of Fame, the Women Who Write the West Hall of Fame, the California State University Hall of Fame, and the Colorado Authors Hall of Fame.*

*Writing with her husband, Michael Gear, their books, short stories, and nonfiction articles have received forty-two national and international awards including four Spur Awards from the Western Writers of America. With close to eighteen million copies in print worldwide, their books have been translated into thirty languages.*

# MARC CAMERON

## MUD AND HATE

### AN ARLISS CUTTER STORY

"WERE YOU BORN a dumbass, or did you have to study up?"

"Long years of practice, my friend," Deputy U.S. Marshal Arliss Cutter said as he moved around the big Roman-nosed bay. He didn't have time to get mad at the younger deputy on the other side of the horse.

Cutter shoved a borrowed .30-30 Winchester in the leather scabbard and gave the end of the buttstock a hearty smack with the flat of his hand, the way he'd seen his grandfather do it—to make sure the rifle was seated and to check the skittishness of an unfamiliar mount. He'd never had a horse of his own, but that same grandfather, a Florida lawman everyone called Grumpy, made certain he and his older brother had plenty of opportunities to ride while they were growing up in his care.

Winchester in place, Deputy Cutter adjusted the length of the off-side stirrup and pulled the fender down, popping the leather—again, to preflight the horse. He wore Tony Lama boots, faded jeans, and a loose white cotton shirt. But for a blue Marshals Service ball cap and the emergency broadcast tone screaming from the phone in the pocket of his waxed canvas trucker jacket, it would have been easy to mistake him for a turn-of-the-century lawman.

A sudden gust, heavy with the smell of creosote bush and rain, whipped across the asphalt parking lot, slamming the gate on the rusted stock trailer. Far from bothered by all the mayhem, the bay lifted its jug head and gave a plaintive nicker.

Even it knew this was a bad idea.

Cutter was a big man—six foot three and two-twenty-five if he didn't eat too much at the buffet in Mesquite twenty miles to the south where the Marshals Service was housing deputies during this ten-week fugitive sweep.

A somber young woman in a yellow rainslicker two sizes too large stepped back as Cutter worked his way around the animal.

Beside the woman, District of Nevada Deputy U.S. Marshal Gabe Manfredi snugged down his own blue ball cap. He stood as tall as Cutter but was much leaner—a distance runner to Cutter's heavyweight boxer. In his late twenties, Manfredi was younger by at least three lustrums—fifteen years in Grumpy-speak.

"This has got to be the stupidest thing I've ever seen," Manfredi said, his words ripped away by the wind. He'd arrived from Mesquite just minutes earlier, about the same time the young woman in the slicker unloaded the saddled gelding from the stock trailer. "I mean, you gotta have some kind of death wish to ride into this storm. It's a dumbass move and I—"

"Don't hold back," Cutter said. "Tell me what you really think."

"You feel that wind swing around?" Manfredi squinted toward the dust boiling over the red-rock mountains to the south.

Chin quivering, Patty Allison glanced up at Cutter, wringing her hands. "He's right, Marshal," she said. "I'm scared for my husband, but this is crazy. That's a...."

Cutter spared her the trouble of explaining. "A haboob. The wind and dust pushed in front of a hellacious thunderstorm."

Another gust whipped at the woman's slicker revealing sweatpants and a baggy T-shirt. She was clearly expecting a baby. Soon.

Cutter's ad hoc fugitive task force was made up of deputy marshals from all over the country as well as local officers from three states. The area expert, twenty-four-year-old Mohave County sheriff's deputy Wyatt Allison, provided crucial knowledge when the teams attempted warrant service in the boonies of northwest Arizona—where online maps just laughed.

Cutter had arrived at the Allisons' home just before six a.m. that morning—a dusty, sad-looking singlewide behind the Travel Plaza Truck Stop near the Beaver Dam Substation. Instead of an eager sheriff's deputy champing at the bit to ruin the day for a bunch of bad guys, Cutter found Patty Allison frantically loading the Roman-nosed bay into a neighbor's trailer in the gray light of dawn. She'd gone to bed early assuming her husband slept in the guest room to keep from bothering her when he left early for work. He never made it home from his evening ride.

Wyatt had spent the night out in the slickrock mesas and canyons, afoot, hurt… or worse. His wife choked up each time she'd tried to explain the dangers. Cutter called in reinforcements from Mesquite, Las Vegas, St. George, and Kingman then followed her to where her husband's pickup and horse trailer were still parked at the Virgin River Canyon campground off Interstate 15. A virtual army was on the way with radios, ATVs, and air support, but they would take time.

Cutter was here now.

"I know, I know," Manfredi wagged his head—a smirk crossing his extremely punchable face. "You're the supervisor, but from where I'm standing, you're on thin ice already. Seems to me you're pushing the limits carrying your granddad's old wheel gun when the rest of us are stuck with Glocks. That lever-action rifle is so far outside policy it's liable to get you fired."

"Probably so," Cutter said. He carried Grumpy's Colt Python, but the "baby" Glock over his right kidney kept him within policy. His M4 carbine didn't fit the saddle scabbard, where the lever-action rifle did, but he saw no reason to explain himself.

The fact that Cutter didn't argue appeared to hit the younger deputy like a slap.

"I want it on record that I am not part of this asinine endeavor."

"Noted," Cutter said.

"I'm not sure how to get this through your thick skull, but any minute the Virgin River is gonna go from peaceful green trickle to a raging slurry of mud and hate."

Cutter chuckled at the dramatic metaphor. He'd known Manfredi a grand total of four days, but that was the way of the United States Marshals Service. On nationwide fugitive ops like this, you were thrown in with lawmen and women who were at best, friends of friends, deputies you'd heard of but had never actually met. You put your life in a stranger's hands. Manfredi didn't seem like a bad guy. He was smart and loud and political. People like him tended to promote fast, but he'd come onboard straight from college and hadn't lived long enough to carry the soul-crushing weight of regret that spurred Cutter to err on the side of action.

Always.

Cutter turned and eyed the younger deputy with a mean mug that rivaled an Easter Island statue.

"You're saying I shouldn't ride out there because I'm TDY from Alaska and not familiar with the desert."

"That is exactly what I'm saying!"

Cutter took a step back from the gelding.

"So, you're gonna do it then?"

Manfredi gave a vehement shake of his head. "I'll go as soon as the guys get here with the ATVs."

"That's what I thought." Cutter looked at Patty Allison. "What's your plan if I don't get on this horse?"

"Ride out and find my husband," she said without a moment's pause.

"There you have it," Cutter said to Manfredi. "Somebody's gonna go. Might as well be me." He grabbed a handful of the bay's mane and swung into the saddle.

Manfredi harangued away. "You can forget about cell service in those mountains. The slot canyons turn a sat phone into a plastic brick—and that doesn't even take into account the storm."

"Like the old days, then." Cutter settled into the saddle and gave a satisfied nod. "Just a deputy marshal and a horse."

"And a hell of a lot of country that wants to kill you. A couple inches of rain ten miles away and this place floods like a...." Manfredi glanced at Patty Allison and checked himself. "We're in for three times that."

"I hear you," Cutter said. "But I want to be on Allison's tracks before the rain gets here."

Manfredi moved in close to the bay and jabbed at Cutter's thigh with his index finger to punctuate his words. "By the time that rain gets here you and this horse will be underwater!"

Ordinarily, Cutter would have broken the man's finger for poking at him like that. But he was in a hurry. Someone else would have to teach the kid manners. Besides, it was one of Grumpy's rules. Two rudes didn't make a right.

Cutter lifted the reins and smooched at the bay, glancing sideways at Manfredi. "I'll radio back with a direction of travel. You come runnin' with the cavalry."

Patty Allison caught Cutter's eye and gave the slightest of nods. A tear dripped from the tip of her nose.

"Thank you."

Cutter groaned inside. The truth would slap her in the face soon enough. What she needed now was hope. He gave it to her on the back of a lie.

"We'll find Wyatt," he said. "I'm sure of it." He wheeled the horse toward the trailhead before she caught the truth in his eyes.

THE BIG BAY seemed to catch the urgency of the situation before they'd sloshed across the river—stepping out quickly in the ankle-deep water. A flash of lightning painted the mountains to the southwest. Cutter counted on the move, making it to four at the crack of thunder. Not even a mile away.

Manfredi's wave of mud and hate would be along any time now. Judging from the old scour marks on the rocks Cutter had work to do to get above the flood line.

He gave the horse its head, bumping the reins just enough to stay on the faint line of sign. Like the bay gelding, Wyatt Allison's horse wore Borium shoes. The tungsten carbide crystals provided grip—and left telltale scratches on the red sandstone.

Lightning flashed and thunder cracked in a never-ending show overhead. It was no longer possible to tell distance or what clap of thunder belonged to which flash. The warm monsoon wind grew cooler by the minute.

Cutter urged the horse into a ground-eating walk. Allison had gone up one of the side canyons. He needed to stay on the tracks long enough to see which one. The smell of something akin to burned matches and chlorine filled the air. The horse's mane began to float straight up from static electricity. They were sitting ducks. Cutter had seen a horse struck by lightning once when he was a boy—the jagged scar of singed hair running from withers to foreleg, the bottom of all four feet blown out by the sudden jolt.

He wondered if he'd die immediately or just lie there in the rain incapacitated until he drowned. They had to get out of the open. At the same time, he needed to reach higher ground to keep from being washed away in a flood. It was a guns-or-knives conundrum. Cutter pushed thoughts of drowning or getting blasted out of the saddle and focused on the tracks.

Allison had ridden east after he crossed the Virgin River, up and over the knee of a low hill before turning due south into a broad wash to the east of the campground. Grit and sand peppered Cutter's rain jacket as he made the turn into the wind. He could still make out the tracks, but green clouds cast dark shadows on the canyons and bluffs.

He called Manfredi on the handheld, got nothing but static in return. He gave his position anyway, speaking in the blind. A series of brooding mesas lay ahead, tall and stark and, unlike the red rock below, gray as if they'd been bled dry.

Mercifully, Allison's tracks bore left, working their way at an angle up a rocky trail that ran along the draw. Cutter noticed something else—sign he couldn't quite make out, barely visible smudges on the rock. In too many spots to be coincidence, the marks left by the Borium horseshoes had been smeared as if rubbed with a finger. Someone or something had walked across them—following Wyatt Allison.

Cutter dismounted twice to study what were essentially shadows on the rocks. He thought he could make out a smear of rubber on sandstone. It looked soft like a tennis shoe, but that could have been his imagination. A hundred yards later he'd convinced himself he was looking at pugmarks left by a big cat. There were mountain lions in this desert. He knew that. And mountain lions hunted people. His rational brain told him that could account for why Wyatt Allison was missing, but he pushed the dark thoughts from his mind. It was far too early to go down that road.

Cutter climbed back into the saddle with a low groan and craned his neck to check his back trail. The hair on his neck stood up—from lightning or a prowling cougar, he couldn't tell. Horses had a particular aversion to big cats. If there was one around, the bay would let him know. So far, it covered the uneven ground like it had been there before, head down, fearless or brainless—characteristics Cutter's boss often used to describe him.

An accomplished man hunter, Cutter's assignment this time was supposed to have been managerial. It would be good for his promotion package, his chief in Alaska had said. He could go out with the apprehension teams every few days, but his primary job was to coordinate the entire warrant operation from the command post—what his buddies in the Ranger Regiment had called a rear echelon pogue.

A sudden clatter to the right sent the bay jigging sideways—a dangerous proposition on the slick rock. Cutter's hand dropped to his Colt as he worked to simultaneously calm the twitching animal and scan the mountainside for a hungry lion.

A nascent waterfall careened down the sheer wall, slapping the loose stones below before continuing to the canyon floor less than fifteen feet below. The newborn river was rising fast. Dozens more spouts and baby falls formed in the following minutes until the entire trail was awash with spray and muddy runoff. He wasn't nearly as high as he needed to be.

The canyon walls came alive with cascading rivulets of water and noisy spouts splashing down from above. The hissing murmur of a downpour filled the air though more than a few real drops had yet to actually fall from directly overhead. All of this maelstrom was from the storm still miles to the south. Even so, any tracks were long gone.

Cutter kept riding up—the only path forward. The trail behind him was surely impassible by now. The deafening torrent in the canyon floor made him hug the wall as he rode. Less than five minutes later, he reined his horse to a stop at a sharp left-hand bend in the trail. Hooves clattered and clomped on the slick rock. The bay gave another soft nicker, ears perked, locked on whatever was around the corner. Something out there smelled bad, and it wasn't just the approaching storm.

It wasn't so much a smell as a feeling—those thousand little things the subconscious noticed before the brain had a chance to suss out the details. Patterned movement, where the world should be erratic. Gentle curves where everything else was made of angles sharp enough to cut your throat. Telltale sounds that didn't quite belong.

The big bay gave an impatient stomp of his foot. Lightning struck high on the mesa to Cutter's right, close enough he could smell it. A volley of rocks skittered down the canyon wall. Then—

Voices, unintelligible barking as if someone was giving orders—followed by a crack of a gunshot.

The bay blew out hard, stomping its foot again.

Cutter nudged the Colt Python revolver on his belt with his elbow, making certain it was where he'd left it. Was it Wyatt Allison firing a signal shot? Cutter thought of the second set of tracks. A lion? Or something worse.

Thunder cracked, almost but not quite covering the report of another gunshot.

The bay began to dance in earnest now, hooves clomping, throwing sparks against the rock. Cutter slid the Winchester out of the scabbard. He thought of the old adage, you could shoot off any horse... once—and decided to dismount. The Colt Python and baby Glock were all well and good, but his lawman grandfather had taught him early and often that handguns were for fighting your way to a rifle. Reins draped over his arm, he levered a round into the chamber, put the Winchester on half-cock, and eased forward.

The voices grew more audible with each step.

He rounded the corner to find three men under a cavelike overhang. All of them peered over the edge, looking at something Cutter couldn't make out because of the angle. One of the three, a slender man with filthy jeans and a faded shirt that was more holes than greasy cotton, knelt and aimed a pistol at something in the draw below.

Cutter recognized them at once. Eight-by-ten color photos of the Nordeen brothers hung on the wall of the command post—mugshots from previous arrests for the younger two, a driver's license photo for Ross, the oldest of the bunch. David, the youngest at twenty-two, had bludgeoned his girlfriend to death with a can of tomato soup three months earlier. She'd apparently committed the unpardonable sin of sharing some of a methamphetamine stash with her cousin. David killed the cousin with the same can of soup, not over the drugs, but because she'd happened to stop by the apartment. The cousin's twelve-year-old daughter witnessed the murders from the doorway and provided Albuquerque PD with the name of the killer. Ross and Callum, the two older Nordeens, had closed ranks around their kid brother, severely wounding two Albuquerque police officers during a gunfight as they fled the city. A multistate manhunt ensued but the brothers had vanished. There were unconfirmed reports that they'd been spotted near Kanab, Utah, hiding out in cabins around the reservoir, then nothing. Wanted posters went out to every law enforcement office west of the Mississippi River. The trail had gone cold—until now.

The men's backs were to Cutter, but he had no doubt the one kneeling and pointing a pistol over the edge was the youngest Nordeen.

"Come on, Sheriff!" David said. "That water's getting high down there. I'll pull you up. I swear." He looked sideways at his brothers. "He's got food in the saddlebags. Not much, but it's something. Probably more ammo, too, if we stop him before he shoots it all at us."

Ross, the oldest, folded his arms and shook his head like he didn't want any part of this. Callum, the middle brother, smacked his fist against an open palm. His dirty blond hair was pulled back in a ponytail like an old broom. "Hurry up then. Kill him and get it over with."

"Sneaky bastard's hiding behind his horse," David said. "I can't get the right angle without getting shot myself." The outlaw came up on tiptoe leaning back while he aimed his Glock pistol over the edge—like a scared kid lighting a firecracker.

Shots erupted from the canyon floor, eclipsing the throaty roar of water that now came from every direction. Bullets slapped the sandstone overhang, sending David scrambling backward.

"Best keep your distance!" The voice rose up from below, strained, with a hint of fear. It was Wyatt Allison.

Ross shook his head. Nearly thirty and sporting a shaggy black beard, he had owned a drive-in oil-change business before he turned fugitive. Blood, it turned out, was thicker than 10W-30 and he'd followed his little brother on this bloody rampage.

"Water's gonna be up to your neck any minute!" Callum's words echoed off the low stone roof. He motioned for David to work his way to the right while he kept talking. "We'll pull you up. You have my word."

David, apparently at a better vantage point now, aimed in.

Cutter threw the rifle to his shoulder and thumbed the hammer all the way back.

"U.S. Marshals!" His voice boomed in the cramped atmosphere of the stone overhang. "Drop the gun, David! Do it now!"

Calling an outlaw by name could sometimes pierce the fog of the moment allowing them enough brain space to comply with orders.

Not today. The problem with people who'd already shot it out with the cops is that they naturally assumed everyone with a badge was gunning for them. When bloody death was a foregone conclusion, they might as well go out like Bonnie and Clyde and grab a little notoriety on the way.

The two older brothers' hands shot into the air as if on puppet strings. David spun, his gun arcing upward.

The roar of Cutter's Winchester shook the stone enclosure. As usual, Cutter didn't even hear the blast. He was far too focused on his target. The round hit a scowling David Nordeen in the center of his chest.

"Drop it!" Cutter might as well have been talking to the wind.

Nordeen staggered backward, vanishing over the edge without so much as a whimper.

He sidestepped toward the edge of the trail, Winchester trained on the surviving brothers. "Wyatt! That you down there?"

Allison's reply came back haltingly, astonished. "M-Marshal?"

"You hurt?"

"My right leg is toast," Allison yelled. "Shattered it when those bastards pushed me and my horse over the edge."

Callum grinned and gave a what-are-you-gonna-do shrug.

"How long you been down there?" Cutter yelled.

"Since a little before dark yesterday," Allison shouted. "It's a compound fracture. Those goons been sitting up there all night, waiting for me to pass out. I think… I think I got the bleeding under control… for now."

Cutter racked his brain for a solution. "How about your horse?"

Callum Nordeen winked at him.

"They killed her," Allison said.

Cutter cast his eyes around the cavelike room formed by the sandstone overhang. Roughly ten by twelve feet and maybe eight feet at his highest point, it was little more than a wide spot in the trail, but the rock above offered some protection from the rain. Two violent prisoners, rising floodwaters, and a badly injured deputy. His list of solutions was a short one.

Ross, the eldest, dropped to his knees. "You ever hear of a warning shot?"

"Don't believe in 'em." Cutter motioned at the sandstone floor with his rifle barrel. "Kiss the ground. Now."

"Are you kidding?" Callum said.

"You've known me all of a minute," Cutter snapped. "Have I given the impression I play games? Now get on the ground!"

Both men complied. Callum glared at Cutter like he was food all the way to the ground.

"Aren't you going to check on David?" Ross said. It was an earnest ask from an older brother. "He mighta survived the fall."

"Emmm," Cutter grimaced and shook his head, unconvinced. "Fall notwithstanding, a rifle round to the boiler room...."

"Cutter!" Allison yelled from below.

"Be with you in a minute," he said. "I need to see to the Nordeens."

"Better be quick," Allison yelled. "It's started to rain. Floodwater's up to my boots!"

"Well, isn't this a hell of a fix." Belly down, Callum turned his head and stared hard at Cutter in the twilight shadows of the overhang.

"You don't seem the type to shoot us and leave us lay," Ross said.

"Not yet," Cutter said, dead serious. "Both of you take out your knives and toss them toward the back of this cave."

"We don't have—"

"Toss 'em!" Cutter barked. Then, over the edge, "How you holding up, Wyatt?"

"Not good," Allison shouted back. "I got another couple of minutes before the water washes me downstream."

"Geez." Callum gave a nasty chuckle under his breath. "Hope his leg doesn't get infected...."

"You two get on your feet," Cutter said.

Cheek to the ground, Callum blew dirt away from his face. "I kinda like it here," he said. "It's restful."

Cutter cocked the rifle.

The brothers stood, hands in the air.

"Wyatt!" Cutter stepped closer, less than two feet from the drop. He tried to get a look at Allison but caught a flicker of movement in the corner of his eye as Ross Nordeen took a step forward.

"Nope!" Cutter said. "Bad idea."

Ross groaned and took a step back.

"Wyatt," Cutter yelled again. "I need you to throw your pistol in the river."

"Are you crazy?"

"Probably," Cutter said. "I have plenty of guns up here. I'm sending these two down to haul you up. Don't want them tempted to take yours."

"You can't make us go down there," Ross said. "That's gotta be against the… I don't know, the Geneva Convention or something."

"This is going one of two ways," Cutter said, voice low and matter of fact. "I kill you now and go save my friend, or you men help me save him."

Callum scoffed. "You're not gonna kill us."

"I'm not?" Cutter said, rifle up. "History is written by the winner. You help pull my friend out of that water and you can report my bad behavior to my boss. If I kill you both… the only report my boss gets is from me." Cutter glanced over the edge again. Allison had pushed himself as far up the shelf as possible, but churning brown floodwaters lapped at his feet, rising rapidly. Cutter aimed the rifle square at Callum Nordeen's chest. "It's a hell of a choice, I know," he said. "But you have exactly ten seconds to make it."

RETRIEVING WYATT ALLISON from the ledge with the help of Cutter's horse was a relatively simple endeavor, made even easier because the Nordeen brothers didn't care if they banged the hell out of his injured leg during the process. The poor guy was sweating profusely and lapsing in and out of consciousness by the time they dragged him up and leaned his back against the sandstone wall.

The Roman-nosed bay lowered its head and sniffed, nickering softly. There was no need to tie the animal. It appeared perfectly happy to stand under the overhanging rock out of the storm.

Cutter had carried an extra set of handcuffs on every fugitive operation since he started his man-hunting career—until this one. Rear echelon pogues didn't need cuffs—not two sets anyway.

He pitched his only pair to Ross then looked down the barrel of his rifle at Callum. "Right wrist to right wrist!"

Ross complied, letting the empty bracelet dangle. Callum gave a violent shake of his head. "But that puts us pointed opposite each other—"

"Fancy that." Cutter swung the Winchester a couple of inches covering Ross Nordeen's chest. "Get to it. I'm in a rush."

Two minutes later, the Nordeens sat cross-legged with Callum pulling the time-out position facing the rock wall. Each had one hand free, but chained as they were, it would be harder for them to mount an attack. At least that was the theory.

Cutter checked Wyatt Allison's self-administered tourniquet. The bone had come out through the shin and then ducked back in, making Cutter worry about infection in addition to shock. The wound was filthy and needed to be cleaned and wrapped. Cutter searched through the saddlebags for the first-aid kit and found the granola bars he'd stuffed in at the last minute. He peeled back the wrapper on one and gave it to Allison with some water, then pitched one each to the Nordeens.

Ross looked at him like he'd gone insane.

"What's this?"

"Food," Cutter said.

"You threaten to shoot us one minute then you give us a candy bar?" Ross shook his head. "I swear...." For a moment, Cutter thought the man might cry. Instead, he got control of himself and ripped open the granola bar with his teeth. Callum finished his by the time his older brother savored the first bite.

The rain came down in buckets now, forming a near-solid curtain of water, throwing the little overhang into deep twilight. It would have been breathtaking if not for Allison's injuries.

"What's your plan, Marshal?" Callum spat over his shoulder. "I could smell the rot on your little buddy when we dragged him up." Ross jerked the cuffs to shut him up. It was no use.

Mohave County would have choppers in the air as soon as the rain stopped. Cutter would be able to make contact by radio then. If the rain stopped. Manfredi had made it crystal clear—most of these summer storms were quick, explosive downpours—but some could go on for hours.

"Take a look at these walls," Callum went on. "See how they're all scoured smooth? What do you think caused that?"

Cutter ignored him, focusing instead on cleaning Wyatt Allison's wound as best he could with the limited kit. Allison winced and gritted his teeth but seemed to lack the energy to complain.

"I'll tell you," Callum said. "Water. That's what caused it. That river is gonna keep rising 'til it takes us all! What are you gonna do with your friend then? Huh?"

A tawny bird about the size of a robin flitted through the curtain of falling water, frantic, as if something was hot on its tail. It fluttered around the protected enclosure a moment, then perched on the saddle horn. The horse cocked an ear backward but didn't seem to mind. The little bird's head twitched back and forth. Its snow-white breast heaved as it caught its breath, a beautiful sight against the harsh realities of flood and stone.

Callum looked over his shoulder, licking his lips like he wanted to eat the thing.

"Mom used to call those rain crows," Ross whispered, eyes gazing far away, remembering. "On accounta they call more before a storm."

"A cuckoo," Wyatt Allison whispered. "Handsome birds, but… murderous little bastards when they're young."

"How's that?" Cutter asked. He wanted Allison to keep talking to take his mind off the cleaning process.

"Cuckoos often lay their eggs in another bird's nest." Allison winced and took a deep breath, steeling himself. "The cuckoo chick hatches first, bigger, stronger. If he can't roll the eggs out, he pushes out all the other babies once they hatch. Like I said, murderous bastards."

Ross Nordeen finished his granola bar. "How do you think they know to do that?"

"Born that way," Wyatt said through clenched teeth.

Cutter finished cleaning Allison's wounds and wrapped them with clean gauze. He was heartened to find a flexible foam SAM splint in the kit.

"How about you?" Cutter looked up from Allison's swollen leg, seething now. This kid had lain there all night while these assholes had taken potshots at him. If the rain didn't stop soon there was a better than average chance he was going to lose his leg—or fall into shock and die. "You been on the run for three months now. We all figured your sister was helping you out, keeping you supplied. Then she got herself arrested for DUI and left you high and dry. I'm thinking you had to start stealing from campers. Taking advantage of everyone around you like that bird over there. It's like you can't help but prey on people."

Ross hung his head.

"Maybe we was just born that way," Callum said. "Like you said, same as the bird."

"So," Ross whispered. "No redemption then? We just are what we are and that's it."

"My experience," Cutter said. "Truly evil men don't change."

"I guess not," Ross said.

"But," Cutter said. "Ninety-nine percent of the folks I've thrown in jail aren't bad people. They've done bad things, maybe something evil, but they were good in the beginning. There are a few, though… that seem to me are just born bad. That kind doesn't change."

"So, it's not our fault," Callum said. Cutter couldn't remember ever wanting to smack the smug off a face any worse.

"More my fault than yours," Ross said. "At least I had a choice."

Callum jerked at the cuffs. "You saying you're better than me?"

"What I can't wrap my head around," Cutter said, "is why y'all would come all the way from Kanab to clear out here."

"Marshal," Ross sighed, exhausted, like the weight of the world was on his shoulders and he was about to let it drop. "We're not even sure where here is. We're just—"

"Shut your mouth," Callum snapped.

"Can you knock it off for one second?" Ross said. "Just stop! I'm sick of your bullshit. It's you got David killed—"

"Don't you even say his name!"

"Knock it off!" Cutter barked.

The brothers rolled into a tight ball, clawing, biting—and falling directly toward Allison.

Cutter roared for them to stop, dragging the wounded deputy sheriff out of the way. At first, he thought it was a ruse so they could mount a coordinated attack, but Callum snatched up the blunt shears Cutter had been using to cut away Wyatt Allison's clothing—and began stabbing his brother over and over in the chest and shoulder.

"I'll cut your throat you piece of—"

Cutter shot Callum Nordeen twice with his Colt. Hands raised in the effort to stab his brother to death, both .357 magnum bullets went in through the man's armpit, destroying his heart and lungs. He pitched forward without another word, piling up face first on the ground, still cuffed to his brother, on his knees with his ass in the air.

The cuckoo flitted around under the stone for a few seconds at the sound of the blast, then returned to her spot on the saddle horn. The big bay stood stock-still as if all this was a foregone conclusion.

"You done?" Cutter said, covering Ross with the Colt.

The last surviving Nordeen heaved a long sigh and fell against the wall beside his dead brother, nodding, panting from the fight. The blunt sheers Callum had attacked him with had shredded what was left of his shirt and gashed his forehead but didn't appear to have cut anything major.

"You… you're a damn good marshal," he said, "but I'm not so sure you're a good man. My brothers were broken, but not all bad." He spit a mouthful of blood onto the rock. "There's not all that much difference between you and them."

Cutter gave a little shrug. "Just enough, I guess…."

The thump of a distant helicopter rattled the rocks. Water still poured from the mountains above, but the rain outside had stopped. Gabe Manfredi's voice crackled across the radio.

Nordeen's eyes flicked from the handheld to Cutter.

"So, it's over…."

"Looks that way," Cutter said.

Nordeen beat his head softly against the sandstone wall. "I can't believe… I mean, you ride in here on a horse in the middle of a thunderstorm blasting away with that rifle… kill both my brothers. Ready to kill us all without a second thought. How do you…? I mean… what kind of man…?"

Wyatt Allison opened his eyes, wincing as he tried to scootch up higher against the wall. "Pretty sure he was just born that way…."

*—Retired chief deputy U.S. Marshal and* New York Times *bestselling author Marc Cameron published his first Western,* Hard Road to Heaven, *in 2005, followed by* The Hell Riders *in 2006 (both under Mark Henry). Since then, he's written seven Arliss Cutter novels featuring a modern-day deputy U.S. Marshal based in Alaska, and eight Jericho Quinn espionage thrillers. Marc is the author of seven Tom Clancy/Jack Ryan novels for the Clancy estate. His short fiction has appeared in* Boys' Life Magazine *and* The Saturday Evening Post. *Originally from Texas, Cameron and his wife have lived in Alaska for twenty-seven years.*

# JOE R. LANSDALE

## UNDER THE MOON OF ARIZONA

I WAS A long way from Arkansas and a long way from my jurisdiction as a marshal, but I was still tracking a man. Or would be in short time. I'd been asked by Hanging Judge Parker to step away from my duties and head out west to Arizona to find the Apache Kid. The Kid was said to have murdered a friend of the judge, and he wanted vengeance—or justice, as he called it—and he asked me to go.

Telegraphing ahead, the judge got it arranged. The 7th Cavalry post out there knew who he was, and they said, "Why not?" and in short time I wasn't marshaling and I wasn't officially bounty hunting. I was going to be a scout for the United States Cavalry. I could follow a trail pretty good, so I'd be okay, though I was hoping to have Choctaw with me in short time. He worked with the marshals as a tracker, and he'd have been glad to come with me, I was sure, but rumor was he'd gone off on a drunk somewhere up in the Ozarks over some gal who left him high, dry, and fifty dollars short.

Choctaw, bless his foolish heart, had been in love. I left word for him to come and find me.

Had I not felt I owed Judge Parker some consideration for taking on a colored marshal, I'd have stayed home with my wife. But here I was, mounting the stage in Willcox, catching a ride on a mail delivery, about to be wheeled out to the hot and beyond they called Fort Grant.

Due to the color of my skin, I figured on having to ride on top of the stage, like a piece of luggage, but the driver, a lean fellow with a mustache a flea could get lost in, seen me, and said, "Toss that bag on top, and sit here with me. Can you handle a shotgun? Shotgunner got stung in the balls by a hornet, so he can't sit for long. He's lying out on his porch with a wet rag on his gadget."

"I can handle most any kind of gun," I said, climbing up and throwing my bag on the roof, inside the railing. The shotgun there was a double-barrel Greener. Oiled and shiny, both the metal and the wood. There was a little well under the seat, and it was stuffed with shotgun shells.

"It's loaded," the driver said. "I'm Warren Earp."

"Nat Love," I said.

And with a yell and a crack of his whip that tore the air like a sheet of paper, we were off and rolling. The bounce of the stage ached my bones. I hadn't ridden on one in a long time. I had come out by train, riding in the back with the porters, of course. They were good company. A lot of lies were swapped.

Truth was, I was getting a little too old for all this business and was considering maybe becoming a porter myself. My wife felt I had been shot at enough, and I was thinking maybe she was right.

"I heard you're helping scout out the Apache Kid," Warren said.

"No secrets out here."

"Nope. Rumors run like wet shit down a hill. It's the boredom. This Kid, you better watch your ass and grow an eye in the back of your head. He's said to have killed more people than smallpox."

We rumbled along, talked as we went. I slowly realized this Earp was a brother to them that was in that shootout in Tombstone near the OK Corral. I was itching to ask him about it, but figured since he wasn't in on it, I'd just get some secondhand tales, all of them polished by the light of a younger brother. It was an itch I decided not to scratch.

Fort Grant was more upscale than I expected. It even had its own lake and fountain. But as I've heard said, dressing a pig in satin doesn't change it into a debutante. And having a lake and a fountain and good construction didn't change the fact that the fort was in the back and beyond, surrounded by heat and hostiles.

I climbed off the stage, leaving Warren with the shotgun, tipped my hat to him, and started across the parade ground.

A young private trooper that looked as if he had just been hatched, his mustache perhaps loaned to him by an adult, hustled up to me seemingly out of nowhere and brought me to the office of 7th Cavalry Commander Colonel Sumner.

Outside the door, I took off my hat, and to look as smart as one could look after riding on a stage eating dust and sweating buckets, I beat the dust out of my hat on my leg, then patted it off my clothes as much as possible. When I felt about half ready, the private let me in and followed after.

The plump colonel sat behind the desk with a fat finger through a coffee cup loop. He looked at me with rheumy eyes. He had an air of someone slightly smarter than the dead. I could tell he didn't like what he was looking at. That being me. A colored fellow who didn't have to salute, bow, or scrape.

"I been told you marshal for Judge Parker," he said. "Ever catch anybody on the run?"

"It's what I do when I'm not eating watermelon."

The colonel studied me for a moment, trying to figure if I had made a joke or a statement of fact.

He took some wanted posters out of a drawer with sketches of the Kid on them, as well as a couple of photos he had on hand. The Kid had been a scout and was therefore in more than a few pictures taken at the fort and roundabout.

"This Apache Kid, he's a bad one. You'll have to try and pick up a cold trail first. You don't have to deal with him alone. I'm going to send someone with you. But listen here, you got to stay sneaky. It's not just the Kid. He's got four others with him, way I hear it. I don't know of but one of them. A half-breed called Happy Jack. He's as deadly as the Kid, but not as smart, and he's got one short leg. The other two Indians are about half as deadly, but mind you, being half as deadly as the Kid and Jack is plenty enough."

"I got a fellow coming to help me track, so I don't need a trooper."

"I was told you were being sent on account of you being able to track?"

"Track better'n most, but not as good as this fellow I'm talking about."

"That fellow isn't here, and that cold trail is getting colder. You'll take a trooper or you'll go home. You come to help, so I can't wait until your help arrives. You'll be assigned a horse, and you'll get started after you have something to eat."

Going home was appealing, but I owed the judge. Also, I didn't really know for sure Choctaw would show. He might still be out in the Ozarks feeling miserable over his lost love.

"Burroughs here will be the trooper," Colonel Sumner said.

It was, of course, the young trooper who had been waiting to lead me into the office. He had been standing stiffly nearby the colonel's desk.

Some saluting went on between Burroughs and the colonel before we stepped outside. He hustled me up some food and brought it over to the corral where I was inspecting the small bunch of horses I was to choose from. All but a couple looked as if they were on the edge of having to be propped up with sticks and fed laudanum with a spoon.

I picked out the better two, and we got the tack and goods we needed for the trip, saddled and packed the horses, and started out. Burroughs even brought his saber, strapped it to the side of the horse, ready to be pulled.

It was warm and it was the dry heat everyone always talks about, which for me is more deadly than wet heat, because sweat tells you you're getting hot. The other can fool you. Next thing you know, they find you in a dry creek bed with sunstroke.

As we were riding out, I seen a bunch of Buffalo Soldiers ride in, and we paused to watch them ride by. They had personalized their uniforms with stripes, and even dusted as they were, the soldiers looked sharp and professional.

Private Burroughs said, "They belong to the Twenty-Fourth. I suppose you could say they are on loan to the fort due to Apache troubles.

Fine soldiers. Tough as nails. I've been under their sergeant before, and between you and me, I prefer him to our fat colonel. Forget I said that."

"Forgotten."

The sergeant broke loose from his troops, rode over, and said, "Looking at those horses, Private Burroughs, you fellas might as well take turns riding each other. Those horses won't last a day out there. Come over to the stables on our side. We can fix you up."

"Thank you, sir," Burroughs said, and we rode over there and were given fresh mounts. As we were swapping our saddles and goods to the better critters, we told him our mission. Then I said, "I was a buffalo soldier in West Texas for a time. Years back."

I didn't mention that I had run off from the fort with a stolen horse, and might even still be wanted by the authorities back in Texas.

"Then you'll be better off out there than some. The Apache Kid, you might not want to find him. He's got a half-breed with him that I reckon is worse than the Kid, it's just the Kid has gotten all the attention."

"We have already been given that warning," I said.

"We been out there hunting for a few days. Cut their sign about five miles out."

He pointed the direction.

"We followed them into the mountains. Come across a homestead with a whole family cut up and strung up. We buried them, spent the night in the barn there. House was too bloody to stay in. Next morning, we decided to say we lost them, even if their trail was visible. Trail like that, they want you to follow. I decided we wouldn't. Don't tell that on me, but way I see it, I'd like to live another forty years. Besides, I figure we was sent out mostly as bait, to pull them out of their hidey-holes."

Burroughs said, "We won't say a word about your decision, will we, Nat?"

Burroughs had taken me into his confidence quickly. But I agreed. Not a word.

I said, "Figure a small group is better to catch a small group than a big group you can see miles off without binoculars."

"You're right about that, I reckon," the sergeant said. "But I won't joke you. That house, those bodies. It put me off my kit for a few days. I'm understanding of them Apache. They lived here before we did, and we've done everything to them but run over them with a train. And maybe that. But that don't mean I want to throw them no picnic. Watch yourself. They ain't much for kidding."

We left out then, the sergeant's words hanging on us like moss. I'm alert most of the time anyway, hunting miscreants and such being my job, but you could bet I didn't relax in the saddle for one moment. It wasn't my first time to deal with Apache.

Late afternoon with the sun beginning to dip, we came to a watering hole with a few struggling cottonwood trees. The shade was nice. I had picked up the Kid and his companion's trail about where the sergeant said we would. Five miles out. They had been here and gone on and come back again. The reason would be the water. I could tell that from the old tracks and the more recent ones. They had cut the throat of a horse and let him fall in the water, spoiling it on purpose to thwart pursuers. They'd also cut some meat out of the horse, and we could see and smell a blackened fire site where they'd cooked it. We could also smell the rotting horse.

I took Burroughs's camp shovel off his pack and started digging about ten feet from where the water hole was. A place where an underground stream might be leaking down from the mountains. It was some serious work. First hole I dug was dry. I tried another spot. Water bubbled up and filled it before I was two feet down. The water was sandy at first, but it was linked with the same spring that had filled the original pool, so it became less gritty in short time. Still, we strained it through a handkerchief and filled our canteens with it.

Burroughs said, "I came out here with no more than a dollar in my pocket to earn my mettle. But truth is, so far all I've earned is dysentery and saddle sores. I'm having suspicions I'm not cut out for the soldiering life."

"It didn't suit me either," I said.

It was a nervous night, and we slept without fire. It was cold in the dark, and we could hear owls hooting in the trees where the mountain range began. For me, there was always something disturbing about the hoots of owls. Probably because during my time in service, dealing with Apache, I learned that what I was actually hearing might not be owls.

When the sun cracked open the night sky, we had already eaten a cold breakfast without coffee, and were mounted, climbing our way up into the mountains on a trail a mountain goat would have refused. But it was the trail they had taken. They hadn't bothered to hide their tracks, except for a bit of brush work. My reckoning was they meant for us to follow them into an ambush.

I told Burroughs we needed to work our way around and surprise them instead of them surprising us. It took a long time, and the fact was, all that working away from the obvious trail ate up the day like a hungry man consuming a hot apple pie.

We were on a little path through the rocks. Wide enough to lead our horses up. When the moon was high it silvered the rocks and made shadows heavy as lead between the cracks in the stones and the clutters of brush and cottonwoods that had grown thicker during our climb.

I remember pausing at one vantage point to sit on horseback and look through some splits in the rocks, and way in the distance, hit by the moonlight, I could see a man on horseback. I hoped he wasn't coming in our direction. If so, the renegades would have them another to cut and burn and steal his goods. But traveling under a bright moon like that made some sense. It wasn't scalding hot, and you could lie up during the day.

It took us a couple hours to rise to a spot where we could have a good look down on the rocky trail where I assumed our killers would be. When we looked, off to the side of the trail, we could see a fire glowing down in the rocks, and we could see bedrolls all around it.

"You did it, Nat. You sneaked up on them."

I studied the bedrolls. They seemed lumpy to me. Lumpier than men. A chill charged up my back.

"There's no one in those bedrolls, Burroughs. They're draped over rocks. I've been outsmarted."

Proof of this arrived almost immediately as a bullet sliced the night and punched a rock near our heads and sent a ricochet of lead and stone shards into the air.

We tugged our horses upward as another shot cut a hole through my hat so smooth it didn't even knock it off my head. They had tricked me good, letting me think I was doing the sneaking, when in fact, it was them that were the masters. It's hard to outsneak an Apache. You might want to write that down.

Still, they hadn't been quite as smart as they thought, having fired on us before they were close enough and certain enough to make sure they got us. We were able to work our way around a large boulder and up a trail so narrow I wasn't sure we or the horses we were leading were going to make it.

Gravel and dirt tumbled down behind us and made thick dust puffs in the air. That dust cloud gave us a shield against their aim, just long enough for us to reach the peak of that spot and find our way into a large cave opening. We led our horses inside and let them wander toward the back.

The cave was both good and bad. Now we couldn't be snuck up on from behind, but then again, we couldn't really go nowhere either. We had an outpost that gave us sight of them that came up the trail, but all they had to do, if they were of a mind, was starve and thirst us to death.

We didn't give the cave a good look-over right off because they came up after us. Emboldened, one of them came up the trail at a crouch with a rifle clutched in one hand, planning to overrun us before we could get situated.

He was a whip-lean fellow with a band of brown cloth wrapped around his forehead, dressed in a dust-coated white shirt and pants. He came up the trail swiftly, holding a knife, and was almost on top of us before I dropped my rifle and pulled my pistol, a move that to me was as natural as swatting a gnat. I fired and he bent backward and rolled down the hill in a flowing wad of dirt and skidded to a stop against a boulder.

Had that Apache been faster by a second or two, he'd have been on us before we could have responded. It was terrifying to think of that kind of courage and determination. Though I don't know if I would have put him in the smart category.

So, there we were, at the mouth of a cave wide as four men and slightly taller than a horse, with a bit of boulder rising in front of the cave mouth, enough we could lay behind. I recovered my rifle, and me and Burroughs lay there on the ground with our weapons propped over the rock barrier, waiting for another fool to try what the other had tried.

I saw a shape pass from one boulder, across the path, to tuck in behind another on the opposite side. He was probably trying to figure if there was a better angle than straight on to shoot at us. Straight on hadn't worked well for his companion. Especially since he tried to take us with a knife, not that it didn't almost work.

We lay there for some time—nobody moving. Finally, I said, "Burroughs, I'm going to check the back of the place, see if there's a way we can slip out, or be sure they don't slip in. Keep sharp."

In the middle of the cave, around a bend of stone, the horses had wandered to a spot where water was leaking through the rocks above, falling into an indention in the floor, making a pool. Moonlight through the cracks gave me enough light to see the water. The reflection appeared molten silver. The horses were drinking their fill. I stopped and tasted the water. It was fresh. The horses would be all right, and if we drank it, so would we.

I took a leather lantern case off of Burroughs's horse, pulled a lucifer from my pocket, and fired it to light. I carried it into the back of the cave where the dark was thick as blood pudding. There was all manner of bones, and I feared I might come upon a bear or a cougar back there, but instead I found a body. It was a woman, and she was certainly an Apache. Long dead, mummified by the elements.

I lowered the lantern so that I could see her better. Her face was withered and her hair had come loose of her skull in spots, but there were still white strands hanging on her head, looking like dribbles of milk. She was dressed all in leather and the leather had greened and darkened, same as her skin. No telling how long she had been dead. Maybe left by an Apache band when she became too old to cut it, and she had found this spot to wait and die. Death had accommodated her and the climate had kept her.

I set the lantern on a rock, fed and hobbled the horses, pulled some jerky out of my saddlebag for the two of us, and hoisting our canteens and about fourteen pounds of ammunition, wormed my way back the mouth of the cave, blowing out the lantern as I went.

I put the goods I had brought aside, dropped down behind the rise of rock in front of the cave, and picked up my rifle. I told Burroughs what I had found.

"My God, how fascinating," he said. "What could be her story? And look. You can see the sky from this angle, through the split in the rocks to the right. That big red spot in the heavens, that's Mars. There's canals up there, Nat."

"Canals?" I said.

Now, don't think that while we talked we didn't rove our eyes over the trail and where the boulders split, being cautious, but I was glad to think of something else other than my possible demise. We spoke softly, but it wasn't like they didn't know where we were.

"A scientist named Lowell says you can see Mars through a telescope quite clearly, and you can make out water canals cut in the soil, running for miles," Burroughs said. "A civilization is possible up there, Nat. Eking out life on the red desert there same as the Apache eke out one here in this beautiful country."

"Do you think Lowell is right? About the canals?"

"I want him to be," Burroughs said. "I want it to be filled with rare and adventuresome people."

"Adventure isn't calling me at the moment," I said, "being right smack dab in the middle of one that might not work out well has satiated me."

"Nothing is promised to any of us," Burroughs said.

"If Mars is rocks and desert like here, I don't think I would like it much. I miss the trees back home in Arkansas."

"If I could wish myself to Mars by willpower alone, believe me, I would let it have me. Trees or no trees."

"In that case, so would I."

"It's funny, how with them out there and us trapped in here, I keep thinking of wonderful things. Mysterious things."

"That's to keep you from thinking of being castrated and cooked over a slow fire with your pecker in your mouth. Apache are inventive."

"They are so interesting. At the fort, I saw beautiful Apache women, wives and daughters of the scouts. Fine figures, fine carriage, and they didn't hide how much they hated us. The men could live off a blade of grass and a spot of dew, if they had to. They impressed me."

"Listen, Burroughs. Do you hear that?"

It was a slight crumbling sound, like stepping on crackers, and then a few figments of rock and dirt tumbled off the top of the cave and coasted downward in front of the opening. In the moonlight, it looked like fairy dust drifting to the ground.

"Someone's on top of our spot," Burroughs said.

A rifle cracked and there was a spitting sound as blood flared in a red mist in front of us, and then there were spots of it on the ground. A rifle slid off the roof of the cave and clattered on top of the blood-specked gravel, followed by a body. An Apache.

The air snapped with more rifle fire from above and from the rocks below. The Apache were shooting at someone besides us, and that someone was shooting back. I recalled the shape I had seen riding in the distance, and then, I realized who it was.

"I'm coming in, Nat," said a voice from above.

"Choctaw," I said. "Don't shoot, Burroughs. It's my friend."

I hadn't even gotten those words out of my mouth when a rifle dropped in front of us, and Choctaw, my longtime companion, swung into the cave like an acrobat. He leaped behind our barrier as shots whistled around us, slapped into the body of the dead Apache, and echoed at the back of the cave. I was glad the horses were around the curve, back near the water so they wouldn't take a bullet.

Choctaw wiggled up between us.

"How's it hanging, Nat?"

"Unsteady, and to the left."

Burroughs reached over the strip of rock and grabbed Choctaw's rifle, then handed it to him. We let go with a bunch of rifle shots, into the rocks, at nothing we could clearly make out right then, though I did see a moon shadow move between the space where we had observed Mars.

"How many of them are there?" Choctaw asked.

"We thought five in the beginning."

"What's left is three. Pretty sure one of them is the fellow you're chasing. The Apache Kid."

"Better be, otherwise I'd have stayed home. Damn, Choctaw. You're hit."

I knew this because blood was leaking on the rock barrier in front of us.

"My shoulder took a ricochet, and I got one in my leg, too. Rock pieces from where the bullet bounced. It don't bother me none at all. I could dance a jig and kick the hat off your head."

"Gentleman," Burroughs said. "They've quit firing."

"We noticed," Choctaw said. "No bullets whistling past our noses, we can figure that."

"Just an observation," Burroughs said.

We lay there for some time. The night was starting to lighten and we could hear birds singing up in the cottonwoods and among the rocks. The air had turned sweet as a lover's kiss.

"They had the bright moon working against them last night," Choctaw said. "Now they got the sun, and its behind us, so that's good for us. You got water, grub? All of my goods was on my horse. I left it behind the rocks last night. Trailed you here, decided to crawl up there to look over them. And what do I discover up there?"

"Let me guess," I said, "the smelly, fly-covered boy in front of us."

"You get the dolly. Should have come up behind them, but thing was, I couldn't manage a spot where I could put the good sneak on them. But I did bag one of them."

As the sun rose higher, the body in front of us warmed, the stench grew, and the flies filled the air with a constant buzz.

By midday, we had listened and drank water and ate jerky and took shits in the back of the cave, and then the day became really hot, even with us in the shade.

"You know, Nat," Choctaw said. "I think they're gone."

"You think that do you?" I said.

"We can't stay here forever," Burroughs said.

"But we can stay a while," I said.

The day crept on along. There wasn't a sound in the rocks, but then Apache rarely make sounds when they don't want to.

The air lost its sweet aroma and acquired a broiled smell, as if guts were being overcooked on a hot rock. By late afternoon, Choctaw said. "I'm going out to check."

"Night would be better," Burroughs said.

"For them as well. You fellas see an Apache on my ass, please shoot him."

Choctaw kind of slithered over the rock and around the edge of it. I expected rifle fire from the Apache, if they didn't catch him and cut his throat, but there was nothing.

We waited there about an hour, I reckon, before Choctaw said, "Don't shoot, you trigger-happy son of a bitches."

Choctaw stepped into view and came into the cave. "They've packed up. All three. Saw their horse tracks. They took my horse, too."

"Why would they quit?" Burroughs said. "They had us trapped."

"We got a good position, and they know they might have to be here for a few days," Choctaw said. "They've lost men. Decided to move on. Left us with their pals. They got some mounts without riders, which will help them cover ground and give them less tuckered out horses when they need them. Or they can eat them. I wouldn't mind a mouthful of roasted horse shank myself right now. We gonna keep trailing them, Nat?"

"That's our job," I said.

Burroughs and Choctaw went and looked at the woman in the back of the cave out of curiosity, and then we loaded up and led our horses down the trail until I felt we could ride them more safely. As for the dead Apache, we didn't want to deny the buzzards dinner, and maybe a good breakfast of leftovers. I know the Apache Kid and his band would have done the same for us.

Me and Choctaw took turns with my horse, me riding, Choctaw holding to a short piece of looped rope rigged to the saddle horn. He'd grip it and run alongside, then I'd swap with him for a while. Running like that, Apache style, the horse sort of boosted you along, bouncing you on your toes. It was surprising how well and for long you could travel that way, once you got used to it, though I wouldn't recommend it as a sport. It might be noted for those without common sense, you wouldn't want the rider to run his horse at a gallop. Burroughs didn't offer to try it out, and we didn't ask him to. It was not a good time to teach that skill.

This time our prey didn't let us see their tracks so easily. They took what military men like to call evasive actions. They ran their horses for a time, then slow-walked them up into the mountains, and pretty soon it was as if they and their horses had turned to smoke.

I was outsmarted, but it's hard to fool Choctaw when it comes to following a trail. He can track a duck fart to a pond a mile away and know which duck among all its cousins had let it fly. He led us cautiously up into the rocks. I was considering maybe we ought to call in the dogs on this hunt and get back to the fort where we could cool our heels. We could brag we had killed a couple and had pursued the others until we lost them.

Instead, we kept at it, Choctaw in the lead. The rocks were hot with the sun. Still, I wasn't sure how much I favored the dying of the day and the purple shadows that lurked over the mountains. That gave us some cooling and possible hiding room, but it gave them a lot of sneaking room. I had heard once that Apaches didn't like to fight at night, but somehow no one had ever told the Apache that.

We found a spot surrounded with rocks, but not high rocks. We could see over them well enough, and there were a number of gaps where we could see out and they could see in. Other places around us were less secure. There was one easy way in, one narrow path, but anyone could climb over our barrier if they took a mind to. In some ways, like the cave, we were better defended, and in other ways we were trapped. It beat the wide open. There were no high rocks above us in that spot, so they couldn't shoot down on us. Thing was, on one side, you climbed over the rocks you better be able to walk on air because the drop was so deep it could kill a bag of potatoes. But the good was, we didn't have to defend that side at all.

There wasn't much in the way of sleeping. We couldn't afford the luxury. We didn't make a fire, and our supper consisted of a jerky and canteen water. My thoughts were, we didn't have problems in the night we'd head back to the fort come crack of morning. I had had enough.

Burroughs took a position behind a rock near the little path in, Choctaw took a spot between the rocks that faced a rocky expanse, and I hunkered down in the same fashion. I was on the side where brush grew thick, like the old-man's beard.

I roamed an eye this way and that but saw nothing. I heard an owl, and I wondered if it was one of our killers sending a signal to another. I heard a hoot back and felt certain that it wasn't a feathered friend.

The wind moved a bush not too far from me, and I thought maybe I heard a dove coo somewhere, another signal perhaps, but no one came over the wall with a wild cry, blazing firearms or flashing knives. I was as nervous as a goat watching a butcher sharpen his cleaver.

The moon began to sink toward the east. I was sinking myself, so I understood its feelings. I noticed the bush in front of me moving in the wind again. It was a slight move. But none of the other bushes were moving. For that matter, there wasn't any wind.

I reckoned the sight of my rifle on the bush and watched carefully. Wasn't it a slight bit closer than before, or was I merely coming down with a case of the jumps?

I had the rifle cocked and ready. I watched the bush for a long time. It didn't move again. I decided to take a chance and fired away. The bush made a noise and fell over.

"What the hell?" Choctaw said.

But before I could make a remark on my fine shooting, the other two came over the wall. The Apache Kid and the one I figured was the breed, Happy Jack. I knew the Kid right off from those poster drawings and the photos. Even in the moonlight, it was easy to recognize that face. Him and the breed had snuck up so smooth and quiet you'd have thought them a cousin to the dark. They both came over where Choctaw was.

I ran to him. Burroughs came too, carrying a rifle in one hand, his saber in the other, but he slipped on a rock and hit the ground with a smack so hard it was as if Morpheus had struck him with a hammer. He didn't even moan, just lay there, knocked out with his nose in the dirt.

Choctaw and the breed, who was sizable, were rolling on the ground. Choctaw had lost his rifle in the struggle, and the other had a knife. I saw Choctaw latch his teeth onto Happy Jack's ear, heard Jack yelp, and then me and the Apache Kid came together like two trains on the same track.

They had chosen knives to sneak easier, without dragging firearms. I still had my rifle, and I fired, but the Kid was on me as soon as the bullet split the air. I missed. I used the rifle barrel to deflect a knife slash and then hit him in the head with the stock.

He took the rifle away from me as easy as taking a rattle away from a baby. But he dropped it. Either butterfingered or intent on cutting my guts out. I grabbed his wrist as he thrust, but he turned his hand and the knife cut the back of my wrist. It wasn't deep, but it made me jerk away and backstep a yard. I squatted, picked up gravel-laced dirt, and threw it in his eyes. It wasn't much, but like the old lady that peed in the ocean, every little bit helped.

I grabbed a rock only a bit smaller than my fist and flung that as hard as I could. The hand of David, the slingshot master, must have reached back from the ages and guided my hand because that rock hit the Kid right between the eyes, causing the knife to fly from his hand. He stepped back, like he had just remembered he'd left something cooking on a campfire, then keeled over.

I ran to help Choctaw, but the Apache Kid had only been playing possum. He grabbed my ankle and I went down on my face and ate a mouthful of dirt and gravel.

We rolled around a bit, me trying to squirm out of his grasp. I managed my knife out of its sheath and stabbed at him, but the tip hit his leather belt and didn't go in deep enough.

Finally, we came loose of one another and scrambled to our feet. In the background, I could see Choctaw straddling the breed, beating him in the head with a rock large enough he had to use both hands.

The Kid recovered his knife, and now he came toward me, not quite at a run, but enough to make me back up. It was only an instant before I realized I was backing toward the rocks that bordered the big drop-off.

The Kid slashed at me, and I blocked by slashing his forearm. It was a good and lucky hit. Hot blood gushed out of his arm and splashed against my face, into my eyes.

I ducked under another slash, blood still flying out of his arm, and tried to cut up into him. He avoided a good hit, but I did slash his ribs. Now we were both gripping the wrists that held our knives, waddling backward against the rocks. I stomped his foot, kneed him in the horse apples, then let go of his knife hand as I dove down and grabbed his legs and lifted him up over me and over the rocks.

I leaned over for a look, saw a flick of moonlit body tumbling into the dark, and then the dark ate him, and I collapsed.

When the sun came up, it found a place to rest against my forehead, and then when I awoke, it drooped into my eyes. I felt like I had been shot at and missed, shit at and hit.

It only took me about a half hour to sit up. When I did, I saw that I had been wrapped in U.S. Army bandages. I saw Choctaw across the way, sitting on the rocks with the dead breed in front of him. Even from there I could see that Choctaw had damn near beat the man's head flat. Choctaw was wrapped so thick in bandages he looked like a pile of rags.

Burroughs was sitting next to him, applying some finishing touches on the doctoring. He had a dark bruise on his forehead.

"Nat," he said, noticing me. "Sorry. So sorry. I can't believe I tripped over a rock."

"I can," I said. "I saw you."

Burroughs turned red. I made myself get up and look over the drop.

I couldn't see the Kid's body down there. Just the rocky floor. What the hell? You didn't come back from that. Had a wild animal dragged him off in the night?

I went over and sat on the boulder beside Choctaw. I said, "Burroughs, tell me the whole of your name so I can remember you by it."

"Edgar Rice Burroughs," he said.

"That's a mouthful," I said.

There's not much to tell after that. We located all their horses, including Choctaw's and the two belonging to them we had killed up near the cave. We loaded the breed's body and the Apache in the bush, stretched them across their horses and tied them on with rope. We considered going back for the other two Apache at the cave, now that we had some time on our hands. But the idea of hauling in those rotting corpses, if animals hadn't already carried them off, left us to the conclusion that it would be wrong to deprive the worms. Happy Jack's body would prove he was dead, and our word might prove the other. But I doubted it.

It took us a few days, hurt as we were. We holed up for two of those days at the water hole I had dug under the cottonwoods. The body of the horse was mostly bones and stink by then, it having been scavenged.

Back at Fort Grant we gave our report, but the colonel wouldn't mark the Apache Kid as dead, as we couldn't prove it. For years there were rumors he was out there. Had been killed here. Been killed there. Died of old age. Murdered this person or that. Diddled someone's dog. You name it, there was an Apache Kid story to go with it.

Me, Choctaw, and Burroughs know better. Something had dragged that body off. I refused to believe the Kid could have survived. Judge Parker was satisfied with my story and felt his friend had gotten some justice. That was good enough for me.

Let me tell you my surprise and delight when plenty of years later, when I had left marshaling, I found a magazine on a newsstand with a story titled Under the Moons of Mars with Burroughs's name on it. It was a rollicking good tale, and I recognized the thing in the cave and the wishful exodus to Mars. He wrote other stories, even a couple with an Apache hero. I read some of them.

Choctaw married a woman mean as a snake, but a lot better looking, and settled in Oklahoma. She had money and a farm.

Me? I worked as a porter and lived with my wife until death took her on a holiday. Being a porter was good, honest, well-paying work, but it didn't match when me and Edgar Rice Burroughs and my good friend Choctaw roamed the Arizona mountains in search of the Apache Kid, then found and killed him.

You can believe me or not.

*—Joe R. Lansdale is the author of fifty novels and four hundred shorter works, including stories, essays, reviews, film and TV scripts, stage plays, introductions and magazine articles, as well as a book of poetry. His work has been made into films, animation, comics, television series, and he has won numerous awards including the Edgar Award, the Raymond Chandler lifetime award, numerous Bram Stoker Awards, the Lifetime Horror Award, and the Spur Award.*

*He lives in Nacogdoches, Texas, with his wife, Karen, and pit bull, Rudy.*

# ANTHONY WOOD

## THE LAST HANGING TREE

*End of August 1944*

"GET HIM DOWN." The two deputies I inherited from the last sheriff gawk up at the body swaying in the breeze like an airstrip wind sock. Art and Jack stand as stiff as the body stretched by a hangman's noose. I can't tell if their reluctance is from fear or disbelief—probably both.

"Do it now!"

They scramble around like two Vaudeville clowns falling over each other trying to get the rope untied from the grand old oak that hosted many a similar display years ago.

"Somebody should've already cut that old tree down." The time for this kind of justice has long passed. At least until now.

I crush the butt of my Lucky Strike smoke under my bootheel and search the packet I snatch from my shirt pocket. Empty. Like my soul. I crumple and toss it into the weeds.

I growl at the comedy of it all but find no humor in it. "One month into the job as Williamson County's newly elected sheriff, and this is my reward? Two knotheads who don't know if they need to wind their asses or scratch their watches." I rub the back of my neck burned by the sun.

Somebody's making a point, and I can't get to the bottom of it. I never thought they'd go this far. Heck, I don't even know who they are. But they're smart, like they've done this before—many times.

I scan the scene. Three—no, four—bodies lie trampled liked ground beef mixed with freshly pulverized dirt among hundreds of hoofprints. Only one thing could've done such a thing—stampede. This is like a bad Saturday afternoon shoot-'em-up matinee in town.

I rub my chin. "Who's got the stones to do this? Hang a man for rustling a few steers?" I kick at what's left of a rustler's body nearly unrecognizable as human. I pull back bloody dust on my boot. "Won't be identifying this one, or any of 'em, for that matter. Too far gone."

My deputies, with work habits and demeanors akin to a Laurel and Hardy comedy show, fumble around with what Grandpa used to call a "hatchet knot" around the hanged rustler's neck. He'd say, "It'll take a hatchet to get it out."

"Just cut the rope, would you? Otherwise, we'll be here 'til Christmas."

Art and Jack finally get the rope loose from the hanged outlaw's neck.

My impatience grows but my dread thickens. I draw in a deep breath and whisper, "All right, let's see who it is."

Art and Jack lay the body on the hood of my patrol car trying to hold their noses with a free hand. It takes only a few hours for bodies to ripen in this scorching Texas sun. I pull my bandana up over my nose.

I study the grooves in the old tree limb where many a man got his neck stretched for cattle rustling. That was back then, though, when Grandpa worked these hills and canyons chasing cattle thieves as a lawman. They hanged who they caught without the benefit or need of a jail, judge, or jury. But this is now, and it won't continue if I can help it.

I point at the severed rope then wave my arm around to include the other bodies crushed in the dust. "This is the third body we've taken from this old hanging tree this month. But the others scattered about? This is a first. Whoever did this took down a whole gang. In a stampede, no less." Surely they did that to cover their own tracks after murdering these men.

The deputies slink back. They know something I don't.

"What's wrong, Art? That body won't bite you." He drops his head, and I ask, "Jack?" I snicker. "What's he got? A rattler in his pocket?"

I ease over to the body dressed in black with a dingy gray flour-sack mask over its head with three holes cut out and wonder who it could be. "All right, get the hood off."

Jack and Art both reluctantly lift the head and slide the mask off, revealing a thick, bushy, though matted, head of dark brown hair. A hot breeze sweeps the hair from in front of the dead man's face.

"What? Oh, heck no!" I slap my hands palms down on the hood of the patrol car. "Please, Lord, no!" I can't take my eyes from his distorted face—the face of a man strangled by a hangman's noose. I can't stand the sight. "Cover it up. Quick."

There he lay. What I had hoped would not be—what just couldn't be, not in my mind. I turn away to bite my wrist and try not to let tears escape. I yank my bandana covering my nose down and puke. Everything within my gut gushes out like a fire hydrant opened up. They step back so as not to get it on their boots. The world turns dark. My knees buckle and wilt. Art and Jack grab my arms. I feel weak as I collapse, but don't faint.

"Get me some water, Jack, will ya?" He splashes a dash of cool water on my face from my canteen. I rinse my mouth out and spit. I wipe my face with my bandana, trying to gather my wits. I gag again, retching up the last bit of bad coffee laced with a splash of whiskey I'd had on the way here. I pull my bandana back up and uncover the hanged man's face again.

Art reaches for the dead man's eyes, but I stop him. "No, I'll do it." I gently pull his eyelids shut. I steady myself against my patrol car. I can't believe it. No arrest and no charges filed. No judge and no jury—just executioners. They hanged him. They killed Tom. They murdered my kid brother.

*One Month Earlier*

I SIT ON a swivel stool at the café breakfast counter, nursing a cooling cup of coffee, pondering my new job. Not sure if I counted the cost on this one. Not sure if I can do it. But I've got to try. There's a problem here in Williamson County, and the people who voted for me believe I can solve it within the law. That I aim to do.

Ever since Tojo and his Japanese red rising sun flag blasted us into the war at Pearl Harbor, meat, especially beef, has become scarcer by the day. It wasn't long after that the government enacted a rationing program that limited every citizen's portion of goods like meat and many other things to support the war effort. God knows the boys fighting the Japanese and Germans overseas need good meat worse than we do, but still, people have to eat. Problem is, if an item becomes scarce or limited, somebody's going to make a buck off of it.

When I was a kid, Pop told stories of Grandpa's anger about how he and his fellow soldiers roasted rats to survive in the trenches of Vicksburg while local businessmen had squirreled away enough food to feed the Confederate Army for another month at the time of the surrender. They sold it on the black market to get rich off other's misfortune and the very men defending them. Grandpa decided on surrender day to leave it all behind. He swam the Mississippi River on a log after the parole and came to Oklahoma to start a new life. Guess he'd had enough of both governments. It's happening again—profiting off of other's misfortune during wartime.

I hold up my cup to the waitress for a refill. If only my eyesight had been better when I tried to enlist, I'd be eating canned beef in some rat-infested foxhole waiting for a *banzai* charge or a *panzer* unit to overrun us. It was hard to watch all my friends march off to war while I stayed behind. Guess I should be grateful that I'm of some use here on the home front. But these damn rustlers are completely out of control. And I'm not sure I can do what needs doing. I stare into my coffee cup that needs a warming up. Waiting for an answer to my own dilemma. Waiting for fresh coffee. Thinking I need a bit of whiskey in my coffee.

The familiar roar of my green Dodge truck picks up speed as it barrels down Main Street, dragging a four-horse trailer and kicking up a cloud of dust. I spin around on my café stool to watch as laughing and yelling, arms waving and unruly hand gestures, and finally a busted beer bottle take center stage in the sleepy little town of Round Rock. I don't have to stretch and strain to see who it is. I know who it is.

I slap the morning *Daily Gazette* down hard on the counter where in big black letters the headline reads, *Cattle Rustling Worst in Decades—U.S. Government Cracks Down.* "Say it ain't so. Surely he didn't borrow my truck for... dang that boy's hide. Surely he wouldn't get involved in...."

I spin back around to snatch up my coffee cup, spilling half of its full contents on the counter. The rumble of my pickup truck trails off into the distance. As I try to contain my anger and not yell, a shapely, middle-aged waitress shuffles over and swats my shoulder with a damp towel she uses to keep the breakfast counter clean.

"Be more careful next time, Sheriff, will ya? Some of us actually work for a living around here, you know?"

Sheriff, I haven't gotten used to that yet. I brush the bit of coffee droplets from my newspaper. "Sorry about that, Madge. I didn't know you'd refilled my cup."

She pops her chewing gum, bounces her hip, and smiles. "Well, you best leave me a good tip for my trouble, you handsome devil." She winks and refills my coffee cup.

I don't respond to her flirt like I usually do with a comical, borderline inappropriate, though harmless remark. We've carried on like this for years. She's my aunt by marriage—a failed marriage, like mine.

Madge leans in. "You all right, Gabe?"

"Not really. I just saw something I didn't want to see."

"Need cream?"

"Yes, please."

She pours a splash into my coffee. "What's troubling you, dear?"

Burnt coffee and stale cigarette smoke hangs thick in the air like suffocating fog. The greasy breakfast I just wolfed down has already sent my stomach to rumbling. I'll be in the john out back soon enough—whether it's the food or nerves, doesn't matter. The result will be the same. Maybe this fresh cup of mud will ease the cramps. I take a sip. It feels good going down. I pull up the local news rag again filled mostly with cattle prices and weather predictions, crop reports and little league scores, local gossip and police records, and any new news about the war.

"I'll show you." I snap open the paper hoping it'll take my mind off my stomach and point at the headline. I read a bit of the article as Madge leans in close to listen. The article talks about how the war caused the rationing of meat, shortages of all kinds, a foiled Nazi plot to steal government beef, and that rustling is the worst it's been in decades.

I whisper as Madge tries to read along, "Says here, that in 1941, Congress passed the McCarran Act to address the cattle rustling problem. It authorized a maximum penalty of five years in prison and a five-thousand-dollar fine for transporting stolen cattle or meat across state lines."

Madge leans back. "Wasn't like that in the old days when your grandpappy hunted rustlers. They caught 'em and hanged 'em right then down by Brushy Creek on the old hanging tree."

"I know, but there's rumors floating around about some vigilantes who're gonna take the law into their own hands and make use of that old hanging tree again."

"I know this is your first week and all at sheriffing, but do be careful, nephew. And for God's sake, find yourself a good woman to help you deal with the stress. You know how you boys find comfort from your troubles that way." She shakes her bottom just a little as she turns to help another customer and gives me another wink. Aunt Madge has always been too nosey about my personal affairs, especially when it comes to women. I don't have time for that right now.

An old codger drains the last of his coffee, laughs, and points at me. "You tin stars should round 'em up and hang 'em all like they did when I was just a chap. I'z just barely out of short britches when I started chasin' rustlers. I 'member some of them boys swingin' high from the old hanging oak down by Brushy Creek. Damn tree's still standin' tall and ready, if'n you find the courage to use her."

I cut my eyes at the old man, careful to choose the right words with other customers all glued to his mocking tone.

"Hell, you can still see the rope burns on that high limb they strung 'em up on. Rustlers didn't last long back in them days. No sir." He gives a snide grin. "So, what'n the hell's your problem, Gabe Griffin? Scared to go rustler huntin' after dark?" Snickers around the room break the silence.

I get up to leave, pick up my hat, and drop a dollar and a quarter on the counter for my breakfast—seventy-five cents for the breakfast and fifty for Madge's tip. "That's Sheriff Gabe Griffin to you... and I wish it that easy, old-timer."

The gray-bearded old World War One veteran scraps around struggling to get up. "Old-timer, you say? Why, boy, I'll take a willer switch up and down both sides of your backside if I can just get out of this damn booth."

"Keep your seat, Carl. If there's going to be any butt whooping, I'll be the one doing it."

Carl settles back down hard, disgusted with himself—unable to bounce right up at a moment's notice like he once did. He grumbles, "Guess that's what happens when you're seventy-two and outlive all your friends. Nobody 'round to help get you up."

I pick up the newspaper and read the first paragraph again. I crush it like a brown paper sack and whisper, "That's what he's doing. I just know it. And he's going to get caught, maybe even go to prison."

I ease over to look out the window, thinking about my next move. Carl shuffles, fusses, and cusses his way out of the café booth like he's trying to climb out of a hole in the ground.

I read the rest of the article and rub my aching eyes. I snicker, "Looks like I've way too many sleepless nights in my future watching roads, pastures, stockyards, really anywhere cattle can be stolen and transported away from in a flash."

A hand takes my arm. "Damn straight, he's gonna get caught, and you better be the one to catch him."

A little startled, I say, "Carl, don't be sneaking up on me like that. Who's gonna get caught and—"

He chuckles. "It ain't me who you need to worry about sneakin' around. It's that—"

I bark in a low tone, "I know who it is, dammit, or who it might be."

He holds his hands up in surrender. I catch the eyes of the entire café crowd on us. "Could you stop talking, Carl, please? You're not helping."

"Sure I am. You just don't know it yet, or even how. I just got everybody who is anybody in this hash house on your side, and they'll be first in line to find you if they run up on any information you might could use."

He's right, and I know it. Dang these old-timers—they still have grit in their gizzards and chew square nails. That included my grandpappy who raised me and my brother after my daddy was killed in the first big war and Momma died trying to have my baby sister, Viola, who didn't survive birthing. Grandpappy was a duly sworn-in rustler chaser of some sort. Hanged a lot of men and shot a few to boot, at least those are the stories still floating around. He never talked about it, not even when he was on his deathbed.

Carl leans in. "I'll be goin' wid ya, Sheriff."

"No, you're not."

"Look, boy, you may have the muscle and can shoot that fancy hip pistol, but you need extra brains that have the experience to go wid 'em to take care of this sitchiashun."

I can't argue with that. I'm already at my wit's end and don't really know where to start. And to make matters worse, the whole town's watching to see what the new sheriff is going to do to resolve the problem. I need fresh ideas and clear eyes to help me see what's going on here, even if they come from a man older than the hills. But taking Carl along who can barely manage himself? That's another matter entirely. I guess there's no harm in him riding along on patrol.

"All right, Carl, go get in the car, if you can manage that. You can ride patrol with me today. No promises after that."

We step out onto the boardwalk shielding our eyes from the sun. "Wait here, I need to get the mail before we go."

"Well, I ain't sittin' in that four-wheeled oven with a steering wheel you call a car." He steps back up on the boardwalk. "I'll wait in the shade over there under the café awning." He heckles. "Watch crossin' the street. You might get runned over."

I start for the post office. I don't even look both ways. No need. A vehicle passes through here maybe once every half hour. As I sort through the stack of envelopes, the familiar rumbling of my Dodge pickup returns. It's not long that raised voices and threatening shouts fill the street.

I peek through the blinds to see Carl wagging his finger at my kid brother, Tom. With a balled fist at his side, Tom will likely strike the old man if he keeps jabbering like a jaybird.

Carl yells like the house is on fire, "I know it's you and those filthy nothin's you run with. You got no morals and not an ounce of pride in you. You steal and sell other men's cattle herds, bed their wives when the menfolk are off workin', slap their kids around if anythin' is said, and you murder for beef cattle. What a sack of low-down rotten snakes."

I grab up the mail and make it out the door just as Tom sasses old Carl. "You best shut up, old man."

"Old man? Son, I ran with your grandfather when he hunted down jackasses just like you. You think I'm afraid of you? Heck, I'll grind your scrawny little jackrabbit ass into cornmeal and serve you up like a corn fritter before the sun comes up in the morning."

Tom raises his fist. "I've 'bout had my fill of you, you mouthy old—"

"You and your wastrel friends here do nothin' but drink and gamble up other families' hard-earned dollars. Pffft, you rascals ain't got a bit of a sense about doin' what's right betwixt ya." Carl holds up his cane. "Get out of here before I—"

Tom giggles like a schoolgirl. "Do what, old-timer? Swing that cane, and you'll find yourself flat on your back." Tom rears back to hit Carl. I trot as fast as I can to stop him.

Carl strikes a pose like I'm sure he did back in his rustler-chasing days. "Son, do your best, 'cause I ain't kiddin'. If you want to play, I'll go over to the drugstore there and buy you a toy. Otherwise, step up and try me." Carl slides his hand around his back to take hold of something, but doesn't pull it. The gleam of a nickel-plated revolver stuffed in his belt glints in my eye.

"Shut up, old man! I'll snatch you bald-headed in a heartbeat if you keep on talkin'." Tom's friends laugh and start to walk past Carl, bumping him with their shoulders in disrespect.

Carl shoves Tom down with a swift push and wags his finger in his face. "Remember this, you prissy little schoolgirl, a young man'll fight ya, but an old man'll hurt ya."

Tom laughs and gets up. He walks to the café door and slings his empty beer bottle at Carl, but the old man catches it with one hand. "I'm warnin' you, son, even now, it won't be easy if you want to try me. Don't take my feeble years for granted." Carl fires the bottle back at Tom and it hits him in the stomach. "You get to feelin' froggy, just go ahead and leap, you worthless tadpole."

I get between them. "That's enough, you two. Go on inside, Tom. I'll be talkin' to you later."

Tom squints and gives an evil grin. "This ain't over, not by a long shot."

Carl grins back without a blink. "Damn straight it ain't over, boy. They finally caught up to old Sam Bass right here in Round Rock. And you sure as heck ain't him. Give it up while you still can."

"Yeah, but what a helluva ride Mister Bass had."

"It only takes one Jim Murphy to rat you out. Then you're done."

"Those are my pards in here, every one." Tom squints and scans his men already seated in the café. "And who was Jim Murphy anyway?"

"His best friend, or so Bass thought. Sold him out and Bass was shot right over there. Died a worthless cuss, just like you." Carl snickers. "Gotcha thinkin', don't I, boy?"

"Well, you sure know a lot about it. You were probably there, old-timer."

Carl raises his cane. "You call me that one more time and I'll—" He stops, lowers the cane, and smiles. "I do know a lot about it, because I was there. Just six years old but I saw it...." Carl drifts back to another time. "They got Sheriff Grimes all right, but they found Bass in a pasture, all alone. He died the next day. On his birthday, no less." Carl starts laughing like he's watching the cartoon before a feature film at the picture show.

Tom barks, "My brother can't protect you all of the time, Carl."

Carl leans in and growls, "He can't protect you all the time either, you worthless sack of snakes."

Tom slams the café door behind him.

WE GET IN the patrol car.

"What was all that about?"

Carl stares into the distance as I drive to a ranch where a small herd was stolen two days ago. Finally, he answers, "Oh nothin', just reminiscing a bit." He holds his hand out to catch the flow of air as we ride along. "Kinda interesting to have the same birth and death date on a man's gravestone with only the years bein' different, don't you think?" He turns and grins. "Sam Bass's stone, that is."

"That true?"

"Go take a look in the Round Rock cemetery. The stone's in the back near the old slave burial ground, or at least what's left of it. His obituary's recorded in the newspaper somewhere, I'm sure."

"Maybe I will. What about these vigilantes I've been hearin' about?"

"Don't guess I know what you're talkin' about, Sheriff."

"Yeah right, I'm sure you don't."

"You're too soft, Gabe."

"Oh, shut up."

"I will not. These boys stealin' beef cattle and sellin' it to the black marketers has got to stop. These are hard times and you best take care of it. Otherwise, you'll be out of a job. Worse than that, folk will lose their ranches over it." Carl spits out the window. "You know who some of those boys are, and they just—"

"And what? They will be caught, one way or another."

Carl turns and squints. "Might be killed. Ain't wrong to take care of business if the law won't do it. Law-abiding citizens have the right to defend life, home, and property."

"Not at the expense of justice."

"That is justice, young man."

"Well, vigilantes ain't gonna run loose in my county."

"Sure 'bout that?"

I say nothing else as we turn onto a bumpy dirt road leading up to an old ranch house that looks to have been built in the late 1800s.

JOHN WIPES HIS sun-wrinkled face with a red bandana. "Yeah, I know who it was, at least one of 'em. That redheaded Simpson boy I saw with the others took my herd. Guess there to be six of them."

"How many'd they steal, John?"

"Whole dang lot. Fifty-four head. Even took my good horse. All I got is my plowin' mule for Sally's kitchen garden." The old rancher wipes the sweat from his brow as his wife clings to his side.

Sally cries, "It's all we got in the world. What're you gonna do?"

The gray-headed man with lines on his face like turkey tracks leans up. "We could lose the ranch over this, Gabe." John looks at Carl and starts to say something else, but Sally tugs on his vest, shaking her head.

"What, you have more information?"

"Naw, that's about it, 'cept, I hope you can get my cattle back."

"You know I can't promise that."

John hangs his head as Sally wilts into his arms. "Then you best get goin', Sheriff. Nothin' else you can do here."

Carl and I head to the car. "What was John about to say when he looked at you?"

"Got no idea, Sheriff."

TWO DAYS LATER, Art and Jack, my nearly worthless deputies, rush into my office in town.

Jack says, "You need to come with us, Sheriff."

"What for? Can't you see I'm busy?"

"Not too busy to go down to the hanging tree, I'm thinkin'?"

"What the heck?" I grab my holster, belting up as I trot to my patrol car.

Carl, sitting on a bench outside my office, obviously heard everything. I bark, "Get in the car." He stumbles a bit but moves quicker than I would think he could.

We pull up to the edge of the small bluff and plain as day, there's a body dangling from the old hanging tree. I nearly fall, stumbling down the short bluff trail to where the ancient oak stands. I stare at the face of the boy with an unmistakable mane of red hair.

"Josh Simpson, dang it."

WE TAKE THE body down, wrap it in a tarp I have for such purposes, and stuff it in the trunk. No one says anything on the trip back to town, except Carl.

"You're too soft, Sheriff."

I want to backhand the old man to show him I'm not. But he's right, when it comes to Tom, I turn a blind eye. Have for too long. And Josh Simpson is one of his best friends.

We stop by the undertaker's office, unload the body, and I go back to the office to call the boy's parents. I send Jack and Art on some meaningless task to get them out from underfoot, but I ask Carl to stay.

"What do you think, Carl, since you're so all-fired-up ready to help?"

He doesn't hesitate. "We'll use their own newfangled methods against 'em. They use trucks and trailers to sneak away. We'll use trucks with headlights to light 'em up and chase 'em down if'n we have to. We'll—"

"You ain't gonna do anything, Carl. Besides, I don't have those kinds of resources. I'm lucky to have two patrol cars and two deputies, such as they are."

"The resources are out there if you but only look... or maybe in this case, turn a blind eye. Why don't you let these heroes, whoever they are, take care of business?"

"Heroes? Really? They're nothin' more'n vigilante murderers. If I find them, I'll arrest them all."

"You need to let 'em take care of these ne'er-do-wells stealing from good folk tryin' to make honest livin's in the middle of a war. They're takin' meat out of the mouths of our boys fightin' that lousy war, for cryin' out loud. Let the vigilantes do their work and be happy about it."

"So… do it like you and my grandpappy did it?"

"Yeah."

"Well, I know one thing I can do."

The old man grumbles, "What's that?"

"Cut down the last hanging tree."

"Oh, no you don't. Too much history and too much blood associated with that tree. You cut it down and the Old West as we know it is gone."

"It's an eyesore and a reminder of what we've left behind."

"Left behind? It's more of a reminder of what's been lost… of days when the law was the law and the outlaws were the outlaws. No sugarcoatin' things back then, no sir. There was a clear line betwixt 'em. Easy to tell the difference."

"We use modern methods now, Carl, and laws have changed."

"Yeah, and look where that got us. Just 'cause they use pickup trucks and trailers don't make 'em any smarter. They're still dumber than dirt." He spits. "Yeah, five years in prison and a five-thousand-dollar fine? That won't stop nobody, and sure as hell don't do nothin' for the families who lose everything."

He wipes spittle from his mouth. "Hell, those boys are laughin' all the way back home from the stockyard with a fistful of cash dollars."

I can't argue with that, but I have to uphold the law as it sits today, not back in the days of the Doolin brothers, Belle Starr, or Butch Cassidy. Times have changed. We've modernized. Why, smart rustlers can grab a herd and whisk it off to another state in the early evening and be home in beds before sunup. One thing Carl has right, though. Rustling is getting worse, and we can't seem to do much about it. I can't seem to do much about it. But somebody is. That Simpson boy left dangling from the last hanging tree is proof.

"Thanks for your help today, Carl." I pitch him a couple of silver dollars. "There's your supper."

He tips his hat and eases the door shut behind him.

I pull the bottle of Four Roses Kentucky straight bourbon from the bottom desk drawer and pour my coffee cup half full. "I gotta do somethin'. And soon."

★ ★ ★

THE AIR, STILL hot and dry, lies still this moonless night. Sweat trickles down my back.

Art points. "There's a light over the hill there."

Jack swallows hard. "The old hanging tree."

I hold my finger to my lips. "Quiet, let's go."

Jack, Art, and I sneak over the ridge, careful not to kick any loose rocks. Cattle are scattered about. We move closer and peek between the boulders above Brushy Creek. Four horsemen gather around a man with a noose around his neck.

"Any last words, you worthless cattle thief?"

*That voice? Where have I—*

I nudge Art and Jack. "When I say go, run down the hill as fast as you can, as quiet as you can." I look again and whisper, "Go!"

We run bent over, dodging between rocks and brush until we're thirty paces behind the five horsemen, rifles resting in the crooks of their arms. We emerge, taking a stance like Wyatt, Virgil, Morgan, and Doc did at the OK Corral.

I shoot a round into the air. "Sheriff Griffin here. Stop what you're doing and drop your rifles." The four hooded horsemen do nothing.

The man sentenced to die, screams, "I ain't done nothin'. They're gonna hang me for cattle thievin'."

I point my sidearm at the condemned. "Oh, shut up, Buck. You've been stealing cattle since you could ride. Just be glad I got here before you swung."

I wait for the horsemen to drop their guns. They don't.

That familiar voice cracks, "He could still swing, Sheriff."

"Is that you, Carl?" Silence.

Another vigilante says, "This man killed Geoff Runnels over near the county line yesterday. His wife recognized him. She yanked his hood off. It's a wonder he didn't shoot her, too. They stole his herd."

"You saw him do this?"

"Yeah, we got there too late to save old Geoff, but in time to see this redheaded varmint shoot him in the face. Dropped dead like a sack of taters. He got away from us, though. We tracked him down to a shack and found him drunk as a skunk." The vigilante sniffles and clears his throat like he's got a lump in it. "Left his wife with no way to fend for herself and the kids. They was just gettin' their ranch goin' good."

I wince. "My goodness."

"This war is takin' a toll on more'n just soldiers and their families, Sheriff. We aim to stop it."

I try to focus. Can't. What to do? These men have saved many a herd and ranch, not to mention lives, with their vigilante justice. But it's illegal. And deadly.

I drop my head. "Finish it."

Art and Jack make no fuss. They've said all along we should let these men take care of business. They have, and now we're in with them.

Carl smacks the doomed rustler's horse's rump. The limb dips and creaks as he swings. One by one, the four horsemen of the apocalypse walk their mounts walk their mounts past me and my deputies. Carl, though still hooded, stops.

"Won't be long before we get the rest. Should be soon, Sheriff."

I ask, "Who… who are they? Please, Lord, don't let it be my…."

The four horsemen melt into the darkness without a sound except an occasional rock stirred by a hoof.

A voice like the sound of a night bird calls from the shadows, "You already know."

MADGE, CARL, AND the band of old lawmen gather around the stack of rocks we'd placed over Tom's grave. It's only fitting he be buried under the tree that took his life. His marker reads…

*Tom Griffin*
*Born August 25, 1924*
*Died August 25, 1944*

Nothing else needed to be inscribed on the small stone.

I gaze up at the grooves in the old tree limb, then at the notches carved into a large old knot protruding from the trunk. I pull my jackknife out to carve one more alongside the recent additions and those from decades ago. I can't do it. I draw my hand back. Carl limps over.

"Do it for your grandpa, son. He was the best rustler catcher in Texas."

I make the mark then nod to Art and Jack to commence cutting down this symbol of Old West justice and death. Carl lays his hand on my shoulder and shakes his head.

Now I understand the importance of the tree. It's not just a symbol of death. It's a reminder of justice long forgotten but still practiced by men who rode the West when it was young and untamed.

"Art, Jack, put away your axes and crosscut saw. I won't be the one who cuts down the last hanging tree."

*—Winner of the Will Rogers Medallion Award and 2024 Arkansas Hall of Fame author Anthony Wood grew up in historic Natchez, Mississippi, fueling a lifelong love of history. After living in Alaska, he served for three decades as an inner-city church planter, inspiring him to pen* Up Close and Personal: Embracing the Poor *about his work in the Memphis inner city.*

*Anthony is a member of Turner's Battery living history group, the Civil War Round Table of Arkansas, and White County Creative Writers, as well as Managing Editor for* Saddlebag Dispatches *Western magazine. A number of Anthony's short stories and poems have been published, as well as nine books released since 2019. He and his wife, Lisa, live in Conway, Arkansas. You can find Anthony on Facebook and Instagram or visit his website at anthonywoodauthor.com*

# JAMES WADE

## THE HARVEST

I.

THERE ARE WAYS to make money if you have something to kill. The girl won't like it because she thinks the shoats are her pets. You'll have to make her understand. You don't want her to hate you because if she hates you she might end up like the Driskill girls and what then? You shudder at the thought.

Outside the rain falls slantwise. Falls thin and cold and the sky like soot. Trees gray behind the curtains of rain and the rain running riotous on the tin roof. You sit in the kitchen listening, holding your coffee hot on the knee of your pants. Homer should be here by now.

Cora tells you there's only ten dollars in the can and you tell her you know.

You know.

You take your coffee on the porch, and her father is there in the rocker and you wonder if the old man ever sleeps and you ask him, "Do you ever sleep?"

"Slothfulness is a sin," he says, as if that explains it. "There ain't but ten dollars in the can, and I need to go into town later and pick me up an Eskimo Pie. Dooley Powell keeps them in stock just for me."

"No he don't."

The old man flicks at you with the back of his hand as if he'll deflect your words.

"I ain't seen it rain this much since ninety-six," he says. "If you hadn't started on that ark, now might be the time."

Where the hell is Homer?

"I ever tell you about McKinley coming down here?" he asks.

"Yes."

"It was that year," he says. "Ninety-six. That's how come me came to think of it."

"You've done told me."

You look up the road. Nothing but gray rain. The country wet and humid. Not even the decency of a north wind.

"Come down here with a mind to do some presidential politicking," the old man says. "Stuck half a dozen wagons in the mud in Angelina County. Another two or three in Trinity before they finally called it quits."

The river has overrun its banks. Swelling, then swollen, then burst. The floodplain was underwater in an hour. It's come up another fifty or so yards since you checked last night. You can see it from where you're standing.

"I remember when there was camels in this country," he tells you and you frown. You've seen what happens when old folks start to fade and it's the last thing you need.

"Don't look at me like that," he says. "There was camels all up and down this river. Guv'ment program. Brung over from Egypt or some such place. Gonna be better than horses, they said."

You hear the girl crying inside. Cora is telling her there aren't any sweet rolls and the girl is screaming and you wonder if it's too late. Poor Dale Driskill.

"You can see how that turned out. Guv'ment programs."

The government would have given you cash money to plow under your cotton. You refused at the old man's insistence. Gonna be a banner season, he told you. And now look. Your whole crop flooded. Drowned, and you right behind it.

You won't make the same mistakes with the pigs. Kill them all. That's the government's answer to most problems, anyway. Plow them under.

The girl appears in the doorway red-eyed. Shoulders tensed up. Her dress is made from a flour sack with blue-printed diamond patterns. Her hair is uncombed and she is barefoot and in her face she looks like you. In her soul.

She appeals to you about the sweet rolls and you tell her maybe tomorrow. You don't tell her about the pigs. Cora sweeps the girl back inside and closes the door.

"They turned loose a mess of 'em right down yonder by the fork." The old man is still talking. "For years you'd be out there hunting your supper and liable to come up on one or two. Right there in the open. Camels."

Cattle are worth more than pigs. Three dollars for a calf. Five dollars for a cow. You wish you had cattle. You wish the old man would stop talking. You wish a great many things.

You look out toward the road and Homer is late in coming, and you know you'll have to huff it. Doc says if the bodies sit too long they're useless. You don't understand but you don't need to. Doc says a lot of things that don't make much sense.

"Think you'd lost every last bit of your damn mind," the old man says. "If you didn't already know they was out there, I mean."

He rocks forward and spits tobacco juice on your porch.

"I knowed it, though," he says and rocks back, satisfied.

You hear the jingle of harnesses. Homer. Finally. You see his Percherons coming over the hill and then the wagon. He's in the middle of the bench seat, sopping wet. You put on your hat and hold up a hand and come down off the porch.

The old man watches you go. You look back and see him shaking his head.

## II.

THE RAIN LETS up and the sky clears. The small day moon hangs pale and bloodless. Jays and wrens and warblers alike all flit among the bare branches of an orchard as you pass by. There is no wind.

You pass along the bridge at Blind Cove, whereon a pair of young boys are skipping rocks across the slime-topped surface, their lines sitting in the bloated brackish backwater. The cove is little more than a flooded crater full up of red dirt and detritus, and what mutant fish might linger in such a slop-mattered underworld are sure to be some breed all their own.

"Simpler times," Homer says, and you both look at the boys as if you might see in them the shade of your former lives. And you both long for the days of cane poles and smooth stones.

You make Oren's place by midmorning and now it's raining again. He's pacing the covered porch.

"Y'all said first light," he calls down to you. "Christ almighty. Y'all said first light, but you weren't here."

"It'll be all right, Oren," Homer tells him.

"Christ almighty," he says.

"Where is she?" Homer asks.

"In yonder in the bedroom."

Oren looks sick.

You pass by him on the porch, and he's chewing his fingernails. Staring off.

"In yonder," he says again. "On the left."

You go inside and the air smells wet. Saturated. You open the bedroom door and the old woman is there and it looks like she's sleeping and the thought does not comfort you.

"Get her legs," Homer says.

You're halfway out the door when Oren changes his mind.

"I changed my mind," he says. "Leave her be."

"Can't do it," Homer tells him. "We had a deal. Doc's done and paid you."

"I don't give a good goddamn what that infidel done. Put her down."

Homer drops the old woman hard on the puncheon wood. Her head does a strange sort of bounce. Oren steps toward her, but Homer is there, and his pistol is out.

"You listen to me now, bud," Homer tells him. "This ain't just about you. Me and Thomas here got a stake in it, too. You understand? What's done is done. You're gonna let us carry her out of here or we'll be loading up two bodies. I know I could sure use the extra cash, how 'bout you, Thomas?"

With you still holding the woman's legs, she looks like some sad twisted wheelbarrow. You don't know what to say, so you just nod your head.

The earth is an oyster with nothing inside. Your brother told you that once.

Oren thinks about it. He turns away and puts both hands on the table and drops his head and starts to cry.

"I'm sorry, Mama," he says.

THE GIRL HAS named the pigs. The little ones. You try to remember them all. No. You try *not* to remember, but it comes anyway. Pinky. Spotty. Pinky Dinky. *Stop.*

DOC OPENS THE door to the alley and ushers you into his office. Your hands are under her shoulders this time and it's heavier work.

"There, on the board," he says. "You're late."

"Ol' Oren held us up," Homer says. "Tried to crawfish on the deal."

Doc isn't listening. The board sits atop a tub of ice in the middle of the office, a ragged blue tarpaulin stretched out beneath. The board itself is a series of cane latticework to allow for the cold from the ice to rise up onto the body.

The old woman is on the board and Doc is ripping away her clothes. He makes a Y-shaped incision along her torso. You didn't know you would be here to see this part. You never have before, but you reckon Doc won't waste any time just on your account.

"Thomas here don't look so good, Doc," Homer laughs and claps you on the back.

"You don't approve, Mister Hargrove?"

You stay quiet.

"Do you know what the rate of hookworm infection is in this county?" Doc asks. "Tularemia? Pellagra? The life expectancy for an American female is sixty-two years. Missus Green is forty-eight. A year ago she began acting strange—stranger than usual. She was confined to bed rest for nearly seven months. And now she's dead. I, for one, would very much like to know why. Might be that the answer to some century-old question is swimming around in her blood right now. Something that could save lives for generations to come. Given her religious beliefs, she would not allow me such a study while she was alive. Now she is not alive, and therefore unable to protest."

You want to leave, but Homer has wandered off, and you look down at the woman, and her leg twitches.

You jump back.

"Cadaveric spasms," Doc says. "Reflexive muscle action. Either can happen up to twelve hours after the heart stops. This woman is dead, Mister Hargrove. Whether you believe she is in heaven or Elysium or come back as a dung beetle, she is not here with us. She does not care. And this may seem barbaric to you, but I assure you, sir, this is how we challenge death. We look it right in the face. We learn its tendencies and we combat them."

You're not sure if you think it's barbaric or not. You're not sure what being not sure says about you.

When your brother hung himself, Doc pointed out the fingernail marks around his neck, the skin under his nails.

"What does that mean?" you asked.

"He changed his mind."

You wonder what Doc found in your brother's blood. Whatever it was, it's in you, too. You can feel it calling to you, even now.

"Homer," you say, and from another room Homer hollers something back that you can't hear. Doc elongates the lines of his incision to reach the woman's armpits at the top and comes near to her groin at the bottom.

"There are so few experiences which we all share, but death is one," he says. "It is the final resting place of every arc, every infinite incurvation. Each individual contributing a unique moment or set of moments to the fecundity of lived experience."

He uses two hands to enter the woman's chest cavity and begins removing her organs one at a time, tying off blood vessels as he goes.

"And yet if you were to follow ten or twenty or even one hundred million individual arcs, they all begin and end with an experience that is anything but singular. An old woman on her deathbed takes her final gasp. A soldier on the battlefield has a bullet rip through his heart. Their experiences differ up until that last second, but then they coalesce. Heart stops pumping. Lungs stop breathing. Brain hangs on a bit longer, a bit longer, then it's gone. They're gone. Their arcs have found that solitary resting place."

"Why challenge it in the first place," you ask. "Death. If it's gonna end that way no matter what."

Doc smiles at you. He likes this sort of thing. The sound of his own voice.

"Because death is natural and we are unnatural," he says. "Our emotions. Our evolution. Our intellect. We defy nature's dance. We care enough to challenge death. To fight it even though we know there is no chance of winning. We fight because we can, Mister Hargrove. Because we must. It is what separates us from the animals."

"Animals don't seem all that bad," you say.

He laughs. "True. But have you seen wolves develop any medicines? Dolphins build a hospital?"

"Nossir," you tell him. "But I hadn't ever seen 'em fire the first shot, neither."

III.

HOMER INSISTS ON stopping at the Rose Room before heading back. You don't have much of a choice. It's either go along or walk home in the mud. And the rain looks like it will start again soon.

A man plays the piano, and Homer buys two whiskeys, and gives you one and you drink it, and he buys another. One of the Driskill girls comes out of an upstairs room and leans on the balcony and looks down at you and smiles and waves. You turn away.

Homer laughs.

"You think she told her daddy?" he asks.

You stand up and walk away as he feigns protest.

You go to the mercantile and buy two packages of sweet rolls and wait for Homer to finish his drinking. You wait well into the night.

When Homer finally drops you at the cabin, everyone is asleep. Even the old man. You're grateful. You put ten more dollars in the can and go quiet down the hall and look into her room.

You watch her. The rise and fall of her small chest. What dreams visit her now? Happy ones, you hope.

It rains all night and into the morning.

IV.

AT DAWN YOU can see the floodwaters no more than a stone's throw from the porch. Animals go forth with wet coats, fleeing the rising water. Raccoons and porcupines. Badgers and bobcats. Coyotes, skunks, and wild turkeys. Entire herds of deer pass beneath the porch and your thoughts attend the Bible as they have not in a good long while.

The old man is awake but he does not seem to notice the exodus. He rocks in your chair.

"Guess you're wishing you took out that crop insurance, ain't ye?" he chides you.

"I didn't have the money for it," you tell him. "I should've let them plow it under. Took the pay off."

"Guv'ment handout," he scoffs. "Your brother never would've considered it. Wouldn't have even give them bastards the time of day."

You close your eyes. You can feel the water rising.

"Eight years, and in all that time my daughter and that little girl never did want for nothing," he keeps going. Keeps pushing. "Provided for his family the way a man's supposed to."

"And look where it got him," you say, calm. In control.

He's just an old man.

He's just an old man.

"I know what you been doing in town," he says.

You stiffen. You can feel the Driskill girl moving under you.

"Grave robbing and the like," the old man says. "Damnable sins in the eyes of the Lord Our God."

You don't know what to say so you tell him we defy nature's dance.

"I was visiting with Dooley Powell at the feedstore yesterday evening," he says, ignoring you. "Oren Green come in there fussing and hollering about his poor old mama. Had himself quite a story to tell. If he were to tell it to the law, I don't imagine they'd stop with that heretic Doc. Probably be pretty bad for you and your buddy Homer, too."

You shake your head.

"Oren ain't gonna tell the law," you hiss at him, looking over your shoulder at the door. "He's the one who sold the body in the first place."

"Maybe Oren don't need to be the one to tell them then," the old man says.

He grins at you. Rocking in your chair. Spitting on your porch.

You look out at the rising water. It will reach the cabin by nightfall.

You open the door and go inside. The girl is eating the rolls and kicking her feet back and forth in her chair. Her feet don't reach the ground.

"Cora," you say. "Get some things together. Take the girl up the hill to Homer Renfro's place. Flood's coming."

"What about Daddy?" she asks.

"Just do what I say. When you get up there, tell Homer I need him down here."

You walk past her. Won't look at her.

"Tell him to bring the wagon," you say.

It's going to be a long winter. It's hot now but the cold winds will come, and without a harvest it will be tough to scrape by. Still, there are ways to make money if you have something to kill.

*—James Wade is the youngest novelist to win two Spur Awards from the Western Writers of America, and the recipient of the MPIBA's prestigious Reading the West Award. His debut novel,* All Things Left Wild, *was listed as one of the most influential Westerns of the 21st century by* True West *Magazine and included in the* Los Angeles Times's 1,001 Novels: A Library of America. *His Southern Gothic mystery,* Beasts of the Earth, *was named a Best Book of 2022 by both* Deep South *Magazine and* The Southern Review of Books. *James is a four-time finalist for the* Austin Chronicle's *Best Writer in Austin award, and his work has appeared in* Texas Highways, Writers' Digest, *and numerous additional publications. James lives and writes in the Texas Hill Country with his wife and children.*

# JACK STEWART

## HAULING THE MAIL

*Cheyenne, Wyoming*
*Winter 1926*

TOM CALLAHAN NEVER cared much what was in the mailbag, so long as it didn't try to kill him.

The job was really quite simple. He just needed to load the sacks, brave the weather, dodge a few mountains, and land his airplane in one piece. No questions, no fuss. But Tom had a sinking feeling that today wasn't going to be like every other day, and he turned up his collar to shield himself from the bitter wind. The tempest kicked up swirls of dust across the open airfield that carried a scent of oil and gasoline and an ominous warning he couldn't ignore.

"Wind's gonna be tricky down the front range," one of the mechanics hollered, handing Tom a rag to wipe the frost from his goggles. "You sure you wanna fly today?"

Tom snorted. "The mail doesn't wait on the weather, kid."

He turned his attention to the sacks strapped into the biplane's forward cockpit with a length of rope he never quite trusted. He gave the rope an extra tug, but it wasn't the mail that worried him. It was the damned weather.

A cold front had rolled in overnight, and the skies overhead were a heavy gray with a chill that made him feel like trouble was already in the air.

"Looks like you've got company."

Tom turned his head. Across the open field, a black Ford Model T rolled to a stop in front of the Colorado Airways hangar. He didn't recognize either of the two men who stepped out, but they weren't hard to identify. They wore long overcoats and moved like lawmen, with measured and confident gaits and polished boots that crunched across the frozen ground.

The older one was graying at the temples with broad shoulders, and his sharp eyes squinted against the frigid wind as he scanned the field before landing on Tom. The younger one had a nervous energy about him, and his fingers twitched at his side as if itching to grab the pistol holstered under his coat.

"You Callahan?" The older man's voice was like gravel.

Tom paused, wiped his hands on his trousers, then turned away from his final preflight inspection to respond. "Depends who's asking."

"Deputy Marshal Frank Hollis." He tugged open his overcoat and revealed a gleaming silver badge pinned to his jacket. Then he gestured to the younger man. "This is my partner, Sam Whitaker."

"What can I do for you, Marshal?"

"The district of Wyoming is in need of your services, son," Whitaker said, his voice tight.

"I just haul the mail, sir."

Hollis reached inside his coat and pulled out a small, leather-bound courier pouch that was sealed with wax. He hesitated for just a moment, then handed it over. "I know. And we need you to make a special delivery."

Tom held the package in his palm. "This feels like trouble."

Whitaker gave a dry chuckle. "That's why we picked you."

Hollis didn't smile. "Deliver it to Marshal William Harper in Colorado Springs. Straight to him. Nobody else. Got it?"

Tom's fingers tightened around the cracked leather. "You mind telling me what's in it?"

"Let's just say there are folks who'd rather it never gets there."

"That supposed to make me feel better?"

Whitaker spoke up again, his voice tight. "If anything happens—if you catch even the slightest hint of trouble—you don't land until you're at that airfield in Colorado Springs. Understand?"

Tom frowned. "You make it sound like I'm flying into a war zone."

"Just watch your six, Callahan."

Tom didn't like that. Not one bit. He hadn't had to watch his six since he followed Billy Mitchell into the skies over Saint-Mihiel during the war. But the marshal's tone made him itch. There was something knowing in it. Something frightening. Something that suggested he wasn't just talking about the weather or the mountains.

Reluctantly, Tom took the courier pouch and dropped it into the rear cockpit of his plane, certain he was going to regret it.

When the marshals turned to leave, Tom noticed a lone figure leaning against a nearby weathered hangar. The man wore a leather flight jacket with his hands shoved in his pockets but kept his eyes hidden beneath the shadowed brim of his hat. As Tom studied him, the stranger shifted his stance and lit a cigarette as if to acknowledge his presence.

Tom swore under his breath. He didn't like this. Not one bit.

He felt the stranger's eyes on him as he climbed into the cockpit and pulled on his gloves. The mechanic spun the propeller, and the engine sputtered to life as Tom pushed the courier pouch aside and tried ignoring the uneasy feeling gnawing at him.

Whatever it was, it sure as hell wasn't just mail.

And it was probably going to get him killed.

TOM ADJUSTED HIS goggles, tightened his grip on the stick, and eased the throttle forward. A tight smile cracked his numb face as he felt each of the Hispano-Suiza's one hundred and seventy ponies prancing across his soul.

The stranger in the hangar's shadows forgotten, he danced on the pedals and steered the nimble biplane down the frostbitten runway. In short order, his wheels lifted off the earth, and the Standard JR-1B climbed into the dawn while the sleepy town of Cheyenne fell away beneath him.

Tom banked and turned south along the snow-dusted foothills of the Front Range, listening to his airplane rattle as it clawed for altitude in the thinning air. He shivered as shards of early morning chill bit through the gaps in his flight jacket. But the weather was holding. For now.

*Just watch your six, Tommy boy.*

Using his scarf, Tom wiped away a thin layer of frost from his goggles and turned to look over each shoulder. To his right, he saw the jagged peaks of the Rockies stretching westward and up into the bleak shadows. To his left, the rolling plains that faded into a low sea of mist where rivers and foothills disappeared into the gray light of morning.

And directly behind him, the dark shape of another airplane trailing him in the distance.

"What the—"

His breath caught when a sudden gust of wind came down off the slopes and caught his wingtip. He snapped the stick to the right and quickly corrected his altitude to prevent the gale from blowing him off course. But the maneuver had given him another opportunity to study his shadow's silhouette.

Twin wings. A long fuselage.

Tom's stomach twisted.

*That's an Airco DH-4B.*

The Airco was a good plane. Too good. Designed by Geoffrey de Havilland, the military surplus two-seat bomber had been retrofitted for airmail work with a 400-hp Liberty V-12 engine and was faster than his JR-1B by a good margin. Tom had his doubts it was still armed with a wartime loadout of two synchronized forward-firing machine guns, but he knew that meant nothing.

A good pilot doesn't need a gun to be dangerous.

With one more glance at the mysterious plane trailing him, Tom turned his attention back to the sky in front of him. He knew that Denver and Colorado Springs were down there, somewhere over the horizon—over the razor-thin line where the Earth met the sky. But as his breath formed a cloud of white that hung in front of his face, those distant cities felt impossibly far away.

Another gust of wind rocked his plane, and Tom exhaled sharply while wiggling his numb fingers to remain steady on the stick and keep his wings level. He suspected he was probably just jumpy from the marshal's last-minute addition of the mysterious courier pouch. But that didn't mean he could ignore the itch.

*The itch is what kept me alive in the skies over France,* he reminded himself.

Tom glanced back once more at the distant shadow, but his heart bolted when he realized that the Airco had crept forward and was closing the distance. The pilot's flying wasn't aggressive—not yet at least—he was just inching closer while saddling in on Tom's six o'clock.

Just the way a fighter pilot does before committing to an attack.

The itch grew stronger.

He had no illusions about outrunning the other plane. It had more horsepower, a better climb rate, and a higher ceiling. If he remained straight and level out in the open, he would be a sitting duck.

Gritting his teeth, Tom tightened his grip on the stick and dove for the foothills, where dozens of ridges and ravines cut through the landscape like scars. His plane shook violently with the whipping of treacherous air currents, but he scratched the itch the only way he knew how—by dropping into the weeds and flying at treetop height through the rough and unforgiving terrain. The land could offer him cover. But only if he played it right.

He glanced back and muttered a curse when he saw that the Airco was still following him.

Tom yanked the stick to the left and dove into an adjacent narrow canyon, his wingtips mere feet from the rocky walls. Despite the cold, beads of sweat formed under his fur-lined leather cap as he held steady against the unstable air that buffeted his wings. He reversed course and banked hard to the right to follow the winding canyon, doing his best to ignore the hammering heart inside his chest. He hazarded a glance over his shoulder.

The bigger plane was still there.

*Damn. This pilot's good.*

The canyon walls began to close in tighter, but Tom spotted an opening to his left and slapped the stick into his thigh. His nimble plane cut through a saddle between two ridges and dropped into the next valley over, skimming low over the ground while he searched the skies for his pursuer.

*Where are you?*

Suddenly, the Airco appeared. Just a moment too late.

The pilot was good, but he had overshot.

Tom seized the moment and yanked back on the stick, climbing hard and fast in a maneuver he had perfected while evading Fokker triplanes. Only, during the war, he had flown over mostly flat terrain and hadn't been forced to evade enemy planes in the mountains. His speed bled off as he reached the ridge, and he rolled inverted to cross over into the next valley.

Scooping out the bottom on the other side, Tom lifted his nose back into the air and spotted the DH-4B in front of him. For the moment, he had turned the tables. The hunter had become the hunted. But the other pilot realized it, too, and his powerful biplane lurched and banked hard to escape.

Tom pressed his advantage and stayed close to the Airco while pushing his own plane to its limits. His engine screamed at him as he rode through the wake of the other plane's turbulence and cut back and forth across his erratic flight path. The other pilot turned to look at him across the fading darkness, but his face was hidden behind frosted goggles and a fluttering scarf.

*Who the hell are you?*

Tom knew an answer was impossible. But he couldn't help but wonder if it was the stranger he had seen lurking in the hangar's shadows back in Cheyenne.

*What do you want?*

Suddenly, the other plane pitched up, and Tom reacted by rolling left and breaking away to avoid a collision. But by the time he had leveled out, the Airco was back on his tail.

This was no ordinary chase. This wasn't some drunk bootlegger on a joyride in a surplus war machine. Whoever was at the controls knew how to fly the damned thing.

*And if I don't lose him soon, I might not make it to Colorado Springs.*

TOM KNEW HE couldn't outrun the other plane, but he couldn't stay in the mountains forever, either. Every second he spent threading the narrow canyons and brushing the tops of golden aspens still clinging to their leaves was a second closer to disaster. One misjudged turn, a suddenly rising rock face, or a dead-end valley with nowhere to go would send him straight into the unforgiving embrace of the surrounding cliffs.

He gritted his teeth and yanked back on the stick to point his nose up at the thick ceiling of clouds blanketing the Front Range. The dense overcast was his only chance at shaking the sleek predator that continued closing in from behind him.

*He can't chase what he can't see.*

Tom glanced over his shoulder and a fresh jolt of adrenaline coursed through his veins. The Airco was matching his climb, and its pilot was spurring the much faster plane to beat him into the clouds. The hunter had guessed his plan and knew that if Tom made it into the overcast first, the chase was over.

"Come on, girl," Tom muttered, urging his plane upward despite its sluggish response.

His airspeed bled away, and the biplane trembled as it strained against the inescapable pull of gravity. The freezing wind tore through the open cockpit and numbed his fingers further even as sweat dampened his collar. Tom hazarded another glance behind him.

*Damn it.*

The Airco was still gaining on him.

*Just a little bit higher....*

Then, in an instant, the world turned to slate. His gambit had worked, and the thick, wintry clouds swallowed him whole. But now a new problem emerged. His sense of direction had abandoned him the moment he lost sight of the ground. Up. Down. North. South. All blended into a featureless haze.

His stomach lurched when he realized he was flying blind in a sky with no horizon, no reference, and no escape. He had purposely turned his plane into a coffin, and now he needed to claw his way out before it sealed shut.

Panic collapsed inward on him, but he forced himself to focus. He pulled the stick back—too much—and the plane shuddered violently on the edge of a stall. He fought against his own instincts and pressed his boot hard into the left rudder pedal until his muscles burned and his leg trembled. But he didn't let go.

And the world spun around him.

*Any second now....*

The gray void whipped past his cockpit, and suddenly—

Mountains. Plains. Mountains. Plains.

Tom's breath caught in his throat as the ground and sky traded places in a dizzying blur. He cut the throttle and the engine choked into silence. Then, with a practiced motion, he reversed his rudder input and pushed the stick forward. At first, nothing. Then the spinning began to slow.

Mountains.... Plains.... Mountains....

Then, finally, just—

Plains.

His trembling leg eased off the rudder pedal as he leveled out with the frozen fields of Monument, Colorado, stretching out beneath him. His heart hammered against his ribs, and his breath was ragged. But he'd survived. And he was right back where he'd started.

His eyes darted across the sky, scanning for the pursuing Airco.

Nothing.

Tom exhaled a shallow, uncertain sigh of relief.

Then his engine sputtered. A weak cough, then another. His stomach sank as he flicked his gaze to the fuel gauge. The chase had taken its toll, and he'd survived being hunted in the skies only to run out of gas before making it to his destination in Colorado Springs.

*Damn it.*

Scanning the landscape beneath him, Tom spotted a fenced-in field beside a sprawling ranch house and barn that looked like a hangar nestled between wooded ridges and open pastureland. It looked more like an airstrip than a cropland with rows of squash and zucchini. It wasn't an airport, but it would have to do. He banked hard and descended fast, barely clearing a stand of pines before his wheels smacked into the earth. A cloud of dust erupted behind him as the JR-1B bounced, skidded, and lurched to a halt near the weathered barn, where the engine coughed one last time, then fell silent as his fuel ran out.

He dropped his chin to his chest and exhaled sharply with relief, only to snap his head up at the unmistakable sound of a shotgun being cocked.

"You always drop outta the sky unwanted?"

A woman stood on the porch, cradling a shotgun in both hands and studying him with piercing green eyes. She wore a weathered duster over a plaid shirt, and her auburn hair was tucked under a wide-brimmed hat.

Tom remained seated and raised his hands in surrender. "Only when I'm fresh outta fuel, ma'am."

"You come alone?"

He glanced up into the skies, but there was no sign of the Airco. "Far as I can tell."

She didn't smile. Didn't lower the shotgun, either. Instead, she scanned the distant tree line and let out a reluctant sigh before tilting her chin toward the barn. "There's a gas can in there. If there's any left, you're welcome to it."

Tom couldn't see any farm equipment that needed gas, but he lowered his hands to the worn leather coaming surrounding the cockpit and pulled himself up into a standing position. He knew better than to look a gift horse in the mouth. He climbed out of the biplane and dropped to the frozen ground.

"Much obliged, Miss...."

"Wilcox," she replied. "Annie Wilcox."

"Thank you, Miss Wilcox. I'll be on my way just as soon—"

"The sooner, the better," she said.

Tom got the feeling she was expecting someone other than an airmail pilot to drop in unannounced, so he gave her a polite nod, trudged across the field, and ducked inside the musty barn. The air smelled of oil and something pungent that he couldn't quite place, and he paused just inside the door, giving his eyes a moment to adjust to the dim lighting and half expecting to see an airplane filling the open space. Though it felt like every hangar he had ever been in, it was mostly empty, except for the fuel can she had promised. He hefted it from the dirty floor and grinned at the sloshing of liquid, believing that luck had finally come over to his side.

But as he stepped back out into the daylight, his stomach twisted into a painful knot. Annie was no longer on the porch. She was standing next to his plane, with one hand holding the shotgun and the other holding the leather courier pouch.

Tom forced his expression to remain neutral and pretended he didn't notice, keeping his head down while lugging the gas can around to the front of the plane. He stepped up onto the wing and balanced himself against the still-warm engine as he emptied the fuel into the nearly bone-dry tank in front of the forward cockpit.

"You're an airmail pilot?" Annie called out.

"Yes, ma'am." He sealed the tank before dropping to the ground.

"Taking this to Marshal Harper?"

The itch was back.

Tom walked around the plane and set the gas can on the ground at her feet, then studied her expressionless features while wiping his hands on a dirty rag. "Why do you ask?"

"Just noticed the federal seal and figured you were on your way from Cheyenne to Colorado Springs," she said, turning the pouch over in her hands before meeting his gaze. "But you trust the wrong lawman out here, Tom, and you're likely to end up in a ditch."

A long silence stretched between them that she broke by tossing the pouch at him. He caught it against his chest and muttered a curse as she strode past him toward the front of the plane.

"I'll give you a start," she said, gripping the propeller. "Then you best be on your way."

The sooner, the better, he thought, somewhat surprised that she knew how to start the biplane.

Tom didn't know what the hell was going on, but he wasted no time. He tucked the courier pouch into his leather flight jacket and climbed into the cockpit just as Annie gave the prop a sharp spin. The Hispano-Suiza engine coughed, sputtered, then roared to life when the fresh fuel worked its way through the lines.

TOM HAD BARELY settled into the cockpit when something flickered at the edge of his vision and drew his attention to the treeline beyond the barn. He squinted into the shadows for several seconds before convincing himself that his mind was only playing tricks—

*Crack!*

A gunshot shattered that hope and splintered a wooden fence post not ten feet from where Annie stood. Tom instinctively ducked low in the cockpit as another shot rang out, its sharp report echoing across the field.

He whipped his head in the direction of the treeline, and his stomach dropped when he spotted riders—four of them—emerging from the shadows like wraiths with their long coats billowing behind them. The rising sun painted them in stark silhouette and glinted off the blued steel barrels of their rifles and revolvers. One of them, a burly figure atop a chestnut mare, lifted a Winchester to his shoulder and fired another shot.

Tom didn't wait to see if the bullet found its mark. He turned back to the house to shout a warning at Annie, but he fell mute when he saw that she was already running, her boots pounding across the frozen earth as she sprinted toward Tom with her shotgun leveled on the riders.

*Boom!*

He flinched at the deafening blast, but Annie didn't stop. She emptied the second barrel into the closest rider, then tossed the shotgun aside.

"Get that damn plane moving!" she shouted.

She didn't need to tell him twice. Tom jammed the throttle forward and the biplane lurched on its spindly landing gear, rattling violently as it picked up speed and bounced over patches of uneven ground. He glanced over his shoulder at Annie, surprised to see her outstretched arms reaching for the plane.

She leaped across the remaining distance and grasped the leather coaming around his cockpit in a death grip. Her feet kicked at the fabric-covered fuselage and—for a terrifying moment—slipped and skipped across the ground.

Tom's breath caught. *She's gonna fall!*

But she didn't. With a grunt, Annie hauled herself up once more.

"Hold on!"

"What the hell else am I gonna do?" she snapped back.

The fence at the far end of the field was rapidly approaching, and they were running out of room. Another gunshot rang out, and Tom yanked back on the stick, narrowly missing the fence at the edge of the frost-covered grass as he launched the biplane into the sky.

Holding the stick steady between his knees, Tom reached over the edge of the cockpit and wrapped his fingers around Annie's wrist. "Climb up there!" he yelled.

She nodded her understanding, then shifted her grip and stretched her right arm for the forward cockpit's leather coaming. But the wind was relentless and continued buffeting her sideways while her feet scraped helplessly against the fuselage's fabric skin.

Suddenly, the plane lurched in the turbulent air, and Tom let go of her to grab the stick and steady them. But the damage had been done.

Her fingers slipped.

She dangled for half a heartbeat over an endless sky yawning beneath her. Tom's heart bolted, and he instinctively jammed the stick forward, causing the biplane to pitch down and launch Annie upward. She seized the opportunity to grip the cockpit's edge just as Tom yanked back on the stick and slammed her down into the forward cockpit with a grunt.

Tom exhaled. "You okay?"

Annie groaned but nodded. "I—yeah."

"Mind telling me how those gunmen knew I was there?"

"You?" She whipped her head around to glare at him. "They were there for...."

But her words were lost on the wind. Tom frowned, then squinted at a dark shape in the distance. Moving fast and coming in low.

A damn Airco DH-4B.

"You've gotta be kidding me."

Annie spun to follow his gaze. "Friend of yours?"

Tom tightened his grip on the stick. "Let's just say he's been real damn persistent."

The Airco roared past and banked hard across their tail to circle around behind them. The damn thing was faster, heavier, and outclassed his biplane in almost every way. The one advantage they had was in maneuverability, and he'd already pushed that to its limits. Tom cursed under his breath.

"You got anything to fight back with?" Annie yelled.

"This was a trainer, not a fighter!"

Tom leaned out to the side and looked around her head, spotting a jagged ridge line in the distance that had been dusted with the winter's first snow. He had already gambled once with using the terrain to even the odds and knew it was time to up the ante. He exhaled through his nose.

"Hold on to something," he yelled.

He shoved the stick forward, and the plane dove for the earth. The wind—and Annie—screamed as they shot almost straight down toward a canyon on the far side of the ridge. Tom felt the itch and knew the Airco was on their tail, but he was focused on their only hope of escape.

"Let's see how good you really are," Tom muttered. He hesitated, then yanked back on the stick as hard as he could.

Annie's head disappeared inside the cockpit as the g-forces shoved them both deeper into their seats, but Tom grunted and continued pulling until the JR-1B had leveled out and was skimming mere feet above the canyon floor. He exhaled nervously and glanced hesitantly at the sheer rock walls rising on either side, funneling them into a corridor that meant certain death if he made even the slightest error.

Behind them, the Airco roared into the canyon's mouth as its pilot raised the stakes.

The canyon walls blurred past as Tom weaved the biplane through the narrow pass, banking hard to the left to avoid a jagged outcrop. Still, the Airco stayed tight on their tail, its engine roaring like an angry beast.

Annie's head popped up, and she stared at him with wide eyes. "Anytime you want to lose this guy would be great!"

Tom gritted his teeth, sweat slicking his palms despite the frigid air. "Working on it!"

The canyon narrowed even further, and Tom knew the Airco would have to slow down to navigate the turns. He jammed the sticked forward and dropped even lower, skimming just feet above the rocky floor.

Annie craned her neck to spot their pursuer. "He's not giving up."

Tom risked a glance. She was right. The Airco still thundered through the air behind them, disregarding the danger as its wingtips came perilously close to the rocks on either side. But the canyon was closing in, and soon, neither of them would have room to maneuver.

Think, *damn it!*

Then he saw it.

A rockslide had carved out a jagged ravine into the canyon floor, just barely wide enough for a plane as small as his.

"Hang on!"

Annie barely had time to suck in a breath before Tom yanked the stick sideways and dove into the crack in the earth. The walls rushed in, and he could hear the wind whipping off the stone.

But the Airco didn't follow. It couldn't.

Instead, its pilot pulled up hard and overshot them entirely as they burst through the other side of the ravine. Tom wasted no time and banked hard to the right and hugged the ridgeline to remain out of sight.

"Do you see him?" Tom yelled to Annie.

She scanned the skies above them for several seconds before shaking her head. "I think we lost him."

Tom let out the breath he'd been holding and flexed his fingers around the stick, but his heart still hammered in his chest. They had avoided being shot out of the sky, but that didn't mean they were out of the woods. He banked the plane left and aimed for the airport in Colorado Springs.

WHEN TOM'S WHEELS finally touched down on the airstrip in Colorado Springs, he felt the knot of anxiety between his shoulder blades begin to loosen. He taxied the JR-1B to a weathered hangar as the sun cast long shadows across the field. But something about the quiet unnerved him.

*No mechanics? No pilots?*

Just a single Ford Model T parked near the hangar and a broad-shouldered man with graying hair and a gleaming badge pinned to his chest.

"That must be the marshal," Tom said.

Annie inhaled sharply. "Remember what I said about trusting the wrong lawman?"

"You have much experience with lawmen?"

"My husband did."

Tom didn't know what she meant but felt the familiar itch as he killed the engine and filled the air with silence. He felt for the courier pouch tucked inside his leather flight jacket and wondered if it had been worth all the trouble.

"You Callahan?" the marshal asked.

Tom nodded. "Yep."

His eyes narrowed as he searched Tom's face, then flicked his gaze toward Annie. There was a moment of hesitation before he spoke again.

"Didn't know the postal service also hauled passengers," Harper said, sweeping back his jacket to expose the pistol on his hip.

"We don't," Tom replied. "Just the mail."

"Then who's this?" he asked, his voice gruff but not unfriendly.

"This is Annie—"

"Fallon," she blurted, cutting him off before he could reveal her last name.

"Pleased to meet you, ma'am," the marshal said, tipping his hat in her direction before sauntering closer to the plane and fixing his gaze on Tom. "I understand you have a special delivery for me?"

Tom nodded and reached into his flight jacket to remove the leather courier pouch, weighing its heft in his hand. Somehow, it felt different. Lighter. He glanced up at Annie and saw a silent plea in her eyes mixed with something else he couldn't quite place. He hesitated, then tossed the pouch to the lawman.

The marshal caught it and turned it over, examining it closely. "You open this?"

Tom shook his head. "No, sir. I just haul the mail."

He held the package up and Tom saw that the wax seal had been broken. "Then, what's this?"

Tom shot a glance at Annie and suddenly recognized the look in her eyes. Guilt.

"Marshal, I—"

The marshal drew his pistol and leveled it at Tom. "Out of the plane."

For the second time that day, Tom raised his hands above his head and climbed out of the cockpit at gunpoint, wondering what he had gotten himself into. He dropped to the ground and stood in front of the marshal, staring off into the distance where the wind was blowing snow off the top of Pikes Peak and carrying it out over the valley.

The marshal emptied the pouch's contents and unfolded the handwritten note contained inside. He read it in silence, his eyes tracing the words, while keeping his gun pointed at Tom.

When he had finished, he fixed Tom with an angry stare. "Where is it?"

"Where's what?" Tom asked.

"The key."

Tom glanced over his shoulder at Annie, who dropped her chin to her chest in defeat. In that moment, he knew she had opened the pouch back on her ranch in Monument.

"I don't know what you're talking about, Marshal," Tom said, praying that the sincerity in his words were enough to convince him.

"How about you, Miss Fallon?" he asked, turning to point the gun in Annie's direction.

The itch was getting worse, and he felt his anger boiling over at seeing the lawman point his gun at a defenseless woman. He lowered his hands and balled them into fists, just as another man stepped out from the hangar's shadows.

"Lower the gun, Sheriff!" he yelled.

*Sheriff?*

Tom froze with indecision when he spotted the newcomer bearing a U.S. Marshals badge on his chest. He didn't want to be caught in the middle of opposing lawmen, but Annie's words of warning rang in his ears.

*You trust the wrong lawman out here, Tom, and you're likely to end up in a ditch.*

As the sheriff spun toward the marshal, Tom cocked his fist and sent it sailing into his face.

TOM WATCHED THE impostor collapse to the ground in a heap at his feet, then lifted his hands in surrender. The newcomer raced across the tarmac and knelt to handcuff the unconscious man.

"You okay, Annie?" he called out.

"Got here just in time, Marshal."

Tom watched their exchange before clearing his throat. "Somebody mind telling me what the hell's going on?"

The marshal gave Tom a wry smile. "Who's your friend, Annie?"

"Just the mailman," she said.

The lawman gestured for Tom to lower his hands. "You must be Tom Callahan."

"How… how'd you know?"

"Because I'm William Harper, and Marshal Hollis told me you were coming with evidence that would put the sheriff away for good."

*"You're* Marshal Harper?"

The marshal nodded at the unconscious man. "The sheriff here's been running a bootlegging operation up and down the Rockies from Cheyenne to Pueblo. He's been blackmailing local ranchers to store and deliver his booze."

Tom glanced at Annie and saw the look of shame on her face. Her voice was quiet as she spoke. "When my husband came back from the war, he took to drinking to drown the nightmares that kept him awake. But Colorado had already implemented prohibition, and Sheriff Carson arrested him for possession of bootleg liquor."

Tom understood all too well about the nightmares. "What'd your husband do in the war?"

"He was a pilot."

"And those gunmen back at your ranch?"

"They were the sheriff's men, coming to collect the money my husband stole from him. When he got sober, he wanted out. So, he locked away the money as insurance and got word to Marshal Hollis up in Cheyenne."

Marshal Harper took over. "The sheriff here was using barnstormer pilots to deliver his contraband booze and got himself a twofer in Annie's husband—"

The thunderous roar of a Liberty V-12 engine cut off the marshal, and Tom flung himself onto the ground as the sleek Airco dove at them from the sky above.

"Get down!" he shouted.

Tom pinched his eyes shut and waited for a machine gun to fire and tear them all to shreds. But after the plane had passed, he looked up and saw a grinning Marshal Harper squatting down in front of him. "That there's my partner, Marshal Tucker."

Tom glanced over his shoulder at the retreating Airco. "Your *partner?*"

The marshal nodded. "He's been shadowing you since Cheyenne to make sure you made it here safely. We had our suspicions the sheriff was onto us, and we weren't going to take any chances. Nothing makes me madder than a lawman who abuses his power."

Tom couldn't argue with that.

The sleek Airco circled the airfield once more, then settled onto the runway and ended the itch that had been clawing up Tom's back since Cheyenne. He took a deep breath and turned to the marshal. "Anything else I can do for the U.S. Marshals?"

Marshal Harper thought for a moment. "We could always use a pilot like you."

"Hell, no," Tom said. "I just haul the mail!"

*—Jack Stewart is a retired U.S. Navy fighter pilot with over two decades of service and multiple combat deployments, including an assignment to the Joint Special Operations Command. Stewart is a graduate of the U.S. Naval Academy, U.S. Navy Fighter Weapons School (TOPGUN), and holds a Master of Science in Global Leadership from the University of San Diego. He is the USA Today bestselling author of* Silent Horizons, W.E.B. Griffin Direct Action, *and the* Battle Born *series. He lives in Dallas, Texas, with his wife and three children.*

# BETSY RANDOLPH

## IF ONLY: A POLICEWOMAN'S HEARTACHE

TWO THINGS HAPPENED when Linda Maddox heard who the Oklahoma beheading suspect was. First, she vomited, throwing up her lunch of tomato basil soup and house salad with blue cheese dressing—all over the faux-wood, ceramic tile floor of Kamps 1910, the lunch bistro where she and her best friend, Mac, were eating.

Second, she screamed what those within earshot wouldn't soon forget. "I should have killed that motherfucker when I had the chance."

Nolen Alvin—part-time gangbanger, full-time turd—was released early from prison. To celebrate, he went on a killing spree at work. Not just killing, viciously beheading fifty-four-year-old Colleen Hammond—wife, mother, grandmother—then sawing on the neck of a second woman, forty-three-year-old Traci Jameson, a single mother of two. The only thing that stopped Alvin from beheading Traci was a 5.56mm, 55-grain FMJ round. It hit him in the right shoulder, spraying pink mist across the Canon copier and all the mailing labels on which Colleen had been working.

Years before, Linda congratulated herself for her self-restraint. She'd done the right thing by not killing Alvin—justified or not. But now, grief-stricken and broken by his horrific acts, she knew… she could have prevented this.

Charlie, lead television studio cameraman, stood behind the teleprompter on Linda's left. He held three fingers up, then folded his ring finger down, then his middle finger, and with his index finger, he pointed at her.

She was live.

"Good evening, thanks for joining us, I'm Linda Maddox with KFIV News at six. Officials with the Oklahoma Department of Corrections confirmed the suspect in yesterday's beheading at Vaughnery Foods in Norman was released from prison early after serving less than four years on assault and battery on a police officer and multiple drug-related convictions."

She took a breath, hoping the nausea cramping her stomach would subside. "Ed O'Donnelly is live in Norman with more. Ed...."

A dark-headed young man, dressed in a white shirt and blue tie, appeared in the small monitor on the Formica-covered news desk Linda sat behind. The Vaughnery Foods sign, in red neon, shone over Ed's right shoulder. Behind him, yellow police tape flapped in the wind.

*"Thanks, Linda. I'm live outside Vaughnery Foods in Norman where yesterday police say an employee—identified as Nolen Alvin—attacked several coworkers, killing and beheading one, and attempting to behead another—severely cutting her neck before Mark Vaughnery, an off-duty Oklahoma County Sheriff's reserve deputy and owner of the Vaughnery Foods—managed to bring the attack to a stop by shooting Alvin. With me is Suzi Roushet, spokesperson for Vaughnery Foods."*

The photojournalist on scene widened the camera's lens, bringing a blonde woman into the shot. She stood next to Ed staring wide-eyed into the camera wearing a red Vaughnery Foods windbreaker, her name embroidered on her chest.

*"Suzi, what can you tell us about Alvin and his employment with Vaughnery Foods?"*

*"Mister Alvin started working here last fall."*

Ed pulled the foam-covered microphone back to his mouth when she didn't say more.

*"Suzi, does Vaughnery Foods make a practice of employing recently paroled inmates?"*

The corners of Suzi's lips pulled down into a frown. Her eyebrows scrunched together. *"Well, yes. We do. We partner with DOC and Probation and Parole to integrate parolees back into the workforce."*

*"Mister Alvin was fired yesterday by Vaughnery Foods before the attack. Can you tell us why he was fired or what perpetuated the attack?"*

A sheen of sweat shone on Suzi's face in the camera light. She swallowed, pausing before answering.

*"Mister Alvin received multiple complaints from coworkers since he began. He'd converted to Islam while incarcerated and tried to get his coworkers to convert, too. He was aggressive and honestly, frightening."*

There it was. *Islam*—beheading.

Linda knew Suzi would likely face the firing squad herself, for answering. Ed asked a few more questions but Linda's mind had already drifted back ten years to her own encounter with the beheading suspect. So much had happened in the years since. She'd quit the police department, gotten her master's degree, hired on as a field reporter with KFIV, and worked her way up to an anchor position.

Ed's voice droned in the background.

*"Linda, would you care to reply? Linda, can you hear me?"*

Charlie stepped out from behind the teleprompter, waving his hand in front of Linda. He pointed to the small monitor.

"My apologies, Ed. Can you repeat that?"

Heart galloping, she grit her teeth, jaw muscles twitching as Ed repeated the question.

*"Suzi asked how you're handling the news of this attack, considering your run-in with the suspect a few years ago when you were a police officer. Would you care to respond?"*

How in the *hell?*

Linda absorbed the question like a fist to the teeth. An eternity passed. Her mind scrambled, searching for an appropriate response. Cotton-mouthed, sweaty, and on the precipice of jumping up and running, Linda swallowed. A beach ball formed in her throat. She stared at the camera, her hopes of flying under the radar gone.

"Not at this time, Ed. No."

Stunned, Ed stared blankly for a moment into the camera. He turned and thanked Suzi for joining them.

*"That's all for now. Live in Norman at Vaughnery Foods, I'm Ed O'Donnelly for KFIV News. Back to you, Linda."*

She curled her fingernails into her palms—her entire body, a spring under pressure. She wanted to punch something, to feel the shearing pain in her knuckles, releasing her explosive anger on anything. She bit down on her tongue until she nearly whimpered, the metallic taste of blood filling her mouth. Forcing herself to keep her shit together, she turned to the lighted teleprompter on her right.

"Thank you for that report, Ed. In other news, police are searching for the driver of a hit-and-run accident which claimed the life of a city man early this morning...."

Twenty minutes later, after commercials, the local weather forecast, state and national sports, and entertainment news, she signed off and stood. The studio lights blasted her like a heat lamp from every angle. She pulled at her blouse, easing the wet fabric from the folds of her underarms. With shaking fingers, she smoothed her skirt and stepped off the brightly painted news desk stage.

"Are you okay? You look sick." Charlie, the seasoned cameraman, held a hand out to Linda as she descended the three steps. The smooth dark skin on his forehead puckered into a wrinkle as his eyebrows raised. Linda patted his shoulder when her feet were on solid ground.

"Thank you, Charlie. Oh, my god! What a train wreck!"

He shooed her comment away with the wave of his hand.

"It wasn't that bad."

C. L. Musgrove, managing editor and sloop-backed, chronic smoker, stepped out of his glass encased office. His thinning brown hair stood on end, as if he'd been running his hands through his hair—or pulling at it.

"Linda, can I see you a minute?"

C. L. turned and disappeared into his office. Linda glanced at Charlie who ran his finger across his throat before realizing the irony of his actions and turned away, embarrassed. Linda followed C. L. into his office. They settled in their respective chairs on either side of his paper-strewn desk. C. L.'s eyes, behind his large horn-rimmed glasses, looked especially large. His mouth, which usually hung open to breathe—thanks to an extremely deviated septum—appeared as one thin line as he pressed his lips together.

"Let's talk about what happened tonight."

"I spaced."

"Yes, I know. But I'd like to know why. Did you have a connection to the beheading suspect like that woman said? If so, why didn't you say anything?"

Linda's stomach dropped. She took her time formulating what came out of her mouth next. She couldn't get a feel on C. L.—hell, she didn't even know what the initials C. L. even *stood* for. No one did. Thick blue veins protruding from his pale forehead said to tread lightly.

"Full disclosure, C. L., when I was a police officer, I fought with the suspect while arresting him. He managed to escape with one of my handcuffs attached to his wrist. KFIV ran a story on it, along with the manhunt that followed. When Norman PD released the suspect's name earlier today, I should've mentioned it. I apologize."

C. L. stood. He paced the worn carpet behind his desk. His bony hands ran through the wisps of hair on his head then rested on his hips as he walked back and forth.

"I need a cigarette. Or a whiskey. Maybe both."

He cut his eyes to Linda. She'd hung her head. Would they suspend her, let her go? Her gut told her to get out in front of this deal from the onset. Why hadn't she? She rubbed at her temples as C. L. returned to his chair. He scooted close to his desk, placing his elbows down on his notes of a feature piece he'd yet to assign to a reporter about a cat coffee shop. He rested fisted knuckles under his whiskered chin, thinking. After a moment, he leaned back in his chair, its squeak had Linda lifting her eyes to his as he placed his hands, palms down, on the desk, knocking papers off the other side. He appeared feverish, sweat accumulating like pimples on his chin and nose.

"We'll write it up as a serial piece... the beheading suspect's connection to you... and the station." He looked up and to the left as if awaiting signals from outer space, then he jerked his head toward Linda. "Search the archives. Pull any video from the manhunt. Were you injured?"

Linda nodded, her eyes instantly landing on her deformed ring finger. A boutonniere deformity, her surgeon had called it. The digits were stiff with the middle joint pointing down, and the tip pointing up—like her finger was constantly poised on a keyboard.

"He yanked the handcuffs out of my hand. Broke my finger, tore a ligament off the bone—had to have my finger reconstructed."

C. L. stared hard at her. He shook his head, holding both hands out in a questioning gesture. "And you didn't think you should mention any of this *before* tonight's newscast? You sat right there in our meeting this afternoon." He pointed at the chair she'd sat in earlier. "You could have mentioned it—at least given me the chance to decide our course of action. I don't need to tell you we're chasing our own tails now. And the owners are pissed."

He sat back in his chair, arms crossed. Linda fell silent. She'd owned up to the mistake and apologized. She wouldn't apologize twice. She balled her fists as she leaned toward C. L.

"I'm surprised you didn't make the connection. You always research suspects once they're named."

C. L.'s face twisted in anger. His hands shook like he needed a bump of coke. Never one to hold back, he jumped to his feet, his reddened face nearly purple.

"Get the fuck out of my office."

Linda strode down the hall, slamming her desk drawer shut after retrieving her black leather handbag with her concealed carry—a .380 automatic—hidden inside. She slung her purse over her shoulder. She made it outside before her phone rang. She hadn't talked to Stacy Ericson in years. His name and picture on her caller ID, caused an A-fib-like flutter in her chest. A crisp northern wind sent shivers across her body as she slid her finger across the phone's surface.

"Hello."

*"That's not how you're supposed to answer. Try again."*

She exhaled with a laugh.

"Whazzz up, yo?"

*"There ya go. That's my girl."*

"Hey, Stacy. So good to hear from you. Didn't know you still had my number."

*"Well, I'm a little surprised you answered, seeing how you're a big-time TV anchor now, and I'm still just a lowly public servant."*

Former Navy SEAL, habitual gym rat, and prolific spearmint gum chewer, U.S. Marshal Stacy Ericson was blessed with the metabolism of a gazelle. He was not just a public servant. He was a good friend. And he looked damn good in ripstop cargo pants. She didn't know why they'd ever lost touch.

"I've missed you, Stace. How've you been."

*"I'll tell you over drinks. Meet me at The Jungle?"*

She drove the thirty minutes to Guthrie, a turn-of-the-century frontier town north of Oklahoma City, in silence. No radio, no other phone calls. Silence. The events of the night replaying over and over in her mind—a needle on a 33 RPM LP record, stuck in a scratch. And what of Stacy? She chewed on the inside of her cheek wondering what he wanted.

As the metro, with its overhead lights, disappeared behind her, the rural darkness closed in around her. Roller coaster hills and valleys, thick with post oak, blackjack oak, and eastern red cedars crowded in on both sides of the interstate.

She pulled into The Jungle's gravel parking lot and stopped, staring at the two-story red sandstone building on the western edge of town where they'd spent many nights together. A string of white lights outlined the building's shape, drenching the exterior of The Jungle in a golden hue. The building itself had seen better days in its one-hundred-plus years. The concrete foundation sunk slightly on one end. Missing mortar between a few bricks sent stair-step cracks racing toward the roof. Earthquakes, caused by fracking, the likely suspect. But the wide-plank porch, stretching out like a lazy cat across the front of the building, welcomed wayward souls.

Linda smiled at the thought.

She pulled her sun visor down and stared at her reflection in the lighted mirror. Excessive hairspray formed her hair into an impenetrable blonde helmet. She poked, prodded, pulled at the bleached strands until they'd softened. Then she blotted her lipstick with her finger, lightening and removing the hard, Plum Passion purple edges. She was still blotting when Stacy pulled in beside her—driver's window to driver's window. He revved the Ford 250's engine as his lips pulled up at the corners. Teal eyes searched her brown ones as his truck window slowly lowered. She flipped her visor up, grabbed her purse, and opened her door. Stacy's eyes traveled over her body as she stepped out of her car.

"Well, well, well. Don't you look snazzy."

Her lips tightened across her whitened teeth—her first genuine smile of the day. She lifted her chin a tick, allowing her lashes to lower as she stared at him.

"Get out. Let me look at you. Please, God, say you're wearing rip-stop cargo pants."

"Whatever, crazy woman."

He laughed and climbed out, holding a leather-covered notebook.

"Uh-oh. That looks serious."

Linda pointed at the notebook, all seduction in her voice dissipating. "And here I thought you were just going to get me drunk and take me to bed."

Stacy laughed and pulled her into a full hug, chest to chest, rubbing his pecks across her breasts back and forth.

"Ummmm-mmmmmm."

Linda pretended to hit him, pretending not to enjoy his warmth or manly scent. They were still laughing as they stepped through the door and entered the dark bar a few minutes later. A bony, silver-headed man with a frayed baseball cap pushed way back on his head, the only patron. He turned on his barstool to stare at them, mug in hand, as they entered. A faceless voice called from somewhere behind the wooden antique bar.

"Sit anywhere. Be right with you."

They chose a booth near the back, sliding in across from one another across the cracked vinyl seats. Stacy's eyes surveilled the wood-paneled room, taking in the dust-covered framed photos of rodeo champions, movie stars, and sports figures. Stale beer and burnt popcorn perfumed the air. He sniffed and turned to Linda.

"This place hasn't changed a bit." He used his chin to point to the man at the bar. "Hell, he was here when we were here last. Wasn't he?"

Linda chuckled. She stowed her phone in her purse and looked back up to see Stacy staring at her. The laughter in his eyes, gone.

"Don't go getting sappy on me, Stace."

"Just worried about you."

"There's no need."

Stacy leaned back, a smirk on his face as the barmaid placed paper menus on the tabletop in front of them.

"Howdy, folks. How y'all doing tonight?"

Before either could answer, she spouted off what she had on tap.

"…and just ignore the spigot handles—hadn't had a chance to change those out yet."

Stacy ordered an IPA. Linda ordered a red wine. As they waited for their drinks, Stacy reached for her hand.

"You know I care about you. This whole beheading deal—it's jacked up. But if you go around second-guessing every decision you made while wearing the badge or let all this bad shit define you and how you see the world, it'll eat you up."

Linda tried not to let him see she was gritting her teeth. Who the hell was he to pass out unsolicited advice? She drew invisible circles on the table with a finger of her other hand, waiting for him to take a breath.

"I've seen officers in your position…."

She yanked her hand free of his and hammered both fists on the tabletop, cutting him off. Stacy's head jerked back, eyes wide.

"What the...?"

She leaned toward him, her teeth sharp against her tongue, a fake smile pulling the corners of her lips up. With two fingers, she drew air circles around his mouth.

"Have I ever told you how pretty your mouth is when it's fucking *shut?*"

Stacy's face registered shock—mouth open, eyes wide. Before he could reply, the waitress placed their drinks on the table and smiled down at Stacy, twirling a strand of her stringy brown hair.

"Y'all need anything else, hon? We have some frozen chicken fingers I can throw in the fryer, if you're interested."

Stacy cut his eyes up to the waitress. "We're good. Thank you."

Linda's fists were still clinched, resting on the table when he looked back. A split second later, she took a deep breath and apologized—Jekyll and Hyde.

"Sorry, Stace. Say what you have to say."

She put the wine glass to her lips, allowing the warm, red wine to flow over every taste bud as she stared at him. He hesitated then opened his leather notebook, pulling out a single sheet of paper. He turned it around where she could read it.

"EMDR—eye movement desensitization and reprocessing—a neurobiological form of therapy, directly addressing the brain's stress or trauma-induced fight, flight, or freeze response. Our trained psychologists will safely guide you through your trauma—whether PTSD, anxiety, depression, or grief."

Linda rubbed her neck. Without saying a word, she lifted her wine glass and emptied it. She cut her eyes back to Stacy.

"A head shrink? Really?"

"Cumulative trauma is something each of us in law enforcement experience, Linda. You can ignore it if you choose. But eventually you'll have to address it."

He slid the flyer across the table toward her.

"I appreciate your concern, but I really don't believe in this hocus-pocus bullshit."

"It's *not—*"

She cut him off again with a raised hand. "I've really got to go. Have an early meeting."

She insisted on paying the tab.

"Why did you quit law enforcement?"

Linda didn't respond.

She signed the check, grabbed her copy of the receipt, and threw the pen on the table. Purse in hand, she marched out the door with Stacy following. Walking in heels in the gravel parking lot threw her off-balance, pissing her off even more. She stopped just long enough to pull her shoes off, then threw them and the flyer into her passenger seat. She slammed the door and tore out of the lot, sending red earth flying.

THE NEXT MORNING, C. L. looked at his watch when she walked into the meeting fifteen minutes late. It wasn't the best start to the day. Moments later, Rhett, a field reporter, knocked his coffee cup over. Linda's blouse and slacks fell victim to sticky French vanilla creamer with just a splash of coffee inside. At lunchtime, a low tire pressure light on her dash flashed red. Instead of eating, she spent the next forty-five minutes getting a tire plugged. So, when the four p.m. newscast finally rolled around, she was a geyser—waiting to blow.

She opened the broadcast, read the headlines, and turned it over to the weather desk. High daytime temperatures met an evening cold front, creating perfect conditions for a November tornado. After midpoint commercials, she came back with breaking news of a shooting in downtown Oklahoma City. She saw the light go out on the teleprompter as the B-roll cut in. But the footage wasn't for the shooting story. It was for the cat café story—cats lounged on chairs, sofas, and counters. Cats climbed carpet-lined towers. A black one licked itself, its back leg stretched toward the sky—rough-tongued paradise à la mode while the woman, a millennial who opened the Cat & Coffee Café, sipped a cappuccino while pretending to read a book.

Linda turned her anger-flushed face to Dave, her coanchor.

"You've got to fucking be kidding me."

Dave opened his mouth to speak but Linda slammed her fist down hard on the news desk. The entire footage of the cats ran as the executive producer scrambled to find the correct footage.

The teleprompter light clicked back on and Linda ground her teeth. She loathed apologizing for someone else's mistake.

"Please excuse that incorrect footage."

She paused, then read almost all of the remainder of her prewritten script on the teleprompter before the chief meteorologist stormed on the weather set, demanding to cut in with a "weather emergency." He slid his foot across the floor like a ballerina as he watched his own reflection on a monitor off to his right. Dancing Mike—the weatherman.

"A tornado warning is in effect for Beaver County in the Oklahoma panhandle. If you live in or near Buffalo, Oklahoma, you need to get below ground now. This is an EF4 tornado, folks. You will *not* survive if you're not below ground."

He pointed at the green screen behind him which viewers saw as a map of Oklahoma. Color-coded splotches indicated where the Doppler radar picked up the tornado's signature hook pattern as the twister touched down, sending modular homes flying and projectiles hurtling.

Weather preempted the remainder of the news, even cutting into *The Late Show.* Thirty minutes past eleven, she stood, stretched, and headed for her desk when C. L. stepped out of his office, holding out his hand like a school crossing guard.

"Have a minute?"

Linda slung her purse over her shoulder, narrowing her eyes at him.

"Actually, I don't."

He handed her a piece of paper with the station's letterhead on top.

"Suspended with pay until further notice. Really? I don't need this shit today, C. L."

"Well, you got it, regardless."

He threw his hands up, walking back toward his office leaving Linda standing in the hallway—where even the worn, chipped tile appeared forlorn.

LATER, COCOONED IN an oversized Pendleton sweater, Linda sat with her arms wrapped around her knees on a less-than-comfortable wicker chair on her back deck. The Oklahoma City skyline, her usual view, glowed eerily through billowy storm clouds. An occasional flash of lightning and rumble of thunder kept her company. She swirled a goblet filled with Knobel Tennessee Whiskey, raising the glass to her mouth just as her phone rang.

"Your timing is impeccable, Stace."

*"That's not how you're supposed to answer."*

"I'm not in the mood. It's been a shit day."

*"Care to talk about it?"*

She laughed then pulled more whiskey into her mouth, hissing as the devil water heated up her insides. "Remember when you told me women have an unlimited amount of words, implying I talk too much?"

*"You're taking what I said out of context."*

"Doubtful. Regardless, I've used up all my words."

*"Noooo. For how long?"*

"Maybe forever. The station canned me."

*"They fired you?"*

"Might as well have, I'm suspended until further notice."

Stacy sighed into the mouthpiece. She envisioned him sitting in bed, shirtless, covers pulled up to his chiseled abs.

"What are you wearing?"

Stacy ignored the question. *"I can't believe they suspended you."*

"Believe it."

Her French doors squeaked as she slid them apart. She sloshed four more fingers of whiskey into her glass, leaning against the kitchen counter as the room spun. Stacy's voice steadied her.

*"Will you please call the police psychologist? You'll really benefit from the therapy. It might just save your career."*

She let the idea sink in.

THE NEXT DAY, head pounding, dressed in a black pantsuit with a white silk top, pearl earrings, and black pumps, Linda walked into Primrose Funeral home in Norman. Fearing she'd be recognized and attention taken away from the victim, she waited until the service started before entering the hushed chapel. Deep maroon carpet muted her footsteps. Bright white walls and white pews held a roomful of people, none of whom Linda knew. A sickly floral scent, Linda associated with death, permeated the air. Organ music pumped out of hidden speakers strategically placed around the ceiling. Queasy and heartsick, she lowered herself onto a pew in the very last row.

All eyes stared at the big screen at the front of the room. The deceased, Colleen Hammond, smiled in every photo from every decade. Colleen as a baby, little girl, teenager, young woman, her wedding day, her daughter's birth, her granddaughter's birth. Each photo pierced Linda's heart—a dagger plunging deeper and deeper. When Colleen's husband spoke, Linda wept openly. Why hadn't she thought to bring any tissues? She looked around on the pews and floor near her but found no tissue boxes. She wiped her eyes and face with her fingers. Then a fist full of Kleenex appeared over the shoulder of a lady sitting directly in front of her. "Thank you," she whispered. She mopped at her tears and snot. When the preacher asked the congregation to stand—indicating the end of Colleen's celebration of life—Linda slipped quietly out of the chapel. She didn't want to be recognized by anyone—especially Colleen's family.

THE NEXT FEW weeks were a blur. After driving to Texas to attend an EMDR session with the Austin psychologist, she received a letter from the TV station asking her to return to work. Life slowly returned to normal. Stacy faded into her past as two weeks, two months, then two years ticked by. He called multiple times but she never answered. He was part of her old life she chose to forget. When the subpoena came in the mail for her to testify—in what had become a capital murder case with the possibility of the death penalty for the beheading suspect—her past became her present.

She arrived early at the courthouse on the day she was set to testify. Nervous and sweaty, she excused herself after checking in with the DA's office. The second-floor women's restroom door slammed against the wall as she rushed inside. Spaghetti and Sprite from the previous night splattered into the porcelain stool. Shaky and damp with perspiration, she stumbled to the sink, scooping water into her mouth and spitting. When she raised her head to look in the mirror, a woman stood behind her. Linda spun around.

"You scared me."

"I'm so sorry."

The woman fidgeted with the ruffled collar of her blouse. Red-rimmed, swollen eyes stared at Linda. A raised, purple scar wrapping around her neck, stuck out like a jagged purple finger. In her hands were paper towels. She offered them to Linda.

"You slipped out of Colleen's funeral before I could talk to you. I handed you tissues. I'm Traci Jameson—the other woman...."

Linda's knees threatened to buckle. Tiny white stars appeared from somewhere overhead, floating around the blue-and-white tiled restroom. Leaning back against the quartz countertop, Linda lifted her hand, accepting the paper towels, queasier than before.

"Didn't realize that was you—that handed me tissues, I mean. I'm Linda Maddox."

Traci touched her arm. "I know who you are."

Linda's eyes dropped to Traci's hand. Bare fingernails, blunt and partially chewed, said Traci's life hadn't been easy. Her eyes were lagoon blue and sorrowful—the saddest eyes Linda had ever seen—and blinked back at her when she looked up.

"Linda, I'm sorry for what he did to you."

"To me? I'm sorry for what he did to you. And what he did to Colleen."

Bound together by an unbelievable tragedy, the women embraced, comforting one another. The large scar on Traci's neck—the nightmare she would never outrun, outgrow, outlive—pressed against Linda's neck as they hugged.

After swearing to tell nothing but the truth, Linda lowered herself into the witness chair on the raised platform in the Cleveland County Courthouse. Her blood pressure pounded behind her right eye, threatening a migraine. Off to her left, at the defendant's table, the maggot, Nolen Alvin, sat with his orange inmate shirt pulled up over his head—hiding. When the district attorney asked Linda to identify the suspect, she pointed at the cowering clown.

"I suppose that's him there hiding in his shirt."

Linda paused and turned to the judge expecting the judge to instruct the defendant to pull his head out of his ass and out of his shirt, to be identified. But the judge never did. Inside, Linda raged. Her lip curled into a noticeable snarl.

*Where's the big, bad, knife-wielding, woman-beheading, jihadist now?*

The DA peppered Linda with previously prepared questions as the State of Oklahoma laid out their case against the defendant. Linda's answers were short and concise, directly from her original arrest report.

"He had two felony warrants out of Oklahoma County for possession of a controlled dangerous substance and for intent to distribute. No bond. Meaning, he'd have to face a magistrate before bailing out of jail."

Linda testified to her injuries, surgeries, and time off work recuperating. The cross examine was lame. The defendant's council couldn't refute any of her testimony.

Once dismissed, she drove home on autopilot, changed into pajamas, and crawled into bed. Her bedside clock showed 1:15 p.m. but her body demanded sleep. Her limbs were cumbersome and heavy. She was physically and emotionally exhausted. But also restless, angry. After thirty minutes of churning from side to side, she threw off the covers and stalked to her library.

Dark red, bur oak shelves lined three walls. Gold framed, painted landscapes of Oklahoma adorned the other. Two steps up her rolling ladder to retrieve a book off a high shelf, she spotted her globe bar across the room. The Last Drop 1980 Buffalo Trace Bourbon swirled in her Glencairn Glass moments later. Swirling the whiskey, she nosed the tulip-shaped glass and inhaled, eyes closed. Without so much as one sip, she sat the glass down and closed the globe bar.

Down the hallway she ran, rushing into her bedroom closet, ripping off her pajamas, and pulling on colorful leggings, a sports bra, and a racerback muscle shirt.

Her running shoes smacked against the asphalt, beating out a steady cadence as she ran. Every fiber in her being, electrified. Tall sycamore trees, with their exfoliating white-and-gray bark, lined both sides of the street in her historic Mesta Park neighborhood. Each tree's canopy cast spots of shade over Linda as she ran. Sunshine on, sunshine off, on again—off again. On. She realized, there would be periods of shade but nothing could stop the sun from shining.

Twelve miles later, she limped into a coffee shop in downtown Oklahoma City. The barista, a pretty girl with gauges in her ears and piercings in her face, nodded when Linda asked to use the landline. Stacy picked up on the third ring.

"Whazzzz up, yo?"

*"Linda?"*

"You know someone else who says that?"

*"Where have you been?"*

"Stace, I need your help."

WHITE PINE HARDWOOD floors covered Stacy's entryway, flowing into the open-concept living room where an impressive river-rock fireplace stretched toward the twelve-foot-tall ceiling. His championship roping saddle sat on a saddle horse, occupying one corner. A vintage Navajo rug, in shades of red, black, and gray, lay at the feet of a white leather sectional sofa.

"Wow! This place...."

"Thanks. Now strip."

Her hands lowered to the hem of her muscle shirt.

"Not here, goose."

"Sorry. I thought...."

He marched her to the bathroom. "Throw out your clothes and I'll wash them." His thumb brushed her cheek. "I'll bring you something to put on. Oh, and use lots of soap."

She emerged thirty minutes later wearing his gray sweats and smelling of his Cowboy cologne. Stacy smiled at her from the kitchen.

"Have a seat. I ordered a pizza. Wine?"

She nodded when he held up a glass. Their eyes locked—teal on brown. He dropped down on the opposite end of the couch.

"Talk to me."

"First off, I know I ghosted you. I'm sorry."

"You damn well should be."

"Stace, I know I've been an ass. Thanks for being my friend regardless. I've been… lost. Somehow, this whole beheading thing really messed me up. I just kept thinking, if only… if only I'd done things differently… you know?"

"Yes. I do know. That's why I…."

She cut him off by scooting closer to him on the couch.

"I saw the shrink. Did the EMDR, went back to work, and tried to forget, tried to forgive myself. And now that I've testified, something inside me has changed."

"How so?"

"I don't know. Up 'til now I've been so angry. So…."

"Pissy."

Her lips pulled up at the corners. "Undoubtedly pissy."

"You're forgiven."

His eyes were soft, his lips—more so. The kiss was more than a peck but less than lusty. She touched his cheek after.

"I'm not content to sit on the sidelines any longer merely talking about people who make a difference. I want back in."

"Law enforcement?"

"Yeah. Don't know where yet but I'm doing it."

She fell asleep on his couch with him rubbing her temples. The half-marathon, the wine, and a full belly finally catching up to her. She woke with a start around four a.m. searching for Stacy. A note, propped against the empty wine bottle on the kitchen island, explained.

*Got called out—fugitive task force. Make yourself at home.*

*Stacy*

*"BREAKING NEWS...."*

Linda's head jerked up to see the KFIV News scroller crawling across the bottom of Stacy's extra-large television screen later that morning.

*"Cleveland County jurors reach verdict in beheading case."*

The video showed the courtroom. The bailiff, a massive man with arms the size of Linda's thigh, unfolded a piece of paper. He read the jury's verdict as cameras panned the courtroom and zoomed in on the defendant who stood, nonchalant, an impassive look on his face, as if bored.

*"We, the jury, have reached a unanimous decision. We find the defendant, Nolen Alvin, guilty on all eight charges, including murder in the first degree, attempted murder, and assault with a deadly weapon, times six."*

The next shot showed Alvin—cuffed and in belly chains, surrounded by U.S. Marshals—shuffling out of the courthouse and getting stuffed into a waiting DOC van—whisking him away to McAlester Prison, death row.

A year later, framed photos of Colleen Hammond and Traci Jameson adorned Linda's desk in her Glynco, Georgia, dorm room. The former police officer, turned television news anchor, turned U.S. Marshal-in-training would never forget them—or her circuitous route back to the fold.

*—Betsy (Byrd) Randolph grew up in Enid, Oklahoma, working in radio broadcasting beginning at age fifteen. She began her law enforcement career in Artesia, New Mexico, as a dispatcher and detention officer with the Artesia*

*Police Department. She retired as a lieutenant from the Oklahoma Highway Patrol in 2020. She dually served twelve years in the U.S. Army Reserves as an MP (Military Police), then as a drill sergeant. She is the past president of Women Writing the West, a former speaker and board member with Victim's Impact Panel of Oklahoma, and an Associate Editor with* Saddlebag Dispatches *Magazine.*

*Her published works include three adult novels and two middle grade readers. She lives with her husband, George, near Guthrie, Oklahoma.*

# HARRY HUNSICKER

## THE BUTCHER OF BOQUILLAS

THEY FOUND THE woman in the cemetery, her throat slit from ear to ear.

Murders didn't happen very often in my part of the world, especially ones like this.

I was a deputy sheriff in Brewster County, Texas, a big place without many inhabitants. Maybe eight thousand people lived here, spread out over a land mass larger than Rhode Island and Delaware combined.

I liked to think there was some reasoning behind the location of the body, some deeper meaning as to why a killer would leave their victim in a graveyard—other than simple convenience.

A balance of sorts. Places for the living and the dead. Maybe an attempt to bury a childhood trauma.

But I'd seen enough in my thirty-six years to know that evil has no wider significance, other than the act itself. Most killers never thought of themselves as bad people. They were just regular folks, going about their business until something snapped.

Some, of course, came out of the womb with their sense of right and wrong twisted. They were the dangerous ones. The best you could hope for with those was to spot them early on and take precautions. If you didn't—well, you better pray your affairs were in order.

The sheriff's squad car idled at the entrance to the old cemetery in

Terlingua, maybe ten miles from the Rio Grande. An ambulance was parked a few yards away by a Cadillac belonging to the justice of the peace—the man who acted as the county coroner.

I parked my pickup next to the sheriff's vehicle.

Terlingua is a strange place, an old mining town next to Big Bend National Park.

The veins of mercury had long since played out, but the mining left a desolate landscape that resembled the surface of the moon. The mercury fumes caused the miners to die early, suffering from a condition that resulted in excessive salivation and insanity. These days, the town was occupied by misfits and drifters—people running from enemies real or imagined.

It was eight in the morning and getting hot, the tail end of summer in far west Texas. I exited my truck and slid on my straw Resistol.

Sheriff Claymore leaned against the side of his car, talking on his Nokia. He was in his fifties, with a round face, ruddy cheeks, and tiny gray eyes. He usually looked like he was laughing at something. Not today, however.

The call ended, and he held up the phone.

"That was the hospital in Midland," he said. "Martha's second round of chemo, she had a rough night. I got to get on up there."

Martha was the sheriff's wife, a kind soul if there ever was one.

"You want me to run point on this?" I asked.

I already knew his answer. I was the best qualified of the deputies to handle a murder. I'd been an MP in the army, an investigator, having served in Iraq and Kuwait. The heat, the desert, dead bodies—I was used to all those things.

The sheriff nodded. "The victim's been dead a little more than two hours. We do have a suspect, though. A Mexican fellow. APB's already gone out."

"That was quick."

"They've been after him for a while on the other side," Sheriff Claymore said. "Supposedly he killed three people in Ojinaga. Couple days ago, he killed two more in Presidio."

Presidio, Texas, was in the county immediately west of us. It had the only bridge across the Rio Grande for almost a hundred miles. The town on the other side was Ojinaga.

"So the Mexicans chased him over here," I said, "and made him our problem?"

Sheriff Claymore didn't reply. His lips puckered into a circle—the expression he got when he had something heavy on his mind.

"I know you don't like to work with other people on something like this," he said. "Or on anything, for that matter."

This was true. I didn't care to partner with others. And they, in turn, didn't care to partner with me.

"But I need you to be a team player this time, Cody." The sheriff paused. "I need you to work with someone from the other side—a *federale.*"

That stopped me for a moment, my mind going through all the permutations of how that would work. A Mexican cop doesn't have jurisdiction here, any more than I did over there. I said as much to Claymore.

"Believe it or not, I do understand how international borders work." The sheriff rubbed his eyes. "Think of this as a professional courtesy."

I didn't reply, working my mind around the notion of being a glorified babysitter.

"Also, this guy's got some powerful friends," the sheriff said. "I already had a call this morning from the governor's office."

That knocked away one of my chief objections. Corruption was always a potential problem with any law enforcement agency operating along the border, ours included. But likely not in this case if the straight-as-an-arrow governor of Texas was making calls for the man. I decided to play my last card.

"What about the Rangers?" I asked. "If we're bringing in help, it should be them."

The Texas Rangers sometimes served as investigative units for smaller departments like ours. Their officers had the training and the expertise, access to the right equipment.

"They're sending a forensics team," he said. "But everybody else is tied up with the feds. A terrorist task force or something."

"So it's me and a Mexican cop?" I crossed my arms.

"That's about the sum of it." The sheriff pointed toward the cemetery. "He's at the scene right now, waiting on you."

"That was fast."

"They're hot to get this guy, Cody. We are, too."

The sheriff stared at the horizon, a faraway expression on his face.

"The killer hurts his victims before he kills them," he said. "Hurts 'em bad. When it's all said and done, I want this son of a bitch in a Texas prison."

THE TOMBS IN the Terlingua cemetery were marked by simple wooden crosses embedded in markers fashioned from rough stones. No polished marble or carved granite to be seen.

Some graves were festooned with strands of colored beads and candles. Others had dishes and pottery artfully arranged around the marker, small pennants fastened to the cross, flapping in the wind.

One grave was decorated with a rusted child's tricycle and empty ammo cans that had been painted yellow.

A knot of people stood a dozen yards beyond the tricycle grave. The Brewster County justice of the peace. Two EMTs I knew. And a man in the blue uniform of the Mexican Federal Police Force, the shoulders of his shirt adorned with epaulets, colorful patches on the arms.

I headed toward the assembled group.

A white tarp covered the victim.

Everyone was silent, the mood somber. Death scenes had that effect on people.

I took my place next to the JP.

"I'm gonna leave now that you're here," he said. "Rangers are five minutes away."

"Show me the body," I said.

The JP shook his head. "Wait 'til I'm gone, will ya? I don't want to be sick again."

He trundled off toward the entrance to the cemetery, muttering to himself.

The man in the blue uniform approached, his hand out. "You must be Deputy Cody Scanlon."

His fingers were soft, his grip strong. He was in his forties, with an angular face, long chin, and a high forehead. His skin was the color of coffee heavy with cream, his hair wavy and dark brown.

"I am Captain Luis Navarro-Diaz," he said. "At your service, sir. Please, call me Luis."

His English was flawless, only a slight accent.

"I hear you know who did this," I said.

Luis wore a gun belt of tooled leather, a Colt 1911 in a matching holster on his hip.

He hitched his thumbs in the belt and stared at me for a few seconds like I was someone he'd once met long ago but couldn't quite remember when or where—or if the encounter had been pleasant.

"How long have you been a police officer?" He arched an eyebrow.

"A good while."

"Who's the worst person you've ever hunted?" he asked.

I decided I didn't like Captain Luis Navarro-Diaz. He was no doubt a fine officer, but I had a murder investigation to conduct. Answering his questions was not helping me catch the killer.

I turned away from him and said to the EMTs, "Show me the body."

They shrugged and lifted the tarp.

She was young—early twenties, Hispanic. The killer had used a knife elsewhere before slitting her throat. The condition of her body was not the worst thing I'd ever seen, especially considering my time in Desert Storm—but it was close.

"As you can see, he is a disturbed man," Luis said. "Alberto Morales is his name."

I knelt by the corpse, careful not to disturb the ground and stared at her face, wondering who her people were. Did she leave children behind? Was there a mother or a father out there worrying about her right now?

Luis pulled a three-by-five photograph from his pocket and handed it to me—a mugshot with vitals on the back.

Alberto Morales was twenty-eight, originally from the Yucatan. He was short—five foot four and a stocky hundred-fifty pounds. His skin was dark, the color of cured tobacco, and he had wiry black hair. Wide cheekbones dominated a broad face.

"Alberto follows an offshoot of the Santa Muerte cult," Luis said, "one known for their violence. They sell their services to certain criminal elements."

"So this has something to do with the drug trade?"

"There are many criminal elements in Mexico," Luis said. "And in your country as well. But yes, in this case, the killings are related to drugs."

In the distance, a group of people made their way toward our location. They wore white disposable coveralls and carried duffel bags. The Texas Rangers forensics team had arrived.

"Who's the victim?" I asked.

"Bianca Moreno. She lived in Ojinaga, worked at a *farmacia* there."

"How come she ended up on this side?"

"Bianca was—what is the American expression?—on the lam. She saw something she shouldn't have."

The forensics team set down their equipment. One of them began taking pictures of the scene.

"The others, too," Luis said. "They witnessed a particularly large shipment of drugs being transported from Ojinaga to Presidio."

Something didn't add up. Smuggling was a way of life on the border. Been that way since there was a border. People witnessed things they shouldn't have all the time. They kept quiet, went about their business, and no one got hurt.

Luis seemed to read my mind. "This was more than just a shipment. The leader of the organization was present as well. A man of certain standing in my country."

Everything started to make sense now.

"Who is he?" I asked. "This man of certain standing."

"A general in the army," Luis said. "His brother-in-law is the minister of defense."

I whistled softly. No wonder people were being killed.

"How many witnesses were there?" I asked.

Luis pointed to the tarp. "Unfortunately, she was the last one."

"The killer's headed back to Mexico, then."

"That is my assumption, yes." Luis nodded.

"How's he getting around?"

"Alberto crossed into Presidio on a motorcycle," Luis said. "An old Honda with New Mexico plates. If I can catch him alive, there is a chance he can lead me back to the general."

"Then we need to stop him before he gets across. No offense to your country, but once he gets on the other side, he'll be a lot harder to find."

Not to mention the fact that Sheriff Claymore and I both wanted this guy in Huntsville.

"None taken." Luis said. "And you are correct. But know this—the border guards in Ojinaga are not part of the military. They are on the lookout for him. Alberto will not cross that way."

"That means he's headed to another crossing point," I said. "We'll get him there."

A surge of excitement rushed through me as a plan came together. We could stop this guy—and maybe take out someone up the food chain.

Brewster County had two places to cross—Lajitas and Boquillas, that last one deep inside Big Bend National Park. Both were informal and saw little traffic. There was no immigration control on either side, just people going back and forth by boat like they'd been doing for centuries.

Two deputies arrived to help secure the scene. I asked the forensics team if there was anything they needed from me. They said no.

I turned to Luis. "My truck is by the entrance to the cemetery."

"Good," he said. "I hope you will drive very fast."

LAJITAS WAS CLOSEST—only fifteen minutes by vehicle from Terlingua, practically across the street in West Texas terms. I made it there in nine.

The crossing was a sandy spot on the river by a wooden shack with a rusted Coca-Cola sign over the door.

I parked by the shack. Luis and I exited my pickup.

The banks on both sides were empty. No boats. No people milling about, waiting to make the journey to a different country.

An old Hispanic man sat on a wooden bench in front of the shack. He wore a Dallas Cowboys ball cap and a shirt two sizes too big. He smiled at us and waved.

"Where are the boats?" I asked him.

He shrugged.

*"Dónde están los botes?"* Luis pointed to the river, an edge to his voice.

*"Ellas no están aquí hoy,"* the old man replied. "They're not here today."

I stared at the water. The Rio Grande was running fast. There must have been rain upriver. The killer wouldn't be swimming across, at least.

"Sometimes the boats come," the old man said in heavily accented English. "Sometimes not."

"Have you seen this person today?" I held up the photograph. "He wants to get to the other side."

The old man's smile slid from his face. He stared at the ground, not answering.

*"Señor?"* I said. "You've seen this person?"

He crossed his arms, obviously afraid. I wondered if he was scared of two men in uniform—or who he'd seen earlier.

"How long ago?" I asked.

Silence.

Luis yanked him from the bench and slammed him against the side of the shack, using so much force the ball cap fell to the ground.

*"Dime lo que sabes, viejo."* He squeezed the man's throat. Tell me what you know.

The old man's eyes were wide, full of fear, his gray hair askew.

*"Por favor,"* he said in a trembling voice. "I don't want trouble."

Luis looked like he was going to strike the old man, a grim expression on his face, his fist reared back.

I grabbed his wrist and pulled him away.

Luis wrenched his arm free from my grasp, eyes alight with anger.

"That's not how we do things here," I said.

He glared at me. "Where exactly do you think this 'here' place is you are talking about, *amigo?"*

"America. You forget what side of the river you're on?"

"The river floods and changes course often," Luis said. "This time next year, we could very well be standing in Mexico."

"Well, we're not in Mexico today." I paused. "And I'm *not* your *amigo."*

"No." Luis shook his head. "I suppose you're not."

I turned to the old man. "We're not looking to cause you any trouble, *señor.* But we need to know how long ago the man on the motorcycle was here. And where he went."

The old man looked between me and Luis.

"Nobody's going to hurt you," I said. "That I can promise you."

A moment passed.

*"Estuvo aquí hace treinta minutos."* He pointed east. "Thirty minutes ago. He went that way."

The killer had gone toward the park. Toward the only other crossing for hundreds of miles.

*"Muchas gracias."* I gave him a ten-dollar bill and got back in my truck.

Luis jumped into the passenger seat.

A thirty-minute head start was bad. It was at least that long to the park's entrance, then another hour to the crossing.

That would put the killer there around ten thirty, us a half hour later—maybe sooner depending on how fast I could go. There was no way to make up a thirty-minute head start, however.

Ten thirty in the morning was about the time tourists started to gather to make their way to the Mexican side. There was never a big crowd trying to get across—the town south of the river barely qualified as such—but there might be enough to make it difficult for us to arrest the killer before he disappeared into Mexico.

We drove in silence. Luis sat with his arms crossed, staring straight ahead. About halfway to the park entrance, he spoke for the first time since leaving Lajitas.

"Don't put your hands on me again, Deputy Scanlon."

"Don't beat up on old men, and I won't have to."

"It's so easy for people like you, living in this land of great wealth," he said. "Easy to tell others how to conduct themselves. The world does not bend to your will."

"The world of Brewster County, Texas, does."

Luis snorted. A moment passed.

"You never answered my question from earlier," he said. "Who's the worst person you've ever hunted?"

I remembered a supply sergeant I'd encountered in Kuwait City ten years before. A timid little man with a scraggly mustache, he'd used the turmoil of war to cover his sexual activity with children. His particular indulgence involved dead or dying preteens. I still had nightmares about what I'd seen when we finally tracked him down.

"I'm a cop," I said. "I've encountered a lot of bad people in my time."

"You're thinking of someone, though. I can tell."

After a moment, I nodded.

"Good," Luis said. "Keep this person in mind as we get close to Alberto. That will keep your reflexes sharper."

Neither of us spoke again until the entrance to the park appeared—a sand-colored stucco building with an American flag flying in front.

At the barricade, I stopped. The park ranger slid open the window.

I pointed to my badge and said, "Have you seen a man come through in the last half hour or so on a motorcycle?"

The ranger nodded. "He wanted to know about the crossing."

"Are the boats there today?" I asked.

The ranger raised the barricade. "There's a line behind you. Can you pull over?"

I looked in the mirror.

Three cars had stacked up to the rear of us.

I jammed on the accelerator and headed toward our final destination.

Big Bend is a majestic place. The Chisos Mountains dominate the middle of the park, rocky outcroppings rising dramatically from the desert floor before the slope toward the Rio Grande began.

I hardly noticed, intent on driving as fast as possible to our destination.

We passed a few cars and RVs, most with out-of-state plates. Families, retired couples, hippie types. Everyone drawn to the rugged beauty of the area.

We entered a stretch of road with massive boulders on either side. As I rounded a bend, Luis slapped the dashboard.

*"Stop!"*

I jammed on the brakes and pulled to the shoulder.

Luis jumped out while the truck was still moving. He ran back the way we came.

I parked and followed him, stopping when I found him fifty yards behind my pickup, standing near a willow tree. The tree grew alongside a small creek by the road. He was staring at something.

I tracked his gaze.

A motorcycle lay on its side by the creek, a few feet from the road we'd been on. It wasn't hidden but it wasn't easily visible either. The bike was an old Honda with New Mexico plates.

"I saw a flash of paint," he said.

I approached the motorcycle. The keys were in the ignition. I tapped the gas gauge.

"Looks like it's empty."

"He's on foot. That's better for us." Luis stepped back onto the road.

I remained by the motorcycle.

Something didn't feel right. I'd learned long ago to respect feelings like that. The tingle at the base of my neck, the hairs on my arms itching.

"Hold up," I said.

Luis turned to look at me.

I drew my gun, crept toward a small grove of cottonwoods ten feet away. They offered a fair degree of concealment.

I aimed at the most likely place a person would hide. Luis came up beside me, gun drawn as well. I pushed aside a branch.

Luis swore and I holstered my weapon.

TWO BODIES LAY on the ground—a woman and a man, their throats slit.

They were in their sixties, wearing shorts and T-shirts, sneakers.

Tourists.

The man had a wallet in his back pocket. According to his driver's license, his name was Fred Erickson, and he lived in St. Paul, Minnesota.

There was a picture in his wallet, too—a snapshot of the dead couple with a boy in the first or second grade. On the back, in a child's handwriting: *To the Best Grammy and Grandpa—Mike.*

Luis and I stared at the picture for several seconds.

I pulled out my Motorola and flipped it open.

No signal. The police radio in my truck was out of range, too.

"We have to find a park ranger," I said. "Report this."

"And what will that accomplish?" Luis asked.

"This is the FBI's jurisdiction. There's a crime scene to process and—"

"And Alberto gets away," Luis said.

"You don't understand. There're procedures for something like this."

"Will these procedures bring Mister and Missus Erickson back to life?"

I didn't answer.

"We need to hurry," Luis said. "This has slowed him down."

He was right. How long was Alberto on the side of the road waiting for someone to come by? Five minutes? Fifteen? Or longer?

The odds that we could catch the killer on this side of the river had increased exponentially.

"But two people have been murdered," I said. "We can't just leave them here."

Luis didn't reply. He took the picture from my fingers, slid it back in the wallet, and placed the wallet in Mr. Erickson's pocket.

"This is not how we do things here," I said.

Luis held out his hand. "Give me your keys, then."

I stared at the dead bodies for a moment. "No. I'll drive."

Thirty seconds later we were back in my pickup, speeding toward the Rio Grande.

A SIGN ANNOUNCED the Boquillas crossing was four miles away. Luis shifted in his seat the closer we got.

"Can you not go faster?" he asked, sounding agitated. "Alberto cannot be allowed to escape."

The tires on my truck screeched with each curve in the road.

"I go any faster, we may not get there in one piece."

"These drug traffickers, they are a cancer eating away at my country." He spat the words out, angry. "Please hurry."

The road straightened and I jammed on the accelerator as the vegetation began to change—creosote bushes and prickly pear cactus giving way to willows and salt cedars. We were getting closer to the water.

Luis seemed to relax a tiny bit the faster we went.

"Have you ever killed anyone before?"

I thought back to the supply sergeant in Kuwait City. I'd finally cornered him. It was just the two of us in a room filled with things my mind had trouble comprehending. My rifle was against my shoulder. His gun lay on a table within easy reach. I ached for him to go for his weapon. *Give me a reason,* I thought. *Just move your hand a fraction of an inch toward that pistol. Save everybody a shit ton of trouble.* That sergeant must have seen what was in my eyes because he slowly backed away before raising his hands.

I replayed those few seconds again for the umpteenth time. "That's a mighty personal question, don't you think?"

"Alberto will have a gun in addition to his knife," Luis said. "I have a right to know if you can defend yourself."

"Let's just find this guy first."

A National Park Service SUV was stopped by the side of the road. It sat next to a sign indicating the parking lot for the Boquillas crossing was just ahead. A park ranger stood by the sign, talking on a walkie-talkie.

Without meaning to, I eased off the accelerator, the murdered tourists weighing on my mind.

"Don't," Luis said. "Please keep going. You must."

I pressed on the gas. He was right.

The parking lot was not full—maybe ten vehicles in total. Campers and sedans, several pickups. And one van with Minnesota plates.

I parked across from the van. Luis and I crept toward the vehicle with our guns drawn. Luis tried the rear door while I kept my weapon raised.

The door opened. The van was empty.

A park ranger approached us as we holstered our weapons—not the same person who'd been by the sign. He eyed our badges and uniforms.

"Did you see the man driving this van?" I asked.

The park ranger nodded. "A short little guy. He was headed across. Listen, you nee—"

"When was this?" Luis asked.

"You guys can't just wave your guns around. We're in—"

I cut him off. "When did you see him?"

"Maybe three minutes ago," the park ranger said.

"He murdered two people in the park earlier this morning," I said. "A man and woman from Minnesota."

"What?" The park ranger's eyes went wide.

"Their bodies are by the creek that crosses the road a few miles back," I said. "I'll explain later."

Luis sprinted toward the river. I followed close on his heels.

The Boquillas crossing was different than the one at Lajitas. It was nestled between two canyon walls, down a path lined with cottonwoods and mesquites. We followed the signs and a few moments later emerged on the riverbank, a flat sandy area that was long and narrow.

There was a similar spot on the Mexican side. The river wasn't very wide here—maybe seventy-five feet—but the currents were swift.

On the Mexican side were several small, flat-bottomed boats. Young men stood watching our side, waiting for a signal that someone wanted to cross. A corral with horses and donkeys was nearby, the animals tended by another group of men.

A single boat was in the middle of the river, heading toward Mexico. A man paddled furiously against the current while another sat in the back.

"That's him," Luis said.

I squinted against the sun. It was hard to tell, but the man in the back appeared to be dark-skinned with black hair.

On the Texas side a few feet away, a boat had just landed on the beach. A couple in their fifties—a man and a woman—were getting off the craft carrying several plastic bags filled with souvenirs.

"Let's go." Luis pointed to that boat. "Alberto doesn't have much of a head start. We've made good time."

I didn't move, staring at the expanse of water.

"We've come this far, Deputy Scanlon. Are you stopping now?"

"I don't have jurisdiction over there. Legally, I shouldn't even carry a gun across."

The tourists trudged toward the parking lot, nodding hello as they passed.

The man piloting the boat looked at us expectantly.

"Boquillas does not have a police department," Luis said. "The nearest town is over two hundred kilometers away. If I am to capture Alberto, I'll need help."

I remembered the supply sergeant when I snapped the handcuffs on him. The shy smile on his face—oops, you caught me. My lieutenant saying to me afterward, "Why didn't you just kill the fucker?"

Because we have rules that need to be followed. Otherwise, we descend into chaos.

"There is an army garrison nearby," Luis said. "If Alberto manages to contact them before I can arrest him, he will be safe."

The supply sergeant was sentenced to ten years in Leavenworth. He was probably out by now. His sentence should have been much longer, but one of my men screwed up the evidence and some of it was inadmissible.

I took a deep breath. "Let's get this son of a bitch."

THERE WASN'T MUCH to the town on the other side—Boquillas del Carmen, a tiny village perched on a bluff overlooking the Rio Grande.

It had once been a mining center, much like Terlingua. Now only a few dozen people lived in the village, their activity centered around a dusty main street lined with crumbling adobe buildings.

The town had a liquor store, a couple of restaurants, one tiny hotel, and three or four places selling tourist tchotchkes. There were no pharmacies, no doctors or dentists like in the larger border towns of Piedras Negras or Ojinaga.

I'd visited several times in the past. Boquillas was hard to get to but a good place to eat a mean and buy inexpensive booze. The few people there were friendly, too.

Alberto's boat reached the other side when we were about a quarter of the way across. I watched him walk toward town, heading up the hill, disappearing around a bend.

A few minutes later, we landed on the Mexican side. A number of tourists were waiting to cross back, which seemed odd to me. It wasn't even lunchtime yet. Most people came just to eat—maybe to shop a little, too. What was happening in Boquillas that could be driving them away?

Luis and I jumped out of our boat. Luis commandeered two horses from the corral, and we trotted toward town, heading up the hill.

We encountered more tourists going the opposite direction. Some were walking. Others were jogging like they were in a hurry.

Luis kicked his horse to go faster. I did the same. A few moments later, we arrived in Boquillas.

The main street was empty. The tourist shops were open—woven baskets and colorful pottery out front—but no customers or shopkeepers were anywhere to be seen.

"What's going on?" I asked.

"I don't know." Luis stopped his horse in the middle of the dirt street.

In the distance came the *whoomp-whoomp* of a helicopter. A few seconds later, a military chopper flew along the south side of town, low and slow.

"We need to hurry," Luis said.

A woman wearing an apron exited a restaurant and stared at the sky.

Luis and I got off our horses and approached her. She looked at each of us in turn before running down the street.

I drew my gun. Luis did the same. We stepped inside the restaurant.

The interior smelled like tortillas and fried onions. A dimly lit dining room opened onto a patio overlooking the Rio Grande and Texas. The dining room was empty except for a cook watching the news on TV.

Luis and I headed to the patio.

Alberto sat at a table with his back to the river, facing us, his attention focused on the plate of enchiladas in front of him.

Luis and I approached him warily. We moved apart, both of us with our guns raised.

Alberto looked up.

"Put your hands on your head," I said in Spanish, aiming at his chest.

"You can't touch me here," he said to Luis. "You know that. Right now, I'm the king of Boquillas."

"More like the butcher of Boquillas," Luis said.

Alberto shrugged and returned to his meal.

*BAM.*

Luis shot him—a single round to the forehead.

I jumped back as Alberto fell face first into his food. My heart pounded in my chest.

Footsteps sounded behind me.

I whirled around. A few feet away, a soldier aimed a rifle at me. Beside him stood an officer—a general.

*"Bueno,"* the general said. *"Está terminado."*

My skin turned cold, a hollowness settling in my stomach.

*"Sí."* Luis holstered his weapon. *"Está terminado."*

"What the hell's going on?" I asked.

"I'm sorry you had to see that," Luis said. "I thought I would need your assistance. But Alberto didn't put up much of a fight."

"Hell, he didn't put up any fight. And you still shot him in cold blood."

"I shot him because he needed to die." Luis glanced at the general and lowered his voice. "They threatened my family if I did not kill him. I had no choice."

I understood finally. Alberto was the last link between the shipment of drugs and the general. And he'd just been killed by a bullet from a policeman's gun, not a soldier's.

Actions always have consequences. Case in point—me crossing the river when I knew that was the wrong thing to do. The rules mattered. And now I was in a bind, stuck between a rock and a bigger rock.

I had to get back across the border. I swallowed my fear, moved away from the general and his soldier, and kept my gun raised.

"No one is going to hurt you," Luis said. "Put your weapon away and you can leave."

The soldier strode to where Alberto's body lay. He pulled a pistol from the dead man's waistband.

The general shook his head. "Nobody's going anywhere right now."

"If you don't let him go," Luis said, "the Americans will ask questions."

"The Americans are too busy with what's happening in New York to ask questions," the general said.

"What the hell are you talking about?" I asked.

The TV in the dining room had been showing a news report. Something about planes flying into buildings. Was that in New York?

"Terrorists attacked your country several hours ago," the general said. "The World Trade Center. The Pentagon."

I fought back the wave of emotion surging through my body. One problem at a time.

The general snapped his fingers, and his soldier fired Alberto's weapon—the bullet tearing into Luis's chest.

Everything slowed down. It took forever for Luis's body to hit the floor.

I used that time to save myself. My gun hand moved of its own accord, aiming and slapping the trigger in one motion as the soldier shifted Alberto's pistol toward me.

I was faster. My bullet hit the soldier's throat right before he fired. His round missed by a wide margin. He dropped, gun clattering on the tile floor.

The general stared at me, one eyebrow raised. "Good shot, *amigo.* But my men are on the street. You have no chance to escape."

"Like hell I don't." I aimed at his face.

I'd been to this restaurant before. The border was a hundred yards away but at least that much distance lower. It would be difficult, but I could scale down the bluff and grab a boat. Row myself back home.

"Put your gun down," the general said. "Don't make this harder than it needs to be."

My arms shook. Sweat trickled down the small of my back. I remembered the supply sergeant and all the choices I'd made that had led me to this place and time.

I pulled the trigger.

The general fell to the ground.

More soldiers appeared from the shadows of the dining room—rifles at the ready.

I kept firing.

*—Harry Hunsicker is the bestselling author of nine crime thrillers and numerous short stories. His latest book,* The Life and Death of Rose Doucette, *was recently shortlisted for a 2025 Thriller Award—his second nomination for the honor. Additionally, his debut novel was a finalist for a Shamus Award. Hunsicker also wrote the screenplay for a recently produced short crime thriller about a hit man with an irritable bowel syndrome. Both the script and film earned numerous accolades.*

# D.P. LYLE

## RED ROSES

*West Texas*
*October 1955*

ROSALEE TUCKER SWIPED the final water streaks from the windshield and stuffed the dingy blue rag into the back pocket of her jeans. She zipped her red-and-black checkered wool jacket higher as the constant cold West Texas breeze kicked up. It was October. Even the noonday sun offered little warmth.

"That'll be two dollars and seventy-eight cents," she said to the man behind the wheel of the dusty black 1948 Chevy Stylemaster. She knew cars. Helped Daddy work on them. She was partial to Chevys. This one a beauty with chrome wheels and whitewall tires.

This plot of dirt, where a farm road with no name spurred off U.S. 84, was called Tucker's Corner. Rosalee felt like it was her corner. And someday it would be. Walton and Martha Tucker, her parents, inherited it from Walton Sr. and now ran the service station, repair shop, and café. Their white clapboard home and outhouse was in back, and beyond that the pecan grove that according to Daddy was a hundred years old. Rosalee pumped gas, served food, cooked, and helped her daddy with car repairs. She liked that best.

While the man sorted through the bills in his wallet, Rosalee smiled at the young girl sitting in the passenger's seat. Rosalee guessed fourth grade, maybe fifth. She had wavy red hair to match Rosalee's. Strawberry blonde was what Daddy called it.

"Who are you?" Rosalee asked.

The girl mumbled something. Rosalee couldn't really hear.

"Tell her your name," the man said.

Without looking up, she said, "Claire."

"She's shy," the man said. "Like her mama."

Rosalee leaned down, capturing the girl's attention. "I love your hair." She fingered her own. "But then I'm partial to red." She smiled.

That got a quick look and a half smile before Claire's gaze again fell into her lap.

The man handed Rosalee three ones, saying, "Keep the change. Buy yourself something special."

"Thanks, mister. I'm meetin' my friends at the movie theater this Friday night." She wadded the bills into her front pocket. "Now I can get the big box of popcorn."

He laughed. "Not much better than movie popcorn."

"Ain't that the truth."

"You know, you two could be sisters," the man said. "Same hair. Same pretty face."

"Thank you, mister."

"What's your name?"

"Rosalee."

"Pretty."

"Yep. I apparently popped out with a mess of red hair. My daddy wanted to name me Cherry. Mama wouldn't abide by that. Said she liked Rosalee better, so that's who I am."

"You're what? Around thirteen?"

"As of today." Rosalee smiled. "It's my birthday."

The man flipped open his wallet again. He pulled out another dollar bill and handed it to her. "Happy birthday."

"Why, thank you. That's mighty nice."

"Use it for fun. Maybe some Milk Duds with that popcorn."

"I just might do that."

"How much farther to Lubbock?" the man asked.

She glanced west up Highway 84, a straight, flat, oiled-gravel road, and nodded that way. "About sixty miles. When it turns to asphalt, you'll know you only got two miles to go."

The man hesitated, then said, "Yeah. My sister and her family. Haven't seen them in a while. Be glad to get there. Me and Claire and this old car are about tired of each other." He grinned. "Not to mention the smell of that oil."

"Yeah." Rosalee glanced back up the road. "They just oiled it last week. Takes a good month for the stink to settle down." She glanced at Claire, then back to the man. "Why don't y'all come on inside? Take a break. Grab something to eat." She looked back at Claire. "You like pecan pie?"

The man laughed. "She does."

"Mama makes the best. Everybody says so."

"Sounds good."

The man guided the car to the side of the café and parked. They climbed out and walked toward her, Claire tugging on a worn gray coat.

The crunch of gravel behind her drew Rosalee's attention. She turned that way.

"Looks like you're fixing to get busy," the man said. "We better get inside and put in our order." He shepherded Claire toward the door.

Rosalee shielded her eyes from the sun's glare with one hand as the Greyhound rolled up next to the two gas pumps. Aluminum with a blue front face, the white lettering in the black destination box above the windshield read *LUBBOCK*. Buses stopped by sometimes, not often, most rolled on west. Daddy liked it when they did. They always needed a lot of gas. And food.

This one was different, and she saw the problem right off. Right front tire as flat as a hotcake.

The door hissed open, and the driver climbed out. Rosalee saw a handful of passengers inside.

"I see you got a garage," the man said. "Any chance you got a tire for this thing?"

"I'll have to ask Daddy. Even if we do, it'll take a while. Your folks should come inside. It's warmer, and the coffee's hot."

"Sounds good."

Rosalee walked inside. "Mama, we got a bunch of folks coming in."

Martha Tucker looked up from behind the counter. She leaned to one side, peered through the large window. "A mess of them."

"I figure a dozen. Where's Daddy?"

"Out back. He's working on that oil filter for Travis."

"The bus's got a flat."

"I'll holler at him. You get these folks inside and see if they want something to eat."

THE POTBELLY STOVE in the corner warmed the café. Something the passengers seemed to appreciate. Rosalee got everyone seated. There were eleven passengers. Ignoring the empty tables, they filled the four booths along the front window. As if to keep their eyes on the bus for fear it might roll away and abandon them. Here, miles from anywhere.

Daddy walked through from the back, out the front door, to where the driver stood. They shook hands and then squatted next to the deflated tire. Daddy ran his fingers around its edge, stopping near the top, as if he'd located a defect. He leaned in for a closer examination.

Rosalee took orders, starting with the booth in the far corner. The one where Claire and her dad sat.

"What can I get you?" Rosalee asked.

"What do you want, honey?" the man asked Claire.

Head down, gaze glued to the faded yellow Formica tabletop, she shrugged. A fleeting glance up toward Rosalee.

"I don't bite," Rosalee said, smiling. "Especially someone who could be my sister." She squatted, bringing herself down the Claire's level. "I ain't got no sister. Brother neither. Wish I did."

"Me too," Claire said.

"Well. We can't fix that, but we can get you fed."

"You want a grilled cheese sandwich and a glass of milk?" the man said.

Claire nodded.

"I'll have the chicken-fried steak with potatoes and green beans, and a couple of biscuits."

"You want any blackberry jam with that?" Rosalee asked. "I make it myself."

"That'd be nice."

She called the order to Mama and then moved from one booth to the next. She loved this part of her duties. Talking to folks from all over who were just passing through. From places she'd never see. Except for pictures in magazines. She'd been to Lubbock and Dallas, once up to Oklahoma City, but that was about it. She found their various accents fascinating and wondered how folks from the same country could talk so differently. Not to mention the rare foreigners. Last year, a couple with their two kids stopped in. From France. Their English sounded like singing.

There was a booth of five—mom, dad, two kids, and grandma. From Baton Rouge, headed to Santa Fe for a family reunion. That syrupy Louisiana rhythm. She loved that one. A couple from Dallas going to Lubbock, and two twenty-five-year-old men from Houston, off to California, looking for construction work. They said California was booming. Rosalee had heard that. Also that California was magical. Another place she'd probably never see.

Mama clanked around in the kitchen, sliding plates through the pass-through window, where Rosalee collected them and served the passengers.

The driver and Daddy came inside, Daddy saying, "Let me make a call."

He went in back where the wall phone hung near the griddle. The driver sat at a table.

Rosalee took his order—a ham and cheese sandwich with coleslaw. She refilled coffee cups and ferried glasses of sweet tea to a few of the customers before retreating to the kitchen to help Mama. Daddy made three calls before nodding to Mama and saying, "It'll be a bit."

Daddy sat with the driver. They talked for a couple of minutes. Finally, the driver scooted his chair back and stood.

"Okay, everyone," he said. "Looks like the tire ain't fixable. Gonna have to bring a new one over from Lubbock." Groans followed. He raised a hand. "Better than coming from Dallas. It'll take a couple of hours and then another to get it bolted on." He glanced at Daddy, who nodded. "So, looks like about three hours or thereabouts, and then we'll be on our way."

OVER THE NEXT hour, the passengers ate, at first quietly but soon the conversations livened, punctuated with laughter as stories spilled out. Everyone making the best of the situation. Rosalee cleared the dirty plates, poured more coffee, refilled glasses, and served desserts—mostly Mama's famous pecan pie, attested by the dozen county fair blue ribbons that framed the doorway into the kitchen.

"I bet you'd like it," Rosalee said to Claire. "I'll heat it up for you. Plop on some ice cream. How's that?" She got a half shrug.

"Make it two," the man said.

A few minutes later, she returned with the pies. "There you go."

The man dug in. The girl hesitated. He aimed his spoon at her. "Better eat it up before the ice cream melts."

She finally took a bite.

"Pretty good, ain't it?" Rosalee said.

The girl gave a nod, took another bite.

"You said you was going to Lubbock. Where you coming from?" Rosalee asked the man.

He hesitated, then said, "Nashville."

He didn't sound like Tennessee. Farther north. More like that couple from Michigan who stopped in a couple of weeks ago.

"That where you're from?"

He nodded. "All my life."

Hmm.

Rosalee heard the front door open. The man glanced over his shoulder. He tensed.

Rosalee looked that way. "Where you been, Billy Wayne?"

Texas Ranger Billy Wayne Morgan looked handsome, as always, in his black Ranger shirt, gold badge, and white Stetson, which he removed as he entered, revealing his thick, blond hair. Dishwater was what Mama called it. Mama had words for every hair color you could imagine. Raven, mahogany, platinum, gunmetal silver, a bunch of them.

"Busy." Billy Wayne smiled. "And hungry."

"Grab a seat."

He settled at the counter, resting his hat on the seat to his left. Mama stuck her head through the pass-through window. "The usual?"

"You bet."

Rosalee walked behind the counter, swiped a cloth across it. She poured Billy Wayne a cup of coffee. The man in the corner booth kept glancing their way. So did Claire, the little girl.

"You're busy," Billy Wayne said.

"Bus got a flat. Daddy's waiting on a tire from Lubbock."

"There're worse places to break down, I reckon." He smiled. "I need to get the filter and oil changed on my car."

"I bet Daddy's got time. It'll be another hour or thereabouts before that tire gets here."

"I'll tell him," Mama said from the kitchen.

"It's been the better part of a week since we seen you," Rosalee said. "Where you been?"

"Up in Amarillo. Working on a case."

"Did you get the bad guys?"

He took a sip of coffee. "Sure did."

"Good." She propped her elbows on the countertop, rested her chin on her fists. "I thought maybe you'd called the wedding off." She grinned.

"No way." He matched her grin. "But you still have a few more years of growing before we get there."

"You always say that. I'm thirteen now."

"I know. Today's your day. I got something for you. Out in the car."

"What is it?"

"You'll see."

Mama carried a plate of eggs, bacon, and pancakes from the kitchen and placed it before him. "After you eat."

Rosalee cleared the tables and tended to the customers while Billy Wayne finished his meal. He then retrieved Rosalee's present from his car. A small box. He handed it to her.

"I got it when I was over in Dallas last month."

She opened it. A gold necklace with a small cross.

"Oh, my." She looked at him. "You shouldn't have."

"Why not? You're now officially a teenager."

"It's beautiful."

Mama hooked it into place, saying, "Billy Wayne, it's too extravagant."

He laughed. "Not for my girl."

Rosalee fingered it. "I'll wear it forever."

"How about some pie?" Mama asked Billy Wayne.

"You bet."

Mama cut an extra-large slice, heated it, and slapped on a hefty clump of vanilla ice cream. She sat it before Billy Wayne. "Extra ice cream. Just the way you like it."

"Martha, you're the best."

"That I am." She swiped the countertop with a cloth. "Walton's got your car in the shop. Said he'll be done in about thirty minutes."

"That'll give me time for two slices of pie." He grinned. "Besides, I'm in no rush to get back on the road. All that fresh oil. But, I hear some rain's a-comin'. That'll help."

"Well, we need it," Mama said. "But, I hope it ain't too much and for sure don't turn to snow. We're harvesting the pecans next week."

While Billy Wayne devoured his pie, Rosalee watched Claire and her dad. He repeatedly glanced over his shoulder toward Billy Wayne. Rosalee could almost feel his discomfort. Why? Was he afraid of the law? Was he in some kind of trouble? Hiding out? She knew Nashville was a lie. No way he was from there. But did that make him a criminal? Mama always said her imagination got the best of her, but if he was some fugitive, that'd be a wild story to tell her friends at the movies this weekend. A desperado right here at Tucker's Corner.

Billy Wayne tossed some bills on the counter and stood. "Martha, that was good." He patted his belly. "Like always. I better go see how Walton's doing."

The man's gaze followed Billy Wayne out the door. So did Claire's.

ROSALEE WIPED DOWN the counter while Mama scraped and cleaned the griddle. The customers settled in, the after-lunch lethargy taking hold. Conversations softened. The grandma in the first booth dozed, her wadded coat a pillow against the window. The two men on the way to California played cards.

Rosalee entered the kitchen where Mama washed breakfast dishes in the trough sink. She dried her hands on a frayed blue towel.

"Everybody out there happy?" Mama asked.

"They are."

"Good." Mama looked at Rosalee. Her brow furrowed. "What is it?"

"Nothing."

"Rosalee Tucker, you know you can't hide nothing from me."

"I don't want to cause no dustup or trouble for anyone."

"What is it?"

"That guy. The one with Claire, the little redheaded girl. There's something odd about him."

"What do you mean?" Mama leaned to peer through the pass-through window.

Rosalee clutched her arm. "Don't look."

Mama stopped and nodded.

"I don't know. Claire seems scared to me." She sighed. "Maybe I'm wrong. Maybe she's just shy, like her daddy says." She shakes her head. "But he gives me a bad feeling."

"What're you saying?" Mama asked. "You think this guy kidnapped her or something?"

Rosalee exchanged a look with Mama. "I don't know. It's just odd."

"Well, I'll just go talk to him," Mama said.

"No," Rosalee said. "It might be nothing."

Mama propped a fist on one hip. "Or it might be something." She stared at Rosalee. "Remember Bonnie Cathers?"

She did. Bonnie had been in her fourth-grade class. She'd disappeared. For three months, until her body turned up buried in the desert near Abilene. Some guy passing through had taken her.

"Of course."

"Then we got to do something."

"I got me an idea," Rosalee said.

ROSALEE COULDN'T SAY why the man with Claire made her uneasy. Maybe Claire was simply shy, like he said. But, it seemed like more. Fear? She couldn't be sure.

Was he really her daddy? What was his name? Did he ever say?

Tightness gathered in Rosalee's shoulders as she approached the corner booth. Claire had cleaned her plate.

"You liked it?" Rosalee asked.

A faint nod.

"Want more? We got plenty."

Claire glanced at the man but said nothing.

"Tell you what," Rosalee said, "our pecans are ready for harvest. Why don't me and you go out back and pick a bag for you to take with you? We got a million of them. Fresh off the trees."

"I take it you're talking about that grove I saw coming in?" the man asked.

"That's it."

The man looked out the window, casting his eyes upward. "Looks like it's getting ready to rain."

"In about half an hour," Rosalee said.

The man eyed her. "You can tell?"

"You live out here in West Texas, you learn what the weather's gonna do."

The man nodded. "Well, that sounds good. A pleasant surprise for my sister. Then, we'd better get on the road."

"Come on, Claire," Rosalee said. "It'll be fun."

Rosalee hoped the pecan gathering might offer a chance to get Claire alone, talk to her, see if there was a problem.

That was the plan.

It didn't go as easily as she had hoped.

The man followed them. They bundled into their jackets and headed out back. Mama said to bring her a bag of pecans, too. She needed to bake a half a dozen more pies. Mama was always good at acting casual.

"This here's where we live," Rosalee said as they veered around her house. "And this's our grove."

They stood at the top of a slight rise, looking down on the haphazard patch of trees that didn't really resemble a grove. Rosalee had seen a few in the area. Like the Crawfords' huge one. Daddy said over two hundred acres. Their trees were in regimented rows. Not so here. A jumbled mess, the trees tightly packed. Her great-grandfather, Rutherford Tucker, whose picture hung over the living room fireplace, had simply stuck the trees in the ground. A hundred years ago. The lack of order and space made harvesting more difficult. Daddy had to tie a strip of cloth around the ones they'd already harvested so they wouldn't lose track. She and Daddy would climb the trees and shake the branches, while Mama spread a tarp out to catch the falling nuts. And round up the ones that bounced away. She called them runners.

Right now, she could kiss Great-Grandpa Tucker. If he weren't long dead and gone. The disorder of the trees might give her the cover she needed to talk to Claire.

The man scanned the trees. "How big is it?"

"Around thirty acres. More than a hundred trees." She looked at Claire. "You ready to pick up some pecans?"

"Do we have to climb the trees?" she asked.

"Nope. Next week we'll shake them out, but a bunch of them have already fallen off. Mama calls them jumpers. All we got to do is scoop them up."

Claire stared ahead but said nothing. She held a cloth bag, an old flour sack, tightly against her chest.

"Don't take too long," the man said. "It's cold out here. And we need to get going."

The breeze had stiffened and gray clouds had rolled in—the cold now damper and more penetrating.

The man tugged a pack of cigarettes from his pocket. He shook one up, lipped it, and then lit it with a Zippo, which he clacked closed and returned to his pocket. "Don't go too far," he said.

Rosalee led Claire into the trees. They weaved in far enough that the man was barely visible. Claire started slowly, hesitantly, as if unsure what to do. But she soon picked up her pace. As if it were Christmas morning, and each pecan a present. Her bag bulged.

Rosalee had moved them ever deeper into the trees. They snatched up pecans along the way. When she felt they were out of earshot, she squatted down. Claire did the same.

"Where did your daddy say you were coming from?" Rosalee asked.

Claire looked down, fisted a couple of pecans, and added them to her bag.

"Claire?"

The girl looked up and glanced toward where the man waited. Rosalee followed her gaze, the man a faint silhouette through the branches. He had lit a second cigarette, and Rosalee could barely see its glow as he tilted his head back and examined the gray sky.

"What's going on?" Rosalee asked.

"Nothing."

Rosalee nodded toward the café. "I been working in the café since I could walk. Waiting tables since I was six. You got any idea how many people I've served?"

Claire shook her head.

"A bunch. And I talk to them. If I don't already know them, I want to know who they are and where they're from. What stories of other places they might have."

Claire stared at her but said nothing.

"I know people. Mama says I'm better at that than anyone. Better than her and Daddy. I know when they're happy, or sad… or scared."

Claire's gaze dropped. The pecan she held rolled from her hand.

"Girls?" the man called to them. "You about done?"

"Almost," Claire yelled back.

"Hurry up."

"Claire?" Rosalee said. "Tell me the truth."

"That's not my name."

"What is it?"

"Rose. Rose Murdoch. I live in Bowling Green, Kentucky." Tears collected in her eyes. "Or I did."

"And this man? Who is he?"

"I don't know. He said he was Roger." She picked up another pecan and held it in her fist. "I don't believe him."

"How'd you end up with him? Out here?"

"Girls?" It was Roger. "Let's get moving."

Rosalee looked his way. "Almost done," she shouted.

"So, Rose, who is he?"

"I never knew my dad. He left right after I was born. That's what my mama said. She married my stepdad but died last year. I lived with him until last week."

"And?"

"He gave me to Roger."

*"What?"*

"He said something about he couldn't take care of me anymore. That I'd be better off with Roger."

"So he gave you to a stranger?"

She nodded. "I think Roger gave him some money."

Rosalee attempted to absorb that. Sure, she had heard of such things, but here? In nowhere Texas?

"My stepdad was mean. He drank all the time. Used to hit me a lot."

Tears streamed down her face. "I thought maybe anything was better than him." She sniffed and wiped away tears. "I was wrong."

"What do you mean?"

"He does things. Roger."

"Touches you?"

She nodded.

"Anything else?"

Another nod.

"Okay. We can help you. Me and my mama and daddy. And Billy Wayne. He's a Texas Ranger."

"He has a gun."

"Billy Wayne? Sure he does. All Texas Rangers do."

"No, Roger. In his coat pocket."

"Let's go, girls." Roger's voice was harsh, demanding.

"Almost done," Rosalee shouted.

"I said now and I mean now."

"He's angry," Rose said. "We better go."

"No. You ain't going back to him."

"I got to. If I don't, it'll be bad. I tried once."

"What do you mean?"

"I ran away. From a motel in Lexington. I didn't even get out to the road. He pulled me by my hair, smacked me with his hand. He stuck his gun in my face. Right up against it. It was cold and hard. He told me if I ever tried that again, he'd kill me." Tears welled in her eyes. "He meant it. No doubt about that."

"That's why you can't go with him."

Rose sniffed and swiped the back of her hand across her nose. "I have to."

"No, you don't. Daddy and Billy Wayne can take care of this."

"They ain't here." She waved a hand. "No one's here to help me."

"I'm here."

"That won't help."

"We'll get to them. Trust me."

She led Rose deeper into the trees, veering toward the far corner.

"Goddammit," Roger said.

Rosalee heard his shoes scrape down the slope, then the sound of him pushing through the trees.

"You don't get back here right now, it'll be hell to pay," Roger said.

"You ain't getting her back," Rosalee shouted.

"The hell I'm not."

"I know what you did."

"Don't listen to her lies," Roger said.

"Daddy!" Rosalee screamed. "Billy Wayne!"

The thick, unruly trees were now an enemy. They ate up her screams. Better to run, hide.

*Pray.*

She heard him scraping branches, snapping pecans beneath his feet, but could no longer see him.

She grabbed Rose's hand and tugged her forward. They snaked through the grove as quietly as possible. The sound of Roger shouldering through the trees closed in. He might be bigger, faster, and stronger, but Rosalee knew this tangle of trees. Knew a deep arroyo made a diagonal cut through the grove toward its back corner. It had nooks where they could hide until Roger gave up the search. If they could get there. And if he gave up.

Rose tried to pull away. "I should go back. I don't want to get you in no trouble."

Rosalee tightened her grip on Rose's wrist and dragged her toward her. They were eye to eye. "You ain't going near him ever again. You hear me? Now be quiet as you can. I got a place we can hide."

Never releasing her hold on Rose's arm, Rosalee slid past trees and ducked beneath the lower limbs. She couldn't do anything about the crunch of pecans beneath their feet.

"I hear you," Roger said. "You can't get away."

They picked up the pace. So did Roger.

"If you don't stop right now, I'll kill both of you." His voice now high-pitched, angry. "I swear to God."

Rosalee jerked to a stop. She shed her red-and-black checked jacket and hung it from a tree limb, arranging it as if someone wore it. The best she could anyway.

"You'll never find us," she shouted.

She and Rose charged forward, then veered left. The arroyo, still sheltered by the thick trees, came into view. She tugged Rose forward, then into the gravelly bed. They shrank into one of the side crevices, where the shadows enveloped them.

Roger continued toward them, scuffing through the trees. Pecans snapped beneath his steps.

Then, a sudden silence.

The gunshot cracked through the trees with frightening sharpness. Both girls flinched. Rose gave a soft yelp, her hand flying to her mouth.

More shuffling.

Then, "Dammit." Pecans crunched. "Clever girl," he said.

His pace quickened. Closer.

More frantic.

Rosalee questioned her choice to hide and not keep running. Wedged in the crevice, no way to escape, their only hope was for him to run by and not see them.

Didn't work out that way.

"Well, well." Roger stood at the arroyo's lip, looking down. The gun angled toward them, its large black hole directly at Rosalee's face. She and Rose hugged each other.

"Go away," Rosalee said.

"Well, little lady, don't you think it's a bit late for that?"

"We won't say nothing. Not about this. Not about Rose. You can get in your car and leave."

"I don't think so."

"Please."

"Come with me. Get in the car and we'll all drive away."

"No."

"Then, I'll kill both of you. And your family."

He leveled the gun.

Rosalee moved to shield Rose.

An explosion ricocheted through the trees. As if it came from every direction.

Rosalee flinched, expecting to feel the bullet. Rose screamed.

The man known as Roger stiffened. His eyes widened. A bright red stain blossomed on his chest. The gun thudded against the ground. He staggered to his left, then toppled facedown.

Billy Wayne Morgan filled the space where he had been, gun in hand, in his black Texas Ranger shirt and white Stetson. "Your mama said I'd better check on you."

ROSALEE WATCHED FROM behind the counter. Rose placed glasses of water on the table where three men sat, then poured coffee for each. The only customers. Midafternoon was always quiet. She scribbled their orders on her pad. After passing the order through the window to Mama, she sat on a stool opposite Rosalee.

"Hard to believe Christmas is next week," Rose said.

"It's going to be a special one." She reached across and grasped Rose's hand. "Now that I have a sister to share it with."

Rose squeezed her hand. "That means a lot."

"You mean a lot."

Rose looked past Rosalee, into the kitchen. "I miss my mama."

"I'm sure. But, you've got a new one now." Rosalee smiled. "And a daddy, too."

Hard to believe it had only been two months. Seemed longer. Seemed forever. Rosalee couldn't remember a time when Rose wasn't here. That she would stay, be part of the family, was never in question. She had no one else. She belonged here.

Billy Wayne came through the door.

"Well, if it isn't my two red roses." He threw a leg over the stool next to Rose and sat. "What are you two up to?"

"The usual," Rose said.

"Which means trouble."

"You got that right," Mama said as she ferried plates to the three men.

"What's new?" Rose asked.

Billy Wayne turned sober. "Not good news."

Mama moved to the end of the counter and leaned on the edge.

The day after the pecan grove events, Rose, who was actually eleven, had detailed her story. After Roger—real name William Shorter, Billy Wayne had discovered—purchased her from her stepfather in Lexington, they headed west. He forced Rose to help him pick up a young girl near Kansas City. Her name was Sofie. Roger changed it to Susan. At first, Rose hoped this meant he'd let her go. Didn't happen, Roger always said Rose was special. She was his girl.

Two weeks later, he left Rose in a motel room for an hour while he took Sofie to a bus station to send her home. Did that mean that someday he might send Rose home, too? Home. She had no home. She considered running. But to where? The motel was isolated along a desolate highway. The manager that checked them in was even creepier than Roger. Roger returned alone, and they were back on the road.

"The girl," Billy Wayne said, "was Sofie Wallace."

"You found her?" Rose asked.

Billy Wayne sighed. "They found her body."

Rose recoiled, her hand flew to her mouth. "No. I helped him grab her."

"No, you didn't. He would've anyway. It's who he was."

"Besides," Rosalee said. "It could've been you instead of her."

A few minutes of silence.

"All the time I was with him," Rose said, "I thought I had to be the unluckiest girl in the world. That something was wrong with me. That it must be my fault my real daddy ran off, my mama died, my stepdad sold me. That he didn't want me. That no one did." She wiped a tear from her eye. "But all that was worth it, if it got me here." She clasped Rosalee's hand. "Here with you."

"I love you." Rosalee said. "We all do."

"Yes, we do," Billy Wayne said.

Rose sniffed. "I see only one problem."

"What's that?" Billy Wayne asked.

She raised an eyebrow. "Which of your red roses are you going to marry?"

*—D.P. Lyle is the Amazon #1 bestselling, Macavity and Benjamin Franklin Award-winning, and Edgar (2), Agatha, Anthony, Shamus, Scribe, Silver Falchio, and* USA Today *Best Book (2) award-nominated author of twenty-seven books—both fiction and nonfiction. He is the co-coordinator of the Outliers Writing University. He has worked with many novelists and with the writers of the TV shows* Law & Order, CSI: Miami, Diagnosis Murder, Monk, Judging Amy, Cold Case, House, Medium, Women's Murder Club, The Glades, *and* Pretty Little Liars. *Find more at www.dplylemd.com*

# TRACY DAUGHERTY

## LATE IN THE STANDOFF

ON A SWIRLING, cold, late December morning in 1968, my grandfather Harry and I split light fog in a big blue Oldsmobile Cutlass, twisting down Route 66 and various side roads, among small farms, bare-twigged meadows, and Civil War battlefields in the woods of eastern Oklahoma. Since the day before, we hadn't spoken to each other except to get our plans straight.

The governor had sent him to a little town called Jay to settle some nasty business, even though Jay was not located in Harry's congressional district. Before our disagreement, I'd asked if I could come along. It was too late to back out now.

The sky looked snowy but nothing fell. The gray morning light dulled the hills' red soil. I stared, glumly, at the peeling Burma Shave signs by the side of the road. Harry switched on the radio. Paul Harvey said John Steinbeck had died.

We were quiet for several miles. Finally Harry, trying to be friendly again, asked, "Did you ever read *The Grapes of Wrath?*"

"They made us read it last year in eighth-grade English," I wheezed. My throat was still scratchy.

"A lot of Sooners didn't like that book when it first came out," Harry said. "Thought it showed poor Okies in a bad light. Longing for the pastures of plenty and all. But I always felt it was a mighty fine novel. He knew the way it was."

"My teacher said he's a traitor."

Harry frowned. "How's that?"

"When he first started writing, he was on the workers' side, right? Anti-capitalist, antiwar. Then he got rich. He supported all the killing."

"I see. We're back to Vietnam, are we?"

I didn't answer.

He took some weight off the gas pedal. "A wise fellow, a former governor, told me once it takes a mature man to see the complexities of our culture, Pancho. To change his mind when he has to. I think Mister Steinbeck must have been a very mature man."

Paul Harvey finished his newscast. The Beatles came on. I didn't much enjoy their music anymore. It no longer seemed innocent or upbeat. The Fab Four looked old now. They'd grown mustaches and beards and, posing for the camera, didn't smile as much as they used to. John Lennon had said they were more popular than Jesus, and a radio station in my hometown had sponsored a "Beatles Record Burning." One of the DJs showed up in a KKK outfit and waved a wooden cross. I didn't destroy my "gear" 45s, but I didn't play them much, either. Instead, I watched the TV news. Mayhem in Chicago. War wounds. Oh boy. The world was a punctured balloon, with all the joy leaking out.

*"...nah-nah-nah...."*

I reached over and turned the music off.

We stopped at a Dairy Queen just off the highway and ate onion rings. Dead rosebushes twitched in the breeze, tapping the mustard-streaked window by our booth.

"So you're disappointed in me, is that it?" Harry said, wiping his fingers with a napkin.

I didn't know what to say. His anger, yesterday, was new to me. "I guess I don't understand you."

"Why?"

"All the stories you've told me... your resistance over the years...." I faltered.

"Like what?"

"Like opposing the draft," I said.

"But I registered, didn't I? Right after the Lusitania. You need to listen harder, Pancho. I followed the law. Everything I did—everything I've ever done—has been legal and proper. That's the point of my stories." He sipped his coffee. "You remind me of my dad—the last of the Okie Reds. He wanted revolution, and he wanted it *now*. Well, that's not the way things work in this country, believe me. I'm mature enough to know that now. It's not realistic."

"All right," I said. "But you don't really support this war, do you?"

He lit a Chesterfield and coughed. Behind him, a woman in orange stretch pants ordered fries for her two fat kids. "I'm a Democrat," he said softly. "Lyndon Johnson was a Democrat. It would be unseemly of me, as a representative of the people, to criticize my president."

"But Tricky Dick's in charge now!"

He batted away my remarks with a cracked plastic spoon. "You've got to be smart." He looked to me vastly tired, a man who'd suffered for years, bearing lost causes all his life. A spent fighter who'd found it easier to just give in.

The woman herded her kids out the door. "Because I say so!" she snapped. The people have spoken! "Now get in the car!"

IF I WAS a young ideologue, it was Harry's own damn fault. As a child, I was as familiar with the Oklahoma House of Representatives as I was with public swimming pools and merry-go-rounds. Along with Mother Goose, I'd been spoon-fed Mother Jones. Before I could read, I was spelling out *Come Hear Harry Shaughnessy, The Boy Orator,* copying into my coloring books fat letters from Harry's old campaign posters. My first drawings were sketches of his face, from pictures on old Socialist flyers he'd shown me—brittle, yellowed, crumbling in my hands.

When the Socialist Party died in Oklahoma, in the patriotic fervor of the First World War, he'd become a liberal Democrat—against his father's still-militant wishes—running for local offices in Cotton County, just north of the Red River in the southwest part of the state. Finally, in the late '50s, he'd been elected to the House.

When the legislature was in session, he stayed in the Huckins Hotel in downtown Oklahoma City. Sometimes my family drove up from Texas to see him. I'd sit in his room with a stack of hotel stationery, copying the latest Herblock cartoons. Harry saved them for me from the *Daily Oklahoman.* Herblock caricatured Nixon by giving him caterpillar eyebrows and a slim, spiked schnoz. Pure evil. I was delighted.

From one of Harry's books I'd trace Bill Mauldin's weary GIs—Willie and Joe. Or I'd draw *Pogo: We Have Met the Enemy and He Is Us.* From the time I could make a reasonably straight line, I wanted to be a cartoonist. I could entertain myself for hours, just sketching.

In '62–'63, when I was seven, Harry brought me often to the House chamber. He knew I was fascinated by the surroundings. I thrilled to his speeches. Normally, visitors weren't allowed on the floor, especially during a vote, but I was a kid, easy to overlook. It pleased Harry to have his little namesake there. I scribbled it all down.

One afternoon I sat in the chamber, in Harry's leather chair, watching the edges of my drawing paper curl in the heat. Harry stood in the aisle jawing with a couple of other reps. They all wore light gray suits and—at least in my memory—ties the bright morning blue of the Oklahoma flag. In the air, the faint smell of sweat and aftershave.

The chamber was a rectangle with green carpet and cream-colored walls. Black, high-backed chairs bumped small wooden desks topped with silver microphones. Up front, a tote board, tallying votes, flashed green-and-red lights behind the House Speaker's helm. From the walls, electric globes cast peach-colored circles across the room's bottom half. The top, an open gallery for newspaper reporters, swam in a cool fluorescent bath.

Young aides in freshly pressed shirts rushed here and there ferrying telephones from desk to desk, trailing long, twisted cords behind them. Once they'd connected a phone to a legislator's desk, the lawmaker would holler instructions into the receiver then the aides would collect the cords and sprint to another desk.

I sketched the scene. Harry hovered near me, jotting names on a piece of notepaper. He handed the list to one of his partners. "We might have some influence with these knuckleheads," he said. "I've already run our road bill by them, but it wouldn't hurt if you paid them one more visit before the vote."

The man nodded.

"No deals," Harry warned him. "We're not in the horse-trading business. Not on this one. Either we have their support or we don't."

In the warm chamber light, his gray hair looked like silk. He sat by me. He tapped my drawing pad with a nicotined finger. "That's very good," he said. "Did you just do that?"

"Yessir. What's a horse-trading business?"

"You know that road north of Walters—that muddy mess out by Harlan Egbert's farm?"

"Yes."

"Well, I'm trying to get the state to pave it. That way, whenever I take you swimming out there, the car won't get stuck. Won't that be nice?"

Years later, looking through his papers, I learned that the Standard Oil Company, which he'd cursed in rallies as a young Socialist, had lobbied him to sponsor a road bill so it could gain easier access to the natural gas deposits in Egbert's fields.

Harry stood, shaking hands with men who passed him in the aisle, waving at others across the room, mouthing, "Fight for me!"

Finally, the Speaker called the vote. Someone proposed an amendment to the bill. "Son of a bitch," Harry muttered. "They'll drain its juice."

I can't say for sure what happened next, but I know Harry crushed the motion without saying a word. People turned to him. He danced behind his desk like a fresh featherweight. Winks, hand jibes, nods. Later, when the tote board flashed and clattered and came up mostly green, I understood that Harry had finessed his way to victory.

"I want to know who managed that bill!" A rangy man with thick black eyebrows approached him. "I hear Harry Shaughnessy managed that bill." He bent to me. "Are you Harry Shaughnessy?"

"Yessir," I said. For I was.

"Well, Harry, you're one fine floor manager."

"Thank you."

"A pretty good artist, too, I see."

Harry told me, "Harry, say hello to Governor Edmonson." I could tell he was pleased with himself, and I was pleased for him. The governor had sought him out! As Harry's namesake, as a privileged visitor to the people's chamber, I thought I must be important, too.

NOW, SIX YEARS later, a new governor, Dewey Bartlett, had called on Harry to resolve an "Indian problem." Recently an article had appeared in *TIME* magazine saying that Oklahoma's Black people had no political clout and the state's Native population was disorganized and ignored. Since then, Governor Bartlett had moved quickly, whenever he could, to erase *TIME's* racist inferences. Bartlett was a Republican, and Harry defended his efforts to assist minority employment. "He's established the Full Employment Commission, whose primary purpose is to loan money to Mexicans, Blacks, and Indians for job training," Harry said in speeches statewide. "He's created the Oklahoma Indian Affairs Commission, and he's appointed the state's first Black judge. What more can he do?"

Bartlett's campaign slogans were *"Bring Back Our Okies!"* and *"Help an Okie!"* His supporters wore Okie pins on their shirts. He wanted to change the Okie image from that of a poor dirt farmer like Tom Joad to that of a small industrialist, like a rubber tire manufacturer or a clothing supplier. I was frustrated with him because he always dodged questions about his stance on Vietnam.

After leaving the Dairy Queen, Harry and I passed through post oak and twisted spikes of Arkansas yucca, heading north through Henryetta, Okmulgee, and Taft, a predominantly Black town, on our way to Jay. There, a dispute had flared between local officials and a loose band of Cherokee, Kiowa, and Creek. The tribes were upset about the arrest and prosecution of a young Cherokee for hunting deer out of season.

The young man had argued that the land belonged to his people. State laws didn't apply to him, he said—he followed the will of his tribe. The debate, Harry explained to me, had escalated into shouting matches on the streets and in the courts.

Finally, one of the Kiowa leaders requested Harry as a mediator. Harry didn't know anyone in Delaware County. He didn't understand why he'd been called, but the situation was urgent, the governor's staff assured him.

Before our fight about Vietnam, I'd been eager to join him. As a boy, I'd accompanied him many times to Indian powwows in Sultan Park, north of Walters, his hometown. I remembered drums thundering beside the park's little stream. Dogwood blossoms drifted around us. The dancers, wearing robes of white feathers and long blue beads, moved in solemn circles beneath quivering willows. I loved the dancers' thick, straight hair, their long cheekbones. They were so much more beautiful and dignified than the actors I'd seen on TV shoot-'em-ups wearing moccasins and buckskin pants. They didn't grunt to communicate or eat raw animals. They broiled deer meat over open fires in the park, cut it into strips, mixed it with vegetable oil and fresh berries. They laughed and sang. Their ceremonies were full of movement, lines, and grace. I sketched them so intently, I always ran out of breath.

But now Harry and I bristled at each other, and I wished I'd stayed in Walters at my grandma's house.

The day before, my parents and I had driven up from Texas to spend Christmas with Harry and Zorah. She loved the holidays. Her tree was the finest of the season, decorated with strings of long thin lights filled with colored water. When you plugged them in, they bubbled.

Zorah doted on me. When I was little, she'd leave dollar bills in pink plastic eggs for me at Easter. She'd slip coins into my coat pockets. The morning Harry and I left for Jay, she caught me at the door. "In case you stop for a treat," she said, handing me a buck.

She gave us two freshly baked gingerbread cookies. Harry had smuggled his into the Dairy Queen to eat with his coffee. I'd saved mine—a reward, later, for surviving this day with a man I no longer knew.

THE TROUBLE HAD started between us when my folks asked me to explain to him why I'd been suspended from school for a week, right before break. I'd drawn a poster of screaming Vietnamese children from pictures I'd seen in *LIFE* magazine. At the top, I'd scrawled in psychedelic lettering *Stop the Bombing!* Late one afternoon, I'd mimeographed dozens of these and taped them to the classroom doors of my junior high.

Everyone knew who did it. I'd always made posters for dances and other school events. My style was distinctive, the vice principal told me dryly as he pronounced my sentence.

I thought Harry would appreciate my convictions—more than the rest of the family. After all, he was a former Socialist, a man who'd opposed the draft as a kid, a man who'd nicknamed me Pancho because my infant face had recalled, for him, smudgy photos he'd seen in history books of the great revolutionary Pancho Villa.

Instead, after I'd laid out my story, he told me, "If you don't like your government's policies, you work within the system to change them. This maverick stuff, Pancho, it's useless and dangerous."

"What maverick stuff?" I said.

"The protests. The campus riots. The troubles in the cities. You're what, fourteen? Fifteen?"

"Thirteen."

"Old enough to have more sense."

What had happened to the Boy Orator, I wondered, humiliated and confused. What had happened to the guy who'd scorned the nation's "industrial giants and munitions makers?" I looked at his sagging cheeks. It's true, he wasn't a boy anymore, not even in spirit. He was seventy now.

But could a person change that much?

I carried a petition with me denouncing America's bombing of North Vietnam. My Catholic "Youth for Peace" group was sponsoring a drive for signatures to mail to the president. Harry wouldn't touch it.

"These radical young priests in the church now, playing politics—

they don't know the first thing," he said. "Ought to stick to chanting and pouring wine."

"I can't believe you," I said.

"And I expect you to straighten up."

That night, helping Zorah trim the tree, I asked her if I'd done something to tick Harry off. It didn't seem possible that my misadventures were enough to upset him so.

"Nope. He's become cautious, that's all." She sprinkled tinsel on a twig.

"He was always a fighter," I said. Framed on his desk he had a promotional photo of Jack Dempsey, acquired somewhere in his travels. Besides the *Pogo* books, it was my favorite thing in his house. "Boxing's not so different from running for office," he'd told me once when he caught me admiring the picture. "The winner's the one who can take the most blows."

Zorah laughed. "He used to be a fighter. These days, it's, 'Agitation's a luxury I can't afford.'"

"What's he mean?"

"He's an insider now. A political veteran, with a reputation to protect. He can't be reckless."

"What do you think? Do you think my posters were reckless?"

"At your age, your grandaddy would have done the same thing."

Did she mean I'd soften, too, in time?

I reached to fit a snowy angel on the tree and experienced a sudden dizzy spell. I was short of breath. This wasn't uncommon. I was asthmatic. Apparently, the pine needles had provoked an allergic reaction in my lungs.

Zorah plugged in the lights. I focused on the bubbles. My inhaler nestled in my pocket, but the bubbles' pulse steadied my breathing and I didn't have to use it.

"Anyhow, don't worry about your granddad. He thinks the world of you. You know he does. What is it he calls you? History Man?"

"History's Keeper."

"This tempest'll pass. And it's not like it's anything new, is it? He's been in that House chamber longer than old Methuselah. Don't let the old goat get to you, okay?"

"YOU REMEMBER COMING up here couple of years ago?" Harry asked me now in the car. We were nearing Jay, climbing through red-and-yellow hills.

"The Civil War field?"

"Exactly," he said. One of his pet projects as a state representative was preserving historic sites, talking landowners into donating significant property back to the state. Sometimes he took me with him. I was a useful prop. "We want our children, like this young man here, to have a clear sense of their heritage, don't we?" he'd ask a farmer whose pastures had witnessed a nearly forgotten bloody skirmish a hundred years ago.

Folks rarely refused him.

"I'm sure you had your tape recorder with you then," he reminded me. "History's Keeper. Didn't we come back through the city that time and stop at Adair's?"

"I think so."

"We wrap up this Jay business pronto, we might do that again. What do you say?"

I feigned indifference. He knew I loved the place—Adair's Tropical Cafeteria in downtown Oklahoma City. He used to take me there after House votes. In Adair's, he'd recruited me to be his personal storyteller. I remembered the way it looked the first time I saw it. It was in a drab shopping center but the neon palm tree just inside the door promised an exotic experience. To a seven-year-old, the bamboo partitions and jungle-themed wallpaper were thrillingly strange. Usually, Harry was in a fine mood at these meals, having just won a floor fight. Over beets, baked halibut, macaroni and cheese, he'd tell me stories of his early days when he traveled the state as the Boy Orator, speaking for the poor. Eventually, I knew these tales by heart.

All my life I'd seen his name—my name—on posters, matchbook covers, emery boards. *Vote for Harry Shaughnessy—He Has Always Been Your Friend!* I believed it.

One day at Adair's, flipping through my sketchpad, he asked me if I liked to write as well as draw.

I hadn't thought about it. "Sure," I said.

"Good. I hope you'll practice hard, Pancho. Pictures and words—a powerful combination." He mimed a boxer throwing a right cross followed by a swift left hook. He leaned toward me, over his pumpkin pie. "Every family needs a chronicler," he said.

"History's our teacher, right?"

"Right." He'd told me so many times.

He winked at me—the kind of comradely signal he'd sent around the House floor. I felt the sway of his charm.

Instead of encouraging me to collect stamps or rare coins, or to start an ant farm, he made his life my project. He had a sense of himself as a unique individual in a particular place and time, in a way that few of us do, and he shrewdly thought ahead. If I didn't pan out as his Boswell, at least I'd have the stories to pass along to someone else someday.

He bought a Norelco tape recorder—a heavy, square machine small enough to fit into his coat pocket. He saved his thoughts for me on mini-cassettes. On my visits, he'd slip the tapes into my suitcase. "History's Keeper," he'd say, patting my head.

The following Christmas he gave me my own recorder, "To go with your pencils and paper." It was the kind of device I'd seen in James Bond movies—a cute gizmo with secret capabilities. Who knew what it could do? Whenever I played Harry's tapes, I remembered our afternoons in the buzzing light of the neon tree, and my mouth watered with the faint taste of slightly scorched macaroni.

ON THE HARDSCRABBLE outskirts of Jay, pickups lined the highway—rusting, door-sprung jobs, some in need of paint, some painted three or four shades of the same basic color. Their back windows were filled with empty gun racks.

The guns were in the hands of the Cherokee, Kiowa, and Creek who flanked the main street into town, in front of hot dog stands, neon beer signs in dark bar windows, gas pumps, signs saying *JESUS IS COMING.* Store windows were shattered. The Native men wore overalls or jeans, leather coats. They cradled rifles or fingered pistols tucked into the tops of their pants. Their hair was long. I didn't see any women.

A few miles from here, the Joads had scraped their sun-cracked acres, but today, with most whites staying out of sight and Indians in charge of the streets, I'd never seen a less Okie-looking town.

Harry parked the Olds by a state trooper's car. He'd gone pale. "Lord. If I'd known they were armed, I wouldn't have brought you," he said, scared or angry or both.

He tossed a cigarette out the window, and we sat there wheezing. Something else we shared, besides a name—neither one of us could breathe worth a damn. Years of tobacco had taken a toll on him. I was a mass of allergic symptoms. My hands still prickled from touching Zorah's tree.

A young white man with short hair and a gray suit waved to us from the side of the road.

When we left the car, Harry told me to stick close.

The young man introduced himself as Michael Van Buren, one of Governor Bartlett's aides. "We're so relieved you could make it," he said.

"When I spoke by phone to your colleague in the city, he didn't prepare me for this," Harry said. "I was under the impression I'd be talking to two or three representatives of the tribes. This looks like war."

"They started coming out of the hills last night. Staking out the streets. No one took them seriously at first."

"The problem, perhaps."

"Right, right. Now we've got a scalping party on our hands." He laughed.

Harry scowled at him.

In the young man's stare, I saw a confused quality I'd noticed lately in many adults. Listening to Harry, I'd begun to understand that America's old rules of civility and order no longer seemed to apply to daily life. The Kennedys and Martin Luther King were dead. Cities were on fire. This may have been Jay, Oklahoma, but it hadn't escaped the nation's troubles.

"Why'd they ask for me?" Harry said.

"Don't know. Won't say. But you're the man they want. Claim they're through wasting time with the locals."

The air was getting colder, but Harry removed his coat and rolled up his sleeves, a flamboyant gesture of openness to the men in the street—I'm hiding nothing. "Where am I going?" he asked.

Van Buren pointed to the courthouse. "The leader's in there."

"Stay put, Pancho. I'll be back shortly."

Van Buren turned to confer with his aides. Quietly, I followed Harry down the road. He was too focused on the men with guns to notice me trailing him. Despite our argument, I wasn't about to let him walk alone through a hostile crowd.

The courthouse resembled a fort. When Harry reached its steps, he spun and saw me, then shook his head. "All right, sit down, Pancho," he said. "Don't move."

The short walk had winded me. My lungs hurt.

The Indians hadn't shifted when we'd passed them in the street. Silent sentries. In the courthouse doorway, a man with skin as rough and dark as a football told us to wait. He slipped inside the building.

"Got your pencil and paper?" Harry asked me.

He knew I did. I nodded.

"May be a good story in this."

A young man wearing black denims and a blue cotton shirt came out of the courthouse. "Representative Shaughnessy. Thank you for coming," he said.

Harry shook his hand. We all shivered in the cold.

"Why me?" Harry asked. "I'm not from this district."

"You have the reputation, statewide, of being a fair and honest man."

I could see this didn't satisfy Harry but he let it go for now. "All right," he said. "Fill me in."

"My name is John Tasuda, from the Kiowa tribe. As you may know, the Kiowa, Cherokee, and Creek live and work harmoniously here."

Harry nodded.

"I've been elected to be their spokesman."

"In this deer hunting matter?"

"In the illegal arrest by the Department of Wildlife of my Cherokee cousin, Louis Chewie."

My chest tightened.

"The hunting laws are clear. Posted well in advance," Harry argued.

"Louis Chewie is a good family man. A farm laborer." John Tasuda scratched his ear through a tassel of long black hair. "You grew up on a farm, didn't you?"

"I did."

"Have you forgotten, while sitting in your nice, air-conditioned office in the capitol, how arduous farm life can be?"

"I haven't forgotten."

"Most of us work in the strawberry fields when we can, but much of the year we're out of work. We do what we can to feed our families."

"Still—"

"The buck in question was killed on the Kenwood Reserve, in the thickest part of the woods. Do you know the place?" John Tasuda asked.

"Yes. I did a little homework before coming here," Harry said. "The government holds it in trust for the Cherokee tribe."

"That's right. So the land belongs to Chewie's people."

"Even so, under federal mandates—"

"What? Is he to be licensed like a dog just so he can feed his children?"

I put a hand to my chest.

Harry rubbed his face. "As one elected official to another, I can tell you, you'll get nowhere with this. I know it doesn't seem fair—" Harry said.

"It's not a question of fairness." Tasuda crossed his arms. "It's a matter of survival. Last September, Chewie's aunt starved to death in her cabin."

"I'm sorry," Harry said.

"Mister Shaughnessy. I heard a long time ago that you believed in equality for Native folks. That's why I've turned to you."

As he spoke, I completely lost my breath. My worst asthma attack in months. It had been building all day, prompted by Harry's cigarette smoke in the car and Zorah's tree. But the timing made my sputtering seem a rebuke to Harry, to John Tasuda's faith in him. I felt it. Harry felt it.

My choking was like a shout. *I don't want to keep your history anymore! You're not who you said you were!*

"Do you have an inhaler?" Harry asked.

"Left it... in the car. I'll be okay. Just let me sit."

I like to believe, now, I was mature enough to compose myself in a crucial moment. I closed my eyes, pictured Zorah's bubbles, and tried to control my breathing.

"We should go," Harry said.

"I'd hoped we could work things out," said John Tasuda.

"I'm fine," I said. "Really."

"Mister Shaughnessy, I've followed your career for many years."

Harry had been watching me. Now he turned to Tasuda. "Why?"

"My grandmother. She used to talk about you. She heard you speak somewhere once. You wouldn't have known her. Just a face in a crowd. But she was a great admirer of yours."

Harry looked slightly bewildered—an old man trying to recall what he used to say. How he used to feel.

"I want you to understand, I don't trust politicians," Tasuda said. "Never have. To you, we're all just faces in a crowd. But I asked to speak to you because I know what'll happen if shooting breaks out. We may win the day, but eventually we'll lose the war. We always do. I figured if I could reason with any white man it might be you. Grandmother believed you were principled and fair."

"He is," I said, still wheezing. The men looked at me. I glanced up at Harry's face. "She was right, wasn't she?"

John Tasuda spread his arms. "We need your help, Mister Shaughnessy. You see for yourself, we'll force change if we have to. We can't go on like this."

Someone sneezed in the street. Rifles shifted. Feet shuffled.

Harry rubbed the back of his neck. "About all I can do is push for the case to be taken to federal court so you're not dealing with locals. It's likely the judges there would be more impartial, more mindful of public opinion, especially in a civil rights case. Your friend Chewie might have a better chance at a fair trial."

"But the local authorities have been adamant—"

*"I'll* handle the local authorities."

"That may not be—"

"Look, all you want's a fair trial for the man, right?" Harry asked.

Tasuda nodded slowly.

"Can you convince your people?" Harry said.

"Maybe. They're cold and tired."

"Well then, you'd better get them the hell off the streets. You said it yourself. They're not helping your cause."

They talked a while longer, making arrangements. I took deeper and deeper breaths. I studied the angles and lines of bodies and guns, the subtle shadings of clothes. I framed individual scenes, up and down the street.

Harry offered Tasuda a Chesterfield. The men held the cigarettes away from my face.

"Where'd your grandmother hear me?" Harry said. "Do you know?"

"It was after a Golden Gloves tournament once, somewhere in the city."

"I remember that. Sure. Long time ago."

"My older brothers, they both boxed."

"Any good?"

"Naw. But they were too big and dumb to fall down, so they usually won their fights."

Harry laughed. "I could use men like that on the House floor."

"So you'll see Chewie through?"

Harry promised, "I'll do what I can."

IT'S TAKEN ME years to see how a good sketch leads a viewer's eye from one figure to the next so the picture appears seamless.

I mean, I've always understood this. But occasionally I've failed to see it.

I guess some lessons we need to keep learning. Sometimes we lose what we know.

In 1921, on the eve of the big Carpentier-Dempsey fight, Harry clipped a cartoon from the *Daily Oklahoman.* It was by an artist named Winsor McCay—I found it in Harry's papers after he died. The caption read *The Kind of Fighting That Pays.* The sketch featured three World War I vets, one missing a leg, another blind, and a third without his arms.

The hobbled fellow is reading about the boxing match in a newspaper. *"Listen to this!"* he tells his buddies. *"The fight is limited to twelve rounds. It may last only one minute or less. Carpentier is to get two hundred thousand dollars and Dempsey three hundred thousand dollars. No matter who wins, or how long the fight lasts, they get theirs!"*

The blind man responds, *"WOW! What do we get for our fighting? Ha-ha-ha! Ho-ho-ho! And a couple of he-he-hes!"*

The third man adds, *"We got ours! Yes, we did. Thanks to an appreciative public."*

The source of the sketch's power is the crippled man's crutches. The crutches' sleek lines lead the viewer's eye down the man's body to his stump. The blind man has planted his cane near the stump. The head of the cane points to his friend's empty sleeves. Simple, smart. A perfectly orchestrated drawing.

I've often thought that a man who tells stories and makes sketches for a living must still be a kid at heart. He's an idealist insisting on symmetry and balance, even when they're hard to find.

Which is to say—I wanted Harry's life to be one straight line.

So did John Tasuda, that day in Jay.

So did Harry, maybe—negotiating the complexities of our culture.

"I COULD USE a soda," Harry said when we returned to the Olds. "How 'bout you? Back to Dairy Queen?"

"Sure."

"Got your breath again?"

"I think so." For good measure, I took a couple hits off my inhaler.

Harry had exchanged a few words with the governor's aide, who still looked confused. John Tasuda was busy addressing his people. They didn't seem happy. They remained in the street with their guns but didn't try to stop us when we pulled away.

We were alone now on Route 66. The road, lined with pumpjacks, had long been bypassed by the interstate.

"That was good," I said after a while. I pinched off a chunk of Zorah's cookie.

"Proud of the old man now? One last time?"

"That was good," I said again. The shadow of a hawk passed over fields.

Harry reached for the radio. *"—bless America and our fine new president,"* someone said. *"And a very Merry Christmas to you all."*

Oh, boy.

"We'll grab some dinner at Adair's?"

"Yeah."

"Then let's go home."

"Yeah, let's go home."

Out the window I waved at the ghosts of the Joads.

*—Tracy Daugherty is the author of over twenty books of fiction and nonfiction, the most recent of which,* Larry McMurtry: A Life, *was a finalist for the Pulitzer Prize in Biography in 2023. He lives in Corvallis, Oregon.*

# MATTHEW V. CLEMENS

## WHAT CAN I DO?

ALTON BURKHART FIGURED he must be the worst deputy in the entire U.S. Marshals Service, even though he allowed that most of the marshals were on active duty in Europe fighting the Nazis or in the Pacific taking on the Japs. After all, Burkhart had been one of those guys once, back at Pearl Harbor, but now he was in the backwaters, the farthest back of the backwaters, working out of the office in Boise, Idaho. If there was someone lower on the marshals' totem pole, Burkhart couldn't think of who that might be.

His first real action in weeks, if it could truly be called "action" was plodding along the Old Oregon Trail highway to pick up two small-time car thieves who had violated the Dyer Act by crossing state lines in a stolen car. President Franklin Roosevelt had set the national speed limit at thirty-five miles per hour to aid the war effort, and that had given the tall, rangy, deputy plenty of time to think. All that cogitating had left him with the conclusion that he was, quite simply, the worst deputy in the service. When he passed a Civil Defense sign that had the words *WHAT CAN I DO?,* his only thought was, *no shit, not much.*

An August heat wave, at least by Idaho standards, raised temperatures into the upper eighties, and though his car's windows were cranked down, it didn't matter. Eighty degrees was hot, whether the air was stagnant or being stirred up in his '38 Ford Deluxe's slow progress southeast.

His dark hair cut in a butch, he looked the part of a fine specimen of a U.S. Marshal at least from the neck up. But now, his white shirt soaked with sweat, and his tie knot loosened, he felt more like a refugee from the hot springs at Yellowstone Park. His charcoal suit coat lay neatly folded on the passenger seat, his gray fedora resting on top of it. His pistol, a Colt 1911 automatic, dug into his kidney where its holster attached to his belt. It was not a department-issue weapon, but out here there was no one to give a shit what he carried. The Colt carried an extra round from the department-issue .38 snub nose and along with his hideout, a .32 automatic holstered to his ankle, they were his only backup.

Pulling the Ford to the curb in front of the Mountain Home, Idaho, sheriff's office, he noticed that even for a hot summer afternoon the streets of the town were bereft of people. There were not a lot of people in Mountain Home, but this main drag looked like a ghost town.

Burkhart used the rearview to tighten up the knot of his tie, then he resisted the urge to use his sleeve and pulled his handkerchief from his pants pocket to wipe the perspiration from his face.

Blowing out a breath, he put on his hat, grabbed his jacket, then stepped out into the blazing sunlight. He slipped the coat on. He needed to look professional, after all. The sheriff's office was a nondescript one-story brick building with a barred window to the right of a half-glass door that had *Office of the Sheriff of Elmore County* painted on it in gold letters. Turning the knob, Burkhart entered. It wasn't much cooler inside than out. A fan sat atop a table in the corner, and while it was doing its best, the fan was doing about as much good cooling the room as a knife at a gunfight.

To his surprise, there were no men in the office. There were four desks, each facing the front door. On the left side of the back wall there was a pebbled glass door with the word *Sheriff* painted on it. To the right of that was a barred door that undoubtedly led back to the jail.

There were also two doors on the wall to his right. Burkhart figured one for a supply room, and the other for the gun room. First there was no one on the street, and now the sheriff's office was abandoned?

Curiouser and curiouser.

Burkhart was just opening his mouth to call out when the nearer door on the right wall opened and a curly haired, blue-eyed blonde—who wasn't Betty Grable but might be her slightly older sister—stepped into the room.

She was holding a mug of coffee and wearing a deputy sheriff's shirt with badge and blue jeans. She did not wear a gun.

"Hello," Burkhart said.

The blonde let out a yip, jumped, but only spilled a couple drops of coffee before she righted the mug and calmed herself. "Jesus, mister, you about scared the life out of me."

"Sorry. I'm Deputy U.S. Marshal Alton Burkhart. I'm here to—"

She held up a hand cutting him off. "I know why you're here, and we ain't got 'em."

"Pardon?"

Holding her arms out wide, gesturing toward the empty room, not spilling a drop of coffee now, she said, "Ain't nobody here but me. They're all out lookin' for your car thieves. They escaped last night."

Burkhart felt her words like a kick to the gut. Long drive for nothing. "Okay, let's back up. Who are you?"

She strolled over to the nearest desk and set down her mug. "Agnes Nesmith."

"Like *Sheriff* Nesmith?"

A nod from her. "My husband. I'm here to answer the phone and take care of any business while Frank and his deputies are out searching for your prisoners."

"When did they escape?"

Agnes plopped down onto her chair. "Come on, you might as well have a seat. I figure we're going to be talkin' for a while. You want a cup of stale coffee?"

Removing his hat, Burkhart walked to the desk next to Agnes and sat down, laying his hat on top of the desk. "Thanks, no." He was hot enough without adding coffee to the equation.

She said, "Happened last night, late. There was only one deputy here. The two prisoners were in separate cells across from each other. One of them...." Agnes checked a piece of paper on her desk. "Jasper Moody, he starts wailing that he's sick and when the deputy came back to see what was wrong, that's when it all went to hell."

"You have protocols, don't you?"

"The deputy, young guy, Adam Colby, is a bright young guy, but he's trusting. He told Moody to step back from the bars, but Moody stayed bent over, clutching his stomach right in front of the door."

"Deputy Colby approached him."

Agnes nodded. "But the kid was on guard for Moody to try to grab him. Moody didn't grab him, though. He pushed him, hard. Shoved him across the hallway to where the other guy, Evan Werner, was waiting. He grabbed Colby from behind and got his pistol out of his holster."

"Shit," Burkhart said.

"Exactly. Werner used the gun to force Colby to unlock his cell then Moody's. Then one of them, presumably Werner, smacked Colby over the head with the pistol and knocked him out. Just to make sure they had more time, they cuffed him, gagged him, and locked him in the cell. Wasn't 'til Frank came in this morning that we found out they were gone."

"Any idea where they went?"

Agnes shook her head.

"Are they armed besides Colby's pistol?"

"Yeah. They got a shotgun and another revolver, a long-barrel .38 like Colby's, out of the gun room."

"Shit."

"Exactly."

Burkhart said, "Okay, what's being done to find them?"

"We've only got Frank and three deputies all together, Marshal. One of them is Colby, and he's still at the doctor's office getting checked out. He's got a hell of a welt on his head."

"I bet."

"Frank's using our family car and the two deputies have the only two prowl cars we have. One of the deputies is driving the town streets while Frank and the other deputy have started searching outside of town."

"Are the prisoners on foot?"

She shook her head. "They stole the same car again."

"Where was it?"

"Hendershot's Conoco. But he doesn't have a garage so the car was parked around back."

"How'd they know where the car was?"

Shrugging, Agnes said, "It's not that big a town, Marshal, and there aren't that many cars. Hell, most people barely use theirs because of gas rationing."

"I have a car," Burkhart said. "Do you have a map? Show me where the others are and where I can help search."

"We appreciate the offer, Marshal, but you ever been to Mountain Home before?"

Burkhart shook his head.

"Know your way around the back roads pretty well, do ya?"

"All right," Burkhart said. "I get you. The sheriff take anything off the two suspects? Write up a report? Anything that I can examine?"

Rising, she went to a nearby file cabinet, unlocked it, then pulled out two manila envelopes. Returning to the desk, she handed them over to Burkhart. "Their personal effects."

Burkhart opened the first envelope. It contained a single onionskin paper booking form, a wallet, and a tie. He held up the red tie.

Agnes said, "Frank took their ties to keep them from using them as a garrote on one of the deputies."

"But not their belts or shoelaces?"

She shrugged. "He didn't want their pants fallin' down, and they were both wearing loafers. Kind of weird, if you ask me."

Setting the tie aside, Burkhart picked up the booking form. There were several places where a typewriter eraser had been used to remove a mistake then typed over. Burkhart, a two-finger typist himself, kept his mouth shut.

He read *Moody, Jasper P.—no aliases—316 Howell Street, Davenport, Iowa.* That was, likely as not, a fake. The birthdate made Moody twenty-four, not even five years younger than Burkhart. *Male, white, blond hair, blue eyes, five-eight, one-forty, no scars or distinguishing marks, and nothing to make the guy stand out. Arrested two days ago for auto theft of a vehicle licensed in Scott County, Iowa.* Maybe the address was legit, after all. Burkhart set the form aside and opened the next envelope.

Evan Werner was only eighteen, and like his buddy not very tall, blond, blue eyes, and not a pound over one-thirty soaking wet. He also had a red tie.

Burkhart now knew about a nickel's worth of knowledge more than when he walked in. Then something about Werner's tie caught his eye. There was a flash of gold. On the back side of the wide tie, stuck up inside the lining was the rest of the gold flash he had seen. Visible on the outside of the tie was a tiny shaft of gold, but when he flipped it over and looked up into the lining, he could see a stickpin. He removed it, examined the trinket with a red enamel oval at the top. Within the oval there was a half circle at the bottom. That half circle contained the letters AV, and rising from the letters were a series of columns atop which rested a gold swastika.

"What's that?" Agnes asked.

Burkhart handed her the stickpin.

She eyeballed it, mouthed "Nazis," then said, "What the hell is *AV?*"

Burkhart had seen the emblem before. *"Amerikadeutscher Volksbund."*

"I don't speak German."

"German-American Bund," Burkhart said.

"Then I was right—Nazis."

"Too soon to say that, but Werner didn't seem to want it known that he was part of the German-American Bund, even though that group disappeared when the war started."

Eyes narrowing, Agnes said, "Roaches always scatter when you turn on the lights."

"Missus Nesmith, can you tell me what these boys were wearing?"

Agnes thought about it, then said, "That's the weird thing about those boys. They almost matched. Each one wore a blue suit, a white shirt, and the two red ties."

"Patriotic," Burkhart said.

She shrugged. "Moody, his suit was a little darker blue, and Werner's had a pinstripe."

"Good. That's something. Most people wear suits around here?"

Shaking her head, Agnes said, "Nope, we're a small town of workers and some farmers come to town now and then. That's the funny part, you would think those boys would stick out like spats on a cowboy. But we haven't found 'em yet."

Burkhart couldn't just sit here. He needed to do something to find his prisoners and get them back to Boise. He considered his options. "Where was the car they stole?"

"Hendershot's Conoco."

"Where's that?"

Agnes pointed east. "Two more blocks you'll see a big white house on the corner, that's Sullivan's Grocery. Sully still lives upstairs. Anyway, there'll be a table out front that's filled with crates of apricots, watermelons, and such. Watermelons are real good this year. You turn right there and Hendershot's is behind the grocery store on Third. You want me to call him and tell him you're coming?"

"No." Burkhart shook his head. "It'll be all right. I'll check back in later, thanks."

Grabbing his hat as he rose, Burkhart handed Agnes the two envelopes.

She said, "I hear from Frank, I'll tell him where you're at."

"I appreciate that. Anything else I ought to know?"

"Just that we need to catch these guys fast. New Army Air Corps base is set to open tomorrow. There will be a bunch of dignitaries hitting town. Some of them are here already, and we can't have Nazi car thieves running loose in town."

"Let's keep the stickpin between us, just the sheriff's office and I know, all right?"

She nodded.

Putting his hat on, Burkhart said, "One day until VIPs show up. Guess I better get going and see if I can find something to help your husband."

The Ford was not any cooler than when he had gone into the sheriff's office, but Agnes had given him good directions. Sullivan's Grocery was easy enough to find with its huge table of fresh fruits and vegetables out front, and Burkhart made the turn even though there was no street sign. Small towns didn't always have all the modern conveniences, like street signs. Behind the store, on the next corner, stood a sign on a metal awning reading *Hendershot's Conoco, Your Mileage Merchant.*

Driving past the two pumps out front, Burkhart parked on a patch of dirt just past the station. By the time he got out of the car a gangly string bean of a man in his forties was walking toward him, wiping his hands on a dirty rag as he approached. Whatever hair the guy had was hidden under his green-and-white-striped Conoco peaked cap. He wore an olive-green uniform of a slightly brighter shade than the soldiers fighting in Europe. There was the red-and-white Conoco logo over the left breast pocket and the name *Jed* stitched in red inside a white oval over the right pocket.

"Can I help you?" the attendant asked with a smile.

Burkhart pulled the little wallet from his coat pocket and showed the attendant his badge. The smile disappeared.

"You're here about the car."

A nod.

"It's long gone."

"What can you tell me about it?" Burkhart asked.

"Blue '36 Ford Deluxe with a rumble seat. Two-twenty-one V8 engine."

Same car as Burkhart's, just two years old and a different color.

"It's in good shape for a seven-year-old car. Except for the right rear tire."

"What's wrong with the right rear?"

Jed said, "Bald." He took off his cap and mopped his skull with the rag. "Bald as me. Come on, I'll show you."

Burkhart followed the tall man back behind the service station.

There wasn't much back here but dirt and stacked near the back of the building a few barrels and cans.

The attendant stopped and held out his arm to keep Burkhart from taking another step. "This is where the car was parked," Jed said. "Look down."

Burkhart did as he was told. He had almost stepped on tire tracks, one of which showed good tread and one where the track look smooth.

"Bald tire," Jed said.

Nodding, Burkhart said, "Yeah, I see that." Looking around on the ground he also saw footprints where the men had approached the car. There were footprints on both sides not far from the rear tire tracks. "They stopped."

Jed nodded. "Good, you've tracked before. You a hunter?"

"Deer, rabbits, and the like back in Wisconsin when I was growing up. I learned to track several animals. Any idea why they stopped right here?"

Giving him a little grin, Jed said, "I already told you."

The penny dropped for Burkhart. "Rumble seat."

"Smart man, Marshal."

"You look inside that rumble seat?"

"I did an inventory of the whole car for Sheriff Nesmith, but when those boys escaped, well, nobody ever came to claim it."

"You want to let me see it?"

"It's in the station, but there's nothing of interest on the inventory except for the bags of fertilizer. Rumble seat would barely close there was so much of it."

"Fertilizer?"

"That's what I saw."

Burkhart saw little white pellets on the ground and bent down to look at them. He touched one, ammonium nitrate fertilizer, all right, and just as he was about to scoop some up, the world spun on its axis. Burkhart stumbled, then fell onto his knees.

"Marshal, you all right?" Jed said, his voice nearly a shriek.

The attendant's hands were on his arms, but Burkhart said, "Just give me a second, I'll be all right."

Even though he was wearing his favorite suit, Burkhart eased into a sitting position in the dirt. The attendant squatted in front of Burkhart. "Look me in the eye, Marshal, you all right?"

Burkhart blew out a breath as the world slowly reset itself. "I was at Pearl Harbor."

"Oh, shit."

"Yeah, I was on the *Raleigh,* a cruiser. First torpedo missed us, the second one hit us square and the ship listed so badly to port that we thought it would capsize."

Jed just stared at him.

"I was a gunner. We kept fighting. Between us we took down five Jap planes, but after we shot down the second one another plane strafed us. He machine-gunned us and we all dove for cover. I hit my head. Got a bad concussion. If I'm not careful when I bend down, I get bad vertigo. Can't serve on a ship like that. They gave me a Purple Heart and sent me home."

"Sorry to hear that, Marshal."

Burkhart shrugged. "Nothin' to be done about it. Give me a hand up?"

Jed held out both hands, and Burkhart let the attendant pull him to his feet.

"Thanks. That's definitely ammonium nitrate fertilizer. Uncle of mine used that on his farm in Wisconsin."

"I don't know if they stole some farmer's car, or if they just stole that fertilizer like they did the car. You know, just because they could. Another crime of opportunity."

Burkhart looked at the attendant. "They steal something from you?"

Jed pointed at the barrels and cans over by the building. "Joke's on them, they stole diesel fuel. They put that in their gas tank they'll fuck that car up something fierce."

"Fertilizer and diesel fuel," Burkhart said, shaking his head. And then it hit him. He knew where the car thieves were going. "Do you have a local map?"

"In the station."

"Let's go."

The inside of the station wasn't much. A glass counter with a cash register on top split the room in two. Inside the door to the left was a spinner rack of maps that Jed perused for just a second before pulling out a map and handing it to Burkhart.

Unfolding it quickly onto the glass counter, Burkhart found Mountain Home, then ran his finger south. Naturally, the new base wasn't on the map.

"How far to the Army Air Corps base, Jed?"

"Ten or twelve miles as the crow flies."

"Is there a road?"

Jed moved to the other side of the counter, studied the map. He pointed at Mountain Home. "We're here, the base is southwest of town. There's a road that ain't on the map yet that the army built. But there's this other road."

Burkhart followed Jed's finger as the attendant traced a faint line on the map.

"More like an old trail, really. Used to be a farm out that way, but they went broke in the Depression. Ghost farm, now."

Picking up the map, Burkhart folded it part way, then he said, "I need you to go to the sheriff's office and tell Agnes she was right about the Nazis."

"Nazis?"

"Don't get excited, she'll know what that means. Also tell her to contact the base. I think they have trouble headed their way."

"What kind of trouble?" Jed asked, already coming back around the counter.

"Bomb kind of trouble."

"Bomb?"

"Yeah. I think they're going to try to sabotage the base opening."

"If I'm going to the sheriff, where are you goin'?"

"To try and stop them."

Leaving the station, Burkhart turned the Ford south and headed for the edge of town. When he got there, to his right he saw the new paved road that led off to the southwest and the new Army Air Corps base. Straight ahead though was a dirt road that, like Jed had said, was little more than a path.

The paved road would be easier, but if he was Moody or Werner, he wouldn't necessarily trust easier. Too much chance of running into someone from the base, or the cops checking the highway as Sheriff Nesmith most assuredly was now. Though he would also be trying to cover the road to Boise, the road north to Bennett, and the road east to Hammett. After all, the sheriff figured those boys were just running to get away, Burkhart figured he was the only one who knew what they were really up to.

For now, Burkhart trusted his gut. He edged the Ford forward onto the dirt track, and as the afternoon sun eased toward the horizon, he went a full mile away from town before he stopped again. This time he got out of the car, then slowly walked forward until he was a few feet in front of his car. Squatting instead of bending over like he had back at the garage, he kept the world from spinning as he examined the dirt of the road.

It took a moment, but then Burkhart picked out a tire track in the dust. Moving closer, looking beyond the impression, he finally saw the edges of another track, this one with no tread. Moody and Werner had come this way.

Rising slowly, careful not to set off his vertigo, Burkhart got back into the car. He would keep going south as long as there was light, but once night fell he would have a much tougher time. Either he would lose the track or he would turn on the Ford's headlights and be visible from God only knew how far away. Lose the scent or make himself a target, neither choice appealed to him.

It wasn't much of a trail, but Burkhart drove as fast as he could while still keeping the tracks in his field of vision. He lucked out and spotted the ghost farm's big barn in the distance. Dilapidated now, the red mostly sanded off by the wind, the building rose from the brown soil at an odd angle like a drunk that couldn't quite get his bearings.

The sun was sliding beneath the horizon like it didn't want to see what was coming. Almost as bad as the lights being visible from distance was the sound of the Ford's engine, so Burkhart cut the motor and let the car coast to a stop. The thieves might be getting away, but Burkhart had to check the farm. If he knew about it, maybe they did. An airfield with more than one runway would be difficult for the Army to guard, even if they could get it fenced in. The farm was only about three miles or less east of the new base, and that might make it the perfect place from which Moody and Werner launch their attack.

Burkhart hated sitting, but he wanted full dark before he approached the farm. He was still a quarter mile away, but he waited a few minutes to let the darkness settle.

Finally satisfied that it was dark enough, Burkhart got out of the car. Even though he drove a Ford Deluxe, the marshals got the standard version and that meant no dome light to worry about. Quietly latching the door, Burkhart stood and listened intently. The Idaho night was as silent as a cemetery, and the task ahead about as inviting, but he was ready for this. There was a sliver of a moon, but the stars seemed especially far off tonight. He'd grown up with country dark and he was used to it. Guys who grew up in the city had to adjust to country dark. There was very little light. Looking toward the farm, Burkhart figured he could see a lamp or lantern if Moody and Werner lit one, but Burkhart saw nothing.

Still, he felt in his gut that he was right. And if he was, there were ways to protect his country that didn't involve him being a gunnery mate on the USS *Raleigh.* Drawing his .45 from its holster, Burkhart started walking in the direction of the farm. He veered a little to his left so he was coming at the place less from the road and more from an angle from which he hoped Moody and Werner wouldn't be expecting him, if they were expecting anyone.

Burkhart moved as quickly as he could even as he tried to remain completely silent. He didn't quite run and he didn't gasp, keeping his breathing even as he came closer to the ghost farm.

At a rail fence he paused and listened again. The house was dark and had the windows broken out, the door sagging open. In front of him was a shed, but the door was on the far side. Beyond that, across a bare dirt yard stood the drunken barn.

Blowing out a breath, Burkhart eased away from the fence, ducking down just in case Moody and Werner were in the house and looking this way. Practically duck walking, he put the shed between himself and the house. He tried to look between the boards of the shed, but it was too dark to see anything. He listened closely. The shed was quiet. Their car wouldn't fit in there so there was little chance the men were. The house maybe, but probably not the shed.

The expedient thing would be to go across the open yard between the three buildings, but expedient was a good way to end up dead. Instead, Burkhart duck walked back the way he had come and used the rail fence as cover until he worked his way behind the house. There was no door back here, no real light, and no sound. If Moody and Werner were in the house, they had to be in the front, silent, and sitting in the dark.

With each slow step around the back of the house, Burkhart became more certain that if his prey were here, they were in the barn with their car. If they weren't here, he was spending valuable time, but he reminded himself the property needed to be checked so it was not a waste, just one more thing slowing him down.

Coming to a window, he looked inside the house. Nothing. Not a sliver of light. Three feet more, a second window. Again, nothing inside. The house was still abandoned. If the farm had guests, they were in the barn.

Loathe to cross that open yard, Burkhart receded into shadows as much as he could and looked for an alternate route. There was the big door on the yard side, and a hayloft door above that, not even a window on the side he could see from the house. Certainly the two thieves had the big door covered and might even have one of them in the hayloft to have the high ground. Not in a rush to make a suicide run, Burkhart decided to circle the barn and see if there was another option.

Staying out of sight of the big barn door as much as possible, even in the dark, he moved away from the safety of the shadow of the house and circled around the windowless side of the barn nearest to him. As he went around the side, he also used the opportunity to get himself up against the wall of the barn as he kept his steps small and silent.

His ears perked up, but he heard nothing. Sweat drenched him now, and his heart pounded in his chest, but his breathing remained calm. His Colt held easily in his hand, he edged forward to the corner then peeked around.

There was another big door on the backside of the barn, but it was closed. No way he could open that without drawing attention to himself. Next to that big door, flopped open and hanging by one rusty hinge was a man door. Now that might just be his ticket into the barn. If they weren't here he was falling farther and farther behind them, but in the darkness it was just as likely that he would have lost their track altogether anyway, so he might as well be thorough. If this failed, it was the last building, and he could get back on the trail.

Creeping forward, Burkhart kept the Colt's barrel pointed at the ground. As he got near the opening, he crouched low, the broken door between him and the black hole that was the barn's interior. It was not the perfect angle for an invisible entrance. He would have to swing out around the door or risk pushing it open which was sure to make noise.

Letting out his breath slowly, Burkhart brought up the .45 and pointed it into the depths of the barn as he tried his best to pick out any shapes in the inky blackness. It only took a few seconds for his eyes to settle on the larger, darker-sloped shape of the '36 Ford Deluxe. Moody and Werner were here, probably in this barn somewhere, but where?

A gunshot splintering the barn wall to his left and just over his head gave him his answer. He fired once in the direction of the muzzle flash he had seen and dove to the barn floor to his right. Immediately the vertigo kicked in, the world spinning off its axis, and he knew he was in trouble. Normally, sitting up and just breathing would eventually clear it, but now he felt like he might vomit. Only the worst marshal ever would die in the line of duty because throwing up gave away his position.

Struggling to find structure in the world, Burkhart dug his fingers into hard-packed dirt and straw beneath him, and he heard one of the guys stage-whisper, "Did you get him?"

"I don't think so."

The first voice said, "We don't know who you are, mister, but we don't want no trouble. Why don't you just come over here by the door and we'll talk. We thought this place was abandoned. If we're trespassing, we're sorry. Let's just talk about it."

Burkhart could hear the two men shuffling toward him, trying to be quiet. He needed to get his feet under him, get control of the vertigo before it was too late. Breathing in through his nose and out through his mouth, he tried to force himself to relax.

As his eyes adjusted to the darkness in here, he realized he was in a stall for some animal. Not good. Crawling on his belly, forcing down bile, he moved out of the stall and farther into the building. Assuming the two thieves were not complete morons, they would be trying to come at him from different directions and get him in a crossfire. Slowly, his head started to clear, but he was still nauseous, and the world still seemed a few degrees short of its axis.

"What's the matter, mister, you deaf? We just want to talk. There doesn't have to be any trouble now. Just come on out."

Judging from the voice, this guy was on the opposite side of the car from him. Did that mean the second one was on this side? Burkhart's hand came to rest on a clod of dirt. One way to find out. Rolling over onto his back, Burkhart controlling his breathing and letting his head clear from the effort, he tossed the clod toward the front wall like he was lobbing a grenade. Even while the dirt was still in flight, Burkhart rolled back onto his belly, swallowed hard to keep from throwing up, and started crawling toward the car. When the clod hit the wall there was a shotgun blast from less than ten feet in front of where Burkhart had lain just a second ago.

Raising his pistol, Burkhart fired toward the muzzle flash he had seen and the vague shadowy shape of a man. As soon as he fired, he was on the move, crawling fast directly toward his target even as the man grunted and the scattergun clattered to the dirt floor. Adrenaline kicked in hard now, and Burkhart felt himself regaining control of his mind and body. He might never serve on a ship again, but he could do this. He had to.

On the other side of the car, the voice, shrill with anger and fear now asked, "Jasper, you all right?"

Lying on the ground now, gutshot and bleeding out, Jasper Moody could only gurgle up blood bubbles.

Now Burkhart knew it was just him and Evan Werner on the far side of the car. Burkhart searched Moody until he found the revolver they had stolen from the jail, and he tucked that into his belt. He picked up the shotgun, and rising to a knee, tossed it out into the yard, hoping to draw Werner's attention in that direction.

Instead, Werner came around the car, coming from the same direction Burkhart had. The skinny man had Deputy Colby's .38 and fired off five wild shots as he charged Burkhart. Staying still on one knee, Burkhart fired twice, both shots hitting Werner in the ticker and he just seemed to run out of gas and topple over, dead before his face hit the dirt.

Next to him, on the ground, Moody weakly grabbed at Burkhart's leg. The marshal turned and looked down at the Nazi. Moody mouthed something but with the noise of the gunfight still reverberating in his skull, Burkhart couldn't hear him. He leaned down closer to the dying man.

"Who are you?" Moody whispered.

Burkhart looked him in the eye. "United States Deputy Marshal Alton Burkhart."

"German," Moody croaked.

"But not a Nazi like you, Moody. You're under arrest."

Moody coughed, flipped Burkhart the bird, then died.

Standing there, knowing he had stopped a Nazi plot within the borders of the United States, and also knowing that no one would ever know that, Burkhart still felt pride at what he had done. Maybe he wasn't the worst U.S. Marshal after all.

*—Matthew V. Clemens is a longtime coconspirator with Max Allan Collins. They have collaborated on thirty novels, nearly two dozen short stories, several*

*comic books, four graphic novels, a computer game, and a dozen mystery jigsaw puzzles. Alone, Clemens's short fiction can be found in the anthologies* Killing Malmon *and* Occupied Earth. *His first Western,* Bloody Hollow, *will be published in 2025.*

IN 1960S TEXAS,
ONE MAN STANDS BETWEEN ORDER AND CHAOS.

# REAVIS Z. WORTHAM

NEW YORK TIMES BESTSELLING AUTHOR

# THE TEXAS RED RIVER MYSTERIES

"REAVIS Z. WORTHAM IS THE REAL THING...."
—CJ BOX, #1 NEW YORK TIMES BESTSELLING AUTHOR

10th Anniversary

www.ingramcontent.com/pod-product-compliance
Ingram Content Group UK Ltd.
Pitfield, Milton Keynes, MK11 3LW, UK
UKHW041841190726
13854UKWH00002B/656